IRON & AQUA

BLOOD, BLOOM, & WATER BOOK THREE

AMY MCNULTY

I would admit that I'd thought my first Halloween with a boyfriend would be a *little* more exciting than sitting on the front porch next to a skull bursting at the seams with wrapped confections—a skull that laughed wickedly anytime anyone stuck their hand into it. Or anytime anyone so much as breathed beside it. Which, with me sitting here within motion-activation range, meant I had to be *very* careful with how fast I moved my fingers over my phone screen if I didn't want the endless chorus of tinny cackles to wear a groove in my head. At least I was rocking a *Carmilla* costume: long, black wig; killer smoky eye makeup; black haphazardly-stitched sweatshirt; and dark, ripped jeans. And, of course, black punk boots embedded with silver studs. I'd pinched the sweatshirt from Ivy's closet. I might not even give it back. We *were* at war.

I could have gone with a black tank top, but it was chilly out. And Ivy wasn't likely to show her face back here anytime soon to find out about it.

Not after everything that had gone down at the fishfolk fortress.

Not after I'd sunk my fangs into her.

True, I'd only sent a *little* venom through her. Though to be honest, that hadn't been my intention.

I'd been convinced turning Ivy into a vampire would be the quickest way to end this war between vampires and merfolk, the best way to avoid worse injuries. But part of me had balked at the idea of making Ivy an undead against her will.

Even if my boyfriend had shown me being a vampire wasn't so bad.

That little bit of hesitance had been enough. I'd panicked and sputtered and ripped my fangs out of her flesh before she could turn.

She was recuperating at Orin's cabin last I knew, something he'd insisted on because he didn't think it would be fair for one champion to outright slaughter the other while she was unconscious and couldn't fight back.

As if I would sink *that* low, world-ending stakes or not. Besides, she knew the truth now. It was only a matter of time before she licked her wounds and came crawling back, ready to surrender.

The skull laughed again.

"Trick or treat!"

I looked up from my phone to see a gaggle of Disney princesses, complete with princess moms in on the act, shoving bags and buckets into my face.

"Help yourself." Smiling, I nodded toward Laughy McBoneFace there. "Just a couple each please!"

The girls dug in with ravenous glee, the skull's incessant noise doing nothing to frighten them away.

"How have you been, dear?" asked a particularly cheery Mom-Belle. "How's your mother?"

Right. Mrs., um, I wanted to say Jeung? She lived somewhere a block or two over. Mom had had all these moms over for a block party or two, though she hadn't extended an invitation to her low-key wedding ceremony last weekend.

"Great." As I grinned, the dark red lipstick I'd slathered all over my lips cracked strangely with the movement. I wasn't used to this much makeup. "She's out Trick-or-Treating with my step-dad and little step-sister."

Mom-Cinderella put a gloved hand to her chest in a very princess-like manner. "That's right! She got remarried! Congratulations!"

"Thanks," I said. The little girls were already heading down the walkway leading to the sidewalk and the next house over. "That's why I'm stuck here," I complained, though I cleared my throat and tried to sound chipper. I didn't bring up the fact that I usually just watched scary movies at Journey's or had her come here to watch them with me anyway—unless she'd been invited to a Halloween party.

I'd gone to one my freshman year and had spent the evening awkwardly cradling some *weird*-tasting punch in the corner, so I hadn't wanted to go again.

"What would she do without you?" asked Mom-Belle. She and the other moms bade me goodbye and headed off after their daughters.

"Hey!" shouted Mom-Snow-White in a very un-Snow-White-like manner. "Did you tell the pretty Morticia *thank you*? Huh?" The girls mumbled something back at me and I nodded at them, but their attention was already focused elsewhere.

Morticia? I did a quick Google search. Morticia Addams. I supposed I kind of looked like her. She never seemed to be out of a clingy black dress, though.

"Trick or treat!" came another set of toothy faces, super-heroes and monsters and cartoon characters. Chipper parents, sullen parents, costumed parents. On and on to the tune of Skullface's never-ending laughter.

Guess who just showed up to my place? read a text message from Journey. She wasn't here, wasn't getting ready with me for tonight's party at the Horne manor. For actual vampires, yes, I could get over my preference to stay home. At least I knew that the refreshments there would be unlikely to be spiked with vodka. Because vampires got everything they needed from human blood.

Who? I typed, knowing poor Journey had been stuck with treat duty, too, since her mom was helping her dad and grandma at the diner. They had a lot of drunks wander into the diner on Halloween and late into the night, so they stayed open all night. Some kind of Slowe family tradition. *Devam?* I hazarded a guess, referring to her boyfriend of around a month.

Oh, please, like I'd act like he was the big surprise, she wrote. *He's going to meet us at the party. He said he'd drive himself.* I could imagine how stiff her shoulders might have gotten as she'd written the words. It was clear that though Journey and Devam had embraced the world of vampires to an extent, they were still arguing over how *far* of an extent they should do so.

I felt bad for dragging Journey into this. And for biting her just a bit on Homecoming night, too. *That* one hadn't been on purpose. Even now I was still getting used to having fangs and a literal lust for blood on occasion.

Journey attached an image. Autumn, my eight-year-old step-sister, hamming it up for Journey's camera. She'd planned on being a *My Little Pony* but had changed her mind at the last minute and had insisted on being Tinkerbell instead. But then she'd added the colorful horse hooves her mom had made for her to wear as gloves and over her boots. I laughed. I'd seen the outfit already, but that girl still cracked me up. She looked like some kind of faery centaur.

She told me she's a faery warrior, wrote Journey. *And that she can shoot vines out of her hooves.*

She's Tinkerbell, I wrote back, chuckling in time with Skull-face's guffaws.

I said that, texted Journey. *She told me it was the only faery costume she could find at the last minute. Then she stuck out her tongue and said she'd refused to wear the wig that had come with the costume because she's not a princess.*

She definitely wouldn't fit in with the neighborhood girls, I wrote back, thinking of the group that had stopped by for candy. I was surprised Mom hadn't *made* her play with them yet, though. She'd always made me when I'd been her age. Though maybe since I'd only ended up actually enjoying myself with her best friend's daughter even after all that hassle, she'd given up on trying to turn introverts into extroverts like her. And Ivy.

Ivy, my step-sister who'd used faery magic to move out of the house as long as we were on opposite sides of this conflict. But that would be over soon. Still, we hadn't heard a peep from either the merfolk or Orin, the faery "referee," so to speak, in days.

Another message dinged and I swiped to see if it was Dean yet—he'd been too quiet over the past couple of hours and I was bored.

I'd wanted him to join me in giving out candy.

He'd claimed he'd needed to help his "aunts" and "cousins" set the manor up for this evening.

As if they didn't have enough people who could do that. I was their champion and I'd kind of ended this war for them— had as good as ended it anyway. Surely, they could spare me a vampire prince to watch over me to make sure no fishfolk tried to retaliate for what we'd pulled off—with Ivy's help no less— over the weekend.

But as I shivered, I realized that having my slim, trim vampire boyfriend's arm around me wouldn't exactly warm me up since his skin was as cold as the dead's. The undead's.

It wasn't a text from Dean, though. It was a Facebook message from Daryl, my older half-brother, whom I spoke to all of once in a blue moon for birthdays and funerals.

It wasn't my or his birthday, so...

I quickly brought the message up.

Hey, little sis, he began. He didn't really call me "sis" much. We hadn't been raised together at all since our dad had left his mom for my mom before I'd been born and Dad had then left *my* mom and he'd been about as present a parent as an old-timey aristocrat with seven layers of nannies and wet nurses between him and his offspring. *Sorry to bother you*, continued Daryl's message, *but have you heard from Dad lately?*

Oh, right. That whole... thing. Since before all this, I'd heard from Dad for the major holidays and that was about it. I assumed it was the same between him and Daryl and that he wouldn't be missed, frankly. He'd only been here a few weeks, since the day after Homecoming, when Mom had summoned him in a monstrous wave of wrath after I'd been found unconscious in a Homecoming fire.

I hadn't had the heart to even come up with an explanation for *that*. Luckily, I hadn't had to as it looked like Orin had used his soothing mind-persuasion abilities to quell any questions Mom might have had.

He's visiting me, I wrote back. *He didn't tell you?* A one-two punch of smugness, then guilt hit me. I'd been jealous at the idea of Daryl even noticing Dad was gone from his normal routine—I certainly wouldn't have before all this—so I'd wanted to ever-so-casually make it seem like this *long* visit had been a planned thing. But that wasn't who I was. I took a deep breath. The vampire inside of me was an angrier girl than I'd ever been.

Human Ember didn't get jealous of her brother. Human Ember sort of liked him, even if they weren't close. So vampire Ember needed to chill.

No, wrote Daryl back after a while. He was typing more and then he stopped, and I got distracted by another wicked cackle and a chorus of "Trick or treat!"

"Hey," said a zombie kid that was probably taller than me. "There's nothing good left."

The skull's cackle in response seemed perfectly timed.

I peered inside. There were some Tootsie Rolls amidst some fruity suckers. Those might have been the dregs of last year's stock.

"Sorry," I said, standing and dumping the old candy into the kid's bucket against his will. "I'll go inside and get some more."

"I don't want this crap," said the kid, pulling his bucket out of the way. "Good stuff only, or we'll be back with a fine collection of toilet paper and eggs." The last of the candy splattered across the stoop and down the steps to the toes of the friend, who was wearing a cheap, horrific mask of some kind of cut-up person oozing fake blood. *Why do the older kids dress up to terrify the little ones out trick-or-treating among them?*

Growling, I pushed down the rage of heat boiling within me as I bent to pick up what was left.

The boys snickered in time with Skullface's endless laughter, the masked one's chuckles muffled and disturbing.

Don't help or anything.

Grabbing my phone, I headed back inside, kicking off my boots, and dumped the candy into the kitchen trash, Skullface's incessant noise ringing out in the empty house the whole time.

Ripping open more of the "good stuff," I poured the bag's contents into the skull one-handed as I scrolled back through my phone.

Dean had sent me a message.

Hey, doll. Can't wait to see your costume. Tonight, we celebrate!

My heart sank just a little. I was hoping for more than that. Not that Halloween was a romantic holiday, per se, but... We'd gone practically a whole day now without seeing each other. I *ached* to be in his arms.

That text could have been sent by my grandma.

Daryl had sent another message, too. *I'm getting married next summer. Did he tell you?*

Really? I shook my head, though no one was there to see it. I hadn't been paying much attention to Facebook lately, hadn't seen some post about Daryl's girlfriend sporting an engagement ring or something. That should have been a "liked" enough post for it to appear even on my timeline, despite the fact that we barely interacted with each other and Daryl rarely used social media anyway.

No, I typed, putting down the empty candy bag and giving my phone my full attention. *Congrats!*

You'll get your invitation in the mail soon, he wrote back as I stopped to help myself to a glass of water. I put the phone in the little indent in the door for getting ice and then opened the fridge door to grab the chilled pitcher. My eyes darted over the cranberry juice Mom kept in there and a sensation of heat burning up from my toes to my throat went wild, my right hand practically sizzling with the need to light on fire.

Red. The color red was enough to tempt me.

Blood... Blood...

Cranberry juice is not blood, genius, I told myself as I quenched my thirst with the water instead. But the glass dropped from my fingers soon afterward, having gone slippery with condensation and steam as my right hand had heated up.

"Dang it," I said aloud as I looked down at the little shards gathered around my feet.

My phone buzzed again. *Dad was supposed to be here last weekend*, Daryl wrote. *To meet Irene's folks.*

Oops. Dad had been interfering with the merfolks' attempts to run a school bus on a Model U.N. field trip off the road by kidnapping a classmate of mine over said weekend. All while Mom was having her (belated) wedding ceremony and I was biting my step-sister's neck after nearly drowning during her plot to kill me.

But I couldn't say all that.

Omg, sorry, I typed back. *He didn't tell me. I think he lost track of time. It's been crazy here.*

No, it's okay, Daryl typed back. *I expected as much from him.* He paused again and I took the opportunity to crouch down and start picking up the glass one-handed. *Irene knows what he's like. Just... glad he's alive, I guess. Thought I'd see if you knew anything.*

Well, he was alive, all right. But not for much longer—not *technically* if I couldn't convince him to get out of town already. It was nice to know that Minnie, Dean's "aunt" and the head of his vampire coven, could entice my dad to do something neither of his kids ever could. Stick around.

My hand full of glass, I stood again and was about to take a careful step when the doorbell went off as if it were trying to keep up with a strobe light in intensity and frequency. I yelped, then growled, then yelped again as my socked foot came down on another chunk of glass with a bone-shattering crunch.

"Where's the candy, goth chick?" shouted the zombie through my front door as he started pounding on the wood.

I uncurled my hand to find that the edges of several pieces of glass had poked fresh holes into my palms in the chaos of those few seconds. Putting my phone back down in the ice dispenser slot, I carefully lifted my foot. There was a single piece stuck up through the bottom of the sock, a small pool of red flowing out and down the clear glass, dripping slowly, slowly to the floor.

The heat inside me went wild, pummeling me from above, from below, making me unsteady on my feet as the *thirst* called to me. It was my own blood, but I couldn't talk myself out of the thirst, the *need*...

That doorbell went off again as Skullface cackled beside me.

Tossing the glass back to the ground and ripping the single shard from the sole of my foot, I launched forward, the heat gathering in my palm, which sweated as I clutched it tightly to keep the fire abated. But with another pounding on the door, I closed my eyes and let the venom surge within me, my incisors growing longer as I pictured the taste of fresh, fresh meaty juices.

Time stopped, the incessant noise cutting out sharply.

I used the short amount of time I could keep things still wisely, ripping open the front door, scary mask's fist halfway to it, then weaving around zombie boy.

The sun was nearly set, but I flinched as the last remaining rays assaulted me from behind, turning quickly to keep my eyes from being burned without sunglasses to ease the rays' effects.

In my distraction, the time pause cut out, leaving me a hissing, snarling vampire full of rage—rage at the boys, at the setting sun, at the lack of blood on my tongue.

They heard me before they saw me, but they noticed the now-open door almost right away.

"What the—?"

I hissed again and they both turned, slowly, slowly, as if their careful movements would protect them.

"Sorry for the wait," I said, holding my bleeding palm up and licking the trickle that had spread down my wrist and forearm. The taste sent shivers down my spine but did nothing to lower the temperature raging within me. *Trick or treat,* I whispered. Baring my fangs, I hissed and launched forward at them, but zombie boy dodged, screaming like a little baby.

"Holy—"

But I didn't hear everything he said, the fire and rage pounding in my head.

Screaming and screaming until their throats went hoarse, the boys darted around me onto my lawn and bolted down the sidewalk, down the block, as far as their feet would take them.

Part of me wanted to rush right after them, to pause time again to catch up, to sink my fangs into that soft, supple flesh.

A dad passing by redirected his children from heading up to my porch, his thin lips pinched as he steered them by with steady hands on their shoulders.

The fire within me drained, and I stood, shaking away the venom within, making it so that even the setting sun didn't bother me. "Hi, Mr. Braga!" I said, waving at them with my injured hand. The blood had smeared down my arm. "Happy Halloween!"

His kids shrieked and escaped from their dad's grip to run down the block ahead of him.

Skullface's cackling traveled out from the kitchen through the open doorway. I shrugged and grabbed the bag and the bucket the older boys had left behind on my front porch. Looks like *I* had gotten the good stuff this year. And I hadn't even had to threaten to resort to vandalism.

CHAPTER TWO

"You had *a lot* of candy left over," said Journey as she pulled up to the Hornes' Victorian manor. It wasn't the biggest house ever, but it was the biggest I'd been in. Though it certainly could have used some renovations, the frozen-in-time aspect of it seemed to suit the vampires, who were in many ways the same. Only they were frozen in a more recent time than their old Victorian home. Though barely more recent.

"Hmm, well, it was busy at first and then I *might* have scared people away?" I admitted. Journey stopped her car at the end of the driveway behind a sleek red restored vintage thing that I knew was Minnie's favorite.

"Did you show anyone your actual fangs?"

"Maybe," I said, not a trace of shame in my voice. Autumn hadn't complained about the mountain of candy left when she'd returned, augmented by the collection those boys had left behind.

Journey cocked an eyebrow. She was in costume as Betty from *Riverdale*, complete with blonde ponytail wig that popped beautifully against her dark skin and a Serpents jacket she'd gotten at Hot Topic. "Tell me you're not seriously scaring children."

I shrugged. "They weren't too much younger than me. And they kind of deserved it."

Journey giggled. "Okay, you're going to have to explain that one."

I promised to later. But right now, we had a party to get to—boyfriends to snuggle and spooky treats to eat. Assuming the bloodbags were having some feast inside courtesy of the full-time bloodbag chef. The vampires themselves did nothing but drink—and not just blood. They were like poster people for hydration.

Two vampires were making out on the front porch. Ernesto and Ruby. Instead of wearing costumes, they just had on fancier attire than usual, though they still looked like they'd stepped out of a black-and-white photo, complete with skin tone far too pale, the brown color sallow but gorgeous on them.

Ruby pulled away first and smiled broadly, showing off her pointy teeth. "Hi-de-ho, champion. And friend."

Ernesto nodded our way.

Nodding back, I hugged my arms tighter to myself as a gust of cold air whipped through the covered porch. Of course, the vampires didn't so much as flinch.

Music echoed out from the manor, along with the dim light of candles—countless, countless candles. These vampires may have been nostalgic for the past of my great-grandparents, but they usually at least settled for a dimmer switch on overhead lights. This was all just for the celebration.

"I'm kind of getting used to these old records," said Journey. The vampires' record player was part of a vintage-looking radio complete with CD and MP3 capability to play their tunes.

Vampires were selectively modern, I found, embracing their favorite parts of the past alongside the most convenient parts of the present.

Journey froze beside me, grabbing hold of my elbow and digging her fingers in so deep, I could feel her nails through the black jacket I'd also *borrowed* from Ivy's closet. "Tell me he didn't get here hours ago."

I followed her line of sight. Devam was there in his base-ball jacket, his hair and most of his clothes disheveled as he let a milky-pale woman—Yvonne—spin him around a makeshift dance floor formed by pushing the dining table to the side of the room. The table was filled with an array of delicately-arranged dishes, plates stacked on one end. The food looked hardly touched, the bloodbags who volunteered to be food for the vampires scattered all over the place, some acting as the vampires' own buffet in dark corners, their limbs tied to mini-mize thrashing, their moans muffled by their own pinched lips as they seemed to both simultaneously enjoy the pain and fear it.

I shivered. I'd gotten used to the feeding rituals by now, but it didn't mean I had to dwell on them. Focusing back on Devam, I did think he was rather... fatigued. "I don't know," I said truthfully. Dean had kept me away from his house for over a day, and he'd even stayed home from school to prepare. "Wasn't he at school?" I asked, referring to Devam.

Journey frowned. "Yeah, but he was supposed to go home and put on his Jughead costume." She practically growled. "Not head right here afterward."

I didn't want to say anything because it was my fault both Journey and Devam were mixed up in all of this to begin with, but Journey was fooling herself if she thought he cared as much about non-vampire things like Halloween costumes as she did. Devam was jittery at school, distracted whenever we hung out in other places. He wanted to be here with the vampires, with the venom... And it was only on my insistence that Minnie and the others were holding back with him, offering him only the slightest bits of venom, because I'd asked them not to turn Journey and Devam.

I didn't want anyone I knew throwing away their future to become a vampire. Not unless they really were sure of themselves.

Journey hardly seemed tempted. Dad and Devam, on the other hand...

But that was the venom, the draw of it. I didn't know if Devam had really thought it through. How was he going to explain this to his parents? Was he willing to skip college, a career, a family, the whole thing? My throat went dry at the thought. I didn't know what *I* was going to do after we officially won. I was already set for college, but if I left, I wasn't sure if Dean would go with me. And there was the matter of a future together, a family... I couldn't have that with him, not unless I joined *his* family.

Journey stomped her feet forward and grabbed hold of Devam's arm, yanking him out of his daze and whispering harshly in his ear. He shrugged and let Journey lead him away from Yvonne, who coquettishly waved at him and smiled her deep red lips broadly as Devam stared back at her with puppy-dog eyes.

My best friend's love life was not going well. And that was *my* fault. "He's young enough to be your son, you know," I spit out to Yvonne as she sashayed by. She was my mom's secretary and had arranged for my mom to meet my step-dad, Easton, I knew now. It was hard to think of her as anything other than "adult."

She paused, her bright, bright blue eyes practically twinkling as she rested a single hand on her hip. "Great-grandson, darling, but I'm not counting." She rolled her shoulder. "Besides, I'm just looking for a bit of a delectable bite to eat and little Devam is quite the ducky shincracker. *You're* the one dating your great-grandfather's contemporary."

My back went ramrod straight as she strutted past. I knew Dean had been a teen in the 1940s. But he looked like a teen still. And so I'd... Well, he was my first real love. My first actual boyfriend. I'd never felt this way before.

He'd never had a champion, a sweetheart, before me.

"Ivy?"

There was something about hearing that deep, smooth

voice that belonged to your boyfriend whisper the name of your more popular step-sister, your mermaid *enemy*, that made your whole body turn ice-cold.

It wasn't just the fact that he'd said it, but the *way* he'd said it. Surprised but... almost happy.

"You showing up here is bad business, doll," he said. "You're lucky you didn't buy the farm the second you showed up. Orin didn't tell us you—"

I whipped around, the long, dark strands of my wig twirling outward like a skirt as the hair shifted askew on my head. I straightened it as Dean's insanely bright blue eyes softened and blinked, a leery smile tugging at the corner of one lip. "Ember, I know it's Halloween, but do you get your kicks by dressing as your sister?"

"I'm *not* dressed as my *step*-sister." A lump was forming in my throat, practically shoving my rapidly-beating heart down as it tried to escape up out of my body. My face pinched and I tried not to show the sudden tautness of my muscles. "I'm Carmilla. The vampire."

"Oh. I've heard of the book," he said after a minute of looking me up and down. "But Gothic novels don't exactly describe characters with jeans and a leather jacket. "

I rolled my eyes. "There's a web series modern version."

"I see." Dean nodded, but he seemed as confused as ever. I bristled. I'd chosen Carmilla *because* she was a vampire, not just because I loved the show.

"It's like a radio serial only with moving pictures on a computer screen," I said in a huff, grabbing his hand and dragging him to the buffet for the bloodbags. "You'd think with eternity, you'd keep up with all the forms of entertainment, do something beyond just embracing texting on smartphones. Doesn't life get dull with the same old, same old?"

Dean looked around. The soft old-timey band music filled the air as vampire and bloodbag alike danced, as the quiet sounds of blood being sucked from veins and the muffled grunts of pain broke through even the soft tunes, coating the atmosphere with the slight scent of iron.

"The faery seems to enjoy all that newfangled stuff," said Dean after a moment. His voice was quiet. "But I don't know if I would."

True, we hadn't really just relaxed on a couch and binged on Netflix or anything. Dean always just wanted to talk, to sit quietly, and that had been fine with me.

It wasn't who I used to be, but spending time with my boyfriend had been just fine with me. We'd had the war to consider.

But with that all winding down...

What did my life look like? What did my relationship with my vampire boyfriend look like when his family got the powers of the consummate lands?

Minnie and Dean claimed they wouldn't do anything *wrong*. That they, unlike the fishfolk, were just fighting for the right to exist, to enlist volunteers to act as sources of blood. Vampires didn't even *need* blood to exist, I'd learned. It was more of an energy boost, a succulent dessert they could hardly resist, one that made them feel fresh and alive.

Sighing, I took in my boyfriend's appearance. I hadn't even tried to costume coordinate—I knew he wouldn't know about *Carmilla*, but I thought I'd be able to explain without this nauseating *feeling* between us. He looked *amazing*, as always—still in a suit, but it was a tux like he'd worn to take me to Homecoming. His tie was a little crooked and I stepped up to straighten it before grabbing a plate. "You look nice." My voice caught on the words.

"You look beautiful, doll, like you always do," he said, his smile broad. "I just think blonde hair suits you better is all."

I raised an eyebrow. "It's a wig, Dean."

"I know." He slipped an arm around my waist. "I made a fool of myself," he whispered into my ear. "Forgive me?"

I wanted to stay mad at him. This might have been our

first fight—if it even counted as one—and so much was bubbling inside me at the thought of being confused for Ivy, for him not even liking my costume, for... Dean kissed the tip of my ear and the rage cooled, my insides turning to jelly. "Only if you find a nice, quiet place I can enjoy some of this food," I said, gesturing to the bloodbags being fed upon in a couple of corners. Nausea hit me like a wave as Minnie came up from a feeding, wiping the blood from her mouth, and I looked down to see my dad's own neck on the divan in front of her.

"What happened here?" Dean asked, not noticing what bothered me and taking my bandaged hand gently into his. I'd just slapped some adhesive bandages across the cuts—they hadn't been that deep or anything, and they didn't even sting anymore. "Not part of your costume, is it?"

"No," I said, going to move a strand of the wig behind my ear, the usually-familiar gesture feeling strange as I found myself tugging on the entire wig. "I cut myself on some glass before I came over."

Dean lifted the hand to his lips and laid gentle kisses on the fingertips. "I should have been there."

I laughed, my breath quickening. "It wasn't *that* big a deal."

Dean tugged my hand closer, practically inhaling the scent of my palm. The scent of coagulating blood? He peeled the bandages off, and I was surprised to find the cuts pretty much healed, perhaps only the slightest remnants of scratches. "You must have turned," he said quietly.

"Into a vampire?" I pulled my hand back. "Yeah, I might have briefly. Not on purpose."

"Becoming a vampire reboots your body, I think." He straightened and his face tightened, though he tried to smile through it. "Not that I have other champions to compare you to. But we don't bleed, so our wounds heal through other means." Taking my plate and piling it high with practically one of everything on offer, he swooped back and grabbed my left hand with his free one, leading me toward the staircase.

I stared at my healed right hand as we moved up to the second floor. My heart beat now. I wasn't a vampire. My wounds would bleed. I wondered if my blood ever tempted him, if there had been some trace of my cuts on the bandages. Though he'd sworn never to bite me.

Not even if I asked.

CHAPTER THREE

"Here," said Dean, draping a second quilt around my shoulders. The finely-stitched threads of the soft plush told me this had been crafted with love and care, but the general mustiness of the fabric that seeped into my nostrils indicated that it had been a long time since such a thing had been needed here in this house.

I put my fork down, having sampled a little of everything on my plate but proving incapable of fitting the entire array in my stomach. Vampires seemed to forget normal human portion sizes.

Dean took the dinnerware from me and put it on a small table beside one of the many beds up here in the house's attic. "Do you need the heater?" he asked, pointing to an electric one designed to look like a flickering black fireplace, complete with a relief made to resemble plastic logs.

I shook my head. The last of the October air was chilly, but not so frigid I needed more than the couple of quilts already draped around me.

Dean slipped back in beside me in the recessed circular windowsill, his back against the wooden shutters that he'd had to use a key to unlock and open. The hinge creaked as he pressed against the wood.

"We used to just nail up boards," he said, playing with the shutter and letting it squeak and creak as he moved it back and forth. "To ensure no sunlight got in. But that got to be a pain in the neck." His eyes seemed to lose focus a moment as he stared out at the neighborhood alongside me. "Bloodbags need fresh air."

We hadn't turned on any lights, so all we had was the moonlight to light the space, the little flakes of dust dancing in its silver beams. "Dad's been staying up here?" It was the first time Dean had taken me to where the full-time bloodbags hung out.

"We picked this place for their safety," said Dean, nodding toward the door leading back into the hallway and the stairs. There were several bolts on the door, though Dean hadn't had to unlock them to open up. "Those locks out there? We installed them long ago to keep the newer vampires from getting in, not to prevent the bloodbags from getting out. Only Minnie and I had keys back in the day. Though now I suppose there aren't really any 'new' vampires to worry about. These days, most everyone can keep their thirst under control. *Usually*." A sparkle lit up his blue eyes, and I wondered if he was joking with me.

"When's the last time you fully turned a vampire?" I'd asked him not to turn Journey and Devam, but I hadn't come out and definitively requested that he also protect my dad.

I supposed a small part of me liked having Dad near—for once. Even if he wasn't really here for me.

"It takes time," said Dean. "The process. If you want to do it right—do it *safely*. Besides, we have a deal going with the faery."

"A deal?"

Dean tugged a little at his tie, like it was choking him. "Yeah. No new vampires till the deed is done." He didn't wait for me to press more, though I had to admit knowing they couldn't turn anyone into a vampire until I'd won this once and for all suited my purposes just fine. "But when the time comes," Dean continued, a smile twitching at his lips, "and it should be any day now, there's the matter of determining which candidates have people who might miss them..."

Daryl's message popped immediately into my mind. "What do you mean?"

"We can't fully turn someone until we're sure they've put their house in order, so to speak. Convinced everyone they're moving to Croatia and are never coming back. Insist they've found a new love who's not interested in connecting with a past family." He wriggled his eyebrows and I thought immediately of my dad—of his devotion to Minnie. "Whatever it takes," he continued. "We don't want gumshoes sniffing around here following up on missing persons reports. Even the blood-bags—we don't keep any of them full-time until we're sure no one will miss them. Change in policy from the old days. It's just too easy to snoop for information in this day and age."

"My dad..." I said, but I couldn't think of what else to say.

"I'm sorry about that, doll." Dean rested a careful hand on my knee. "I didn't know Minnie would go after him. I would have told her not to."

Shrugging, I stared back out at the neighborhood, at the orange-colored lights and flicking jack-o-lanterns dotting the porches in the distance. "He was smitten the moment he saw her," I said. "There was no stopping it."

Dean squeezed my knee and pulled back, leaning against the shutter and causing another spooky, haunted-house-like squeak to echo out in the cavernous attic.

"I guess it's a good thing Dad was 'between gigs,' as he often is," I said, feeling a bit of Mom's bitterness trace my own tongue. "Still. He may not have had a lot of friends, but he has my brother and me."

"Has your brother said anything to you?"

"Dad missed an important meeting with Daryl's fiancée's parents. He's getting married next summer."

Dean frowned. "We'll have to decide what to do about that. Minnie thought he was a pretty good candidate."

"Oh, he's a good candidate, all right." A heaviness pervaded my body. "Though I'd feel bad if he doesn't at least make it to my brother's wedding."

"Well, we can talk to Minnie about that," said Dean. "And your father."

"He won't care," I spat. "Maybe he would have once—a *little*. But now, he's... He's..."

Dean scooched in beside me on what little room we could share on my side of the windowsill, his arm around my shoulder. "He'll still be a part of your life once this is all over. If you want to stay here. With us. With me."

"If I want to be a vampire?" The muscles in my thigh started getting quite twitchy. We hadn't talked about this yet.

Dean kissed the top of my head, but I couldn't really feel it through the wig. "You don't have to become a vampire," he said quietly. "Don't ever think that you have to."

"I am, though," I pointed out. "A vampire. At will."

He chuckled. "Better to become a vampire at will than to be one permanently." He pointed at the moon, which hung high and nearly full. "The moonlight can be lovely, but you can kiss tropical beach vacations, suntans, and catching the sunrise through anything but thick-lensed sun cheaters goodbye."

Snuggling against his chest, I flicked a hand at my pale face. "Do I look like I do a lot of sunbathing?" His body was cold, even through the layers of his suit, but I didn't flinch, the inner fire within me coming out in soothing trickles to combat the chill.

"Touché," he said. "But I want you to think about it. *Really* think about it. You're just a kid, and you have your whole life ahead of you."

I pulled away, resting my bandaged palm on his chest. "Don't treat me like a kid."

The slightest tip of his incisor poked out from beneath his upper lip. "Right. But you still have a life ahead of you. I don't want to be responsible for taking that away."

"But I don't want to lose you."

"As long as you're my champion, I'm your prince," he said quietly. That didn't resolve the issue of what would happen once I was no longer his champion, but when I opened my mouth to speak more, he leaned forward. His lips mere inches from mine, the stillness of him, the lack of breath, was hard for me not to notice as my own breaths grew more shallow.

He kissed me, the iciness of his lips practically sending a jolt to my head like brain freeze, and then he pulled away too quickly. "We should get back to the party," he said, standing and reaching a hand down to me. "You're freezing up here."

I was the one who was cold to the touch?

A car pulled up on the curb and distracted me when the engine cut out. Someone was parking here, not just driving by.

I leaned back out the window to look below. A tall, tanned blonde in a Wonder Woman costume—minus the dark hair— stepped out of the driver's side of the vehicle and shivered, bouncing in place as she rubbed her bare arms. A shorter girl with dark hair and light brown skin got out of the passenger's side, not wearing a costume at all, not hesitating to shiver or talk or anything.

"Rae! Babe!" shouted the blonde.

Ah, of course. Raelynn Kelly and her girlfriend, Lyric something or other, one of Ivy's best friends. At least before all this.

"Will you slow down?" shouted Lyric, taking hold of Raelynn by the elbow, forcing her to whip around and look back at her, though Raelynn's head kept turning to the house behind her, to the party below Dean and me.

"You've been acting weird ever since the accident," said Lyric. She said something more, but her voice had gotten lower, softer, and I strained to pick up their conversation. Dean joined me back at the window again, peering down, his hand digging into his pocket and pulling out the coin I knew he fumbled with when his hands sought something to distract themselves with.

"Our hostage, home to roost?" he said quietly to me.

I nodded. Once we'd kicked some butt at the fishfolk fortress and gotten Journey safely away, I'd insisted on Minnie and Dad and the other vampires letting Raelynn go.

One of the vampires—Leopold—had bit her once by then. He'd had to, he'd said, to keep her quiet, to make it so she'd stop fighting. He'd barely injected any venom. They wouldn't do that to someone who wasn't a volunteer, Minnie had insisted.

But Raelynn didn't look like a girl who'd just *barely* had a taste.

She ripped herself out of her girlfriend's grip and shouted, "Just let me go already!" She poked a finger at Lyric's chest. "You're always so clingy."

Lyric looked as if she'd been slapped. "*I'm* clingy? Have you looked in the mirror lately?"

Raelynn turned on her heel at that, storming toward the manor and out of sight.

"Rae! I'm sorry!" Lyric disappeared after her.

"Looks like Auntie invited some fresh blood to the party," said Dean with a flick of his coin in the air.

I side-eyed him. His dad humor might be funny if it didn't involve more of my classmates in actual danger.

"Shall we?" asked Dean, the crook of his arm extended. I took it, slipping my arm through his, wishing I'd thought to dress up in a vintage ballgown instead of going the traditional Halloween costume route. The last gown Dean had bought me had been ruined by water and combat and ice balls ripping it to shreds. He grabbed the plate on our way out, walking with me arm-in-arm down the entire length of the long, long staircase, even though it was cramped and forced us to huddle against one another, his soft chilled form giving me comfort all the way. He handed the plate to one of the bloodbags who lived here with my dad full-time, who worked as a servant until the day he got enough venom to become one of the coven himself. If he even *could* depending on this "deal" Dean had mentioned.

"Ember, dear, I had no idea you'd arrived," said Minnie, coming around the corner from the dining room, the band music almost trumpeting her appearance on cue. "You should have said *hello* to me." Her red eyebrow arched at her "nephew" at my side.

"You seemed… busy," I said, thinking of her taking a bite out of my father in the dark corner.

"Nonsense," she said. "I always have time for my prized champion. I *love* the costume. A modern, punk vampire, might I guess?"

"So to speak," I said, sending a *see-not-so-hard-to-guess* look at my boyfriend, who smiled slyly and didn't look to meet my gaze. "A modern adaptation of *Carmilla* from a streaming show."

"Oo, sounds delightful," she said in her squeaky voice. The sounds of an argument broke out from behind her. "Oh, dear. Time to rein in some uncouth guests."

Dean and I followed after her to find vampires and blood-bags alike slowing their dances to stare at Lyric in her Wonder Woman costume with her hand over her mouth. "Gross!" she said through her muffled fingers. "I don't care if it's Halloween. It looks like they're actually *biting* people."

"Oh, dear," said Minnie under her breath, running her manicured fingers together.

Journey popped out from the sitting room, Devam stumbling behind her.

"Journey!" said Lyric, dropping the hands from her face. She looked nauseated. "Please tell me this is some kind of sick joke—"

"Ladies, please," said Minnie, laughing gently as she stepped forward to stand between Lyric and the dark corners of the dining room. Lyric was plenty tall enough to see over the shapely petite woman's head, though. "It ruins the All Hallows' Eve atmosphere if you do more than just gape and scream a little at it." She nodded over her shoulder for the others to keep dancing, to keep *feeding* if that was what they were up to beforehand. "You have to forgive our *sense of humor*, dear," said Minnie, putting a gentle hand at Lyric's back and guiding her to where Raelynn sat at a bay window in the sitting room Journey and Devam had just walked out of.

"Ember?" asked Lyric as she looked around. "What are you doing? I thought you were Ivy for a second."

Dean elbowed me in the side gently. *Touché.*

"It's a costume," I spat, falling in line behind her alongside Journey and Devam. The music grew softer and we joined Raelynn in the relative peace of the darkened sitting room.

"There! All my best and brightest Union High students together," said Minnie brightly. "Why don't you chat a bit and I'll have someone bring you some food from the buffet." She pinched her lips and nodded at Lyric. "I know our *Halloween décor* can be a bit gauche for the faint at heart. No sense in having you exposed to it for a moment longer."

"Halloween décor?" muttered Lyric. "That's like one of those live art gallery exhibits."

Dean leaned away as Minnie spoke to him in a hushed voice before she departed.

Tugging on the hem of his suit jacket, Dean straightened. "So you came back, eh, doll?"

It took all of us a moment to realize he was speaking to Raelynn, who sat in that window seat, staring out at the dark street.

Before she could say anything, though, Lyric stepped between her and Dean. "Yeah, *about that*. I get news she and Journey are in an accident, I go to the accident site, I call up every hospital within driving distance, and nope, they didn't get a Raelynn Kelly or Journey Slowe. Then I get a call *hours later* that she's recuperating here?" She gestured wildly around her, the lasso of truth hooked at her belt whapping around as she moved.

I locked eyes with Journey and nodded.

"Ember's dad and Dean's... uncle were nearby," Journey said. "They offered us a lift."

"And you came here," said Lyric, turning her ire on Journey. Journey actually shrunk back. "Instead of home? Instead of letting your loved ones know?"

"We were... tired," said Journey softly.

"Tired," Lyric repeated. She would make a good mother someday, the kind who saw through a teenager's excuse with surgical precision.

"Lyric, enough," said Raelynn quietly. "I'm glad I came," she added more quietly.

Lyric huffed and slid in beside her girlfriend in the window seat. She cupped Raelynn's cheek and then moved her hand to her girlfriend's forehead. "But you haven't been the same since," she said more quietly. "I wish you'd see a doctor—"

Raelynn swatted Lyric's hand away. "I'm fine."

A couple of servants came in so quietly, I practically screamed when they set down plates of food on the coffee table by the sofa behind Devam. He stared after them as they walked away, then he started slowly shuffling after them.

"Hey," said Journey, taking hold of his wrist, keeping him in one spot. She let out an audible breath.

No one moved to eat any of the food offered to us.

"Anyone hungry?" Dean took his coin out of his pocket and leaned against the wall, flipping it just as high as his shoulder.

"Ember, have you heard from Ivy lately?" asked Lyric, her change of track so sudden, I practically stumbled. "I checked in with her yesterday and I haven't heard back." Her eyes pierced through me accusingly. "Paisley reminded me she's living with her mom full-time now, which *I don't really get*, and that doesn't explain why—"

Raelynn snatched Lyric by the elbow, her eyes riveted on the street.

Dean and I exchanged a look and shuffled closer to see out the bay window. There was a dark pickup truck out there, idling in front of Horne manor.

"Who's that?" murmured Lyric quietly.

But I knew. I recognized the truck, and then I vaguely

recognized the people in the back of it as they stood and jumped out of the truck bed.

"Is that Bay and Laguna?" asked Lyric aloud. "I think that's Laguna's brother—he was at the wedding—and another chick."

I wanted to know how she was close enough to them that she knew two of them by name.

Dean pulled me to him, his cold lips brushing my temple as he moved to whisper in my ear. "They're just playing chicken," he said. "Grasping at straws. Afraid of what will happen when Ivy surrenders."

"Ivy and Calder," added Lyric, leaning back from the bay window as the truck went still and two figures climbed out of the cab.

Dean's fingers dug into my hip.

So he hadn't known Orin had let her go, either.

CHAPTER FOUR

Dean shot out through the dining room to head to the front door, Leopold and Zelda slipping in behind him before I could catch up.

"They've got moxie," said Zelda, her lips curling as she stared out the front door.

"They're about to go extinct," said Minnie, and I hadn't even noticed her appear behind us. Perhaps she'd made use of the vampire ability to pause time. "That makes them reckless —fearless even. Unless they know the jig is up."

It was a surprise to find my mouth opening to speak, the words forcing out even through the dryness in my throat. But I knew. Somehow I *knew*. "I don't think they would deliver Ivy here to surrender."

All vampire heads turned toward me. Minnie was the first to move again. She spoke to a servant bloodbag behind her— Rick, I remembered, from my unfortunate first encounter with him—and he crossed through the dining room to the sitting room, where the other Union High students were gathered, looking our way. He said something to them and tried to usher them back into the sitting room—back toward the rear of the house, away from the bay window. Devam and Raelynn complied easily, though the snarl on Lyric's face indicated she had objections aplenty. Journey met my eye before speaking softly to the towering Wonder Woman, leading her out of sight.

A chill met the fire starting to bubble within me. Minnie had sent them away in case this turned into a battle.

And I really didn't think the merfolk expected Ivy to willingly put an end to them on the vampires' front porch. Unless she'd smoothed things over with them and was leading them on, giving them a false sense of security.

Of course. That *had* to be it. Ivy wouldn't be foolish enough to let the fishfolk have any sort of chance, to let them flood the world and kill off humankind.

"Be careful, doll," said Dean in my ear as I headed for the door. "Let me go first."

Instead of holding the door for me as he usually did, Dean stepped outside and held a hand out behind him, keeping me at bay. I didn't let it stop me from slipping out beside him. It was like he'd forgotten that women *could* open their own doors if they needed to.

"Our party is invite only, I'm afraid," said Dean as he strolled down the front steps. "So why don't you take a powder?"

Leopold, Zelda, and Minnie poured out behind me, followed by Herbert, Yvonne, Ernesto, and Ruby. The whole coven of full-fledged vampires.

I tried to put a scowl on my face to meet all of theirs, but as I looked out at the teens—their purple and gold Central letter jackets, their jeans and T-shirts and blouses—something sharp snapped inside me. Calder stood beside Ivy, hovering near enough to touch her, but his hands were jammed into his letter jacket pockets, one sleeve pushed up slightly to reveal crisscrossing bandages.

I didn't *know* those other merfolk, but I knew him. At least a little. And if Ivy surrendered to me, he was *dead*. Knowing him before all of this as just another teen made it all a little more real somehow.

Biting my lower lip, I was surprised to find myself drawing blood, the fire surging within me as I let the venom pierce through my veins.

I had to do this. I had to be okay with this. For Dean. For all of humanity.

"Ember?" asked Calder.

And then there was his soft, gentle voice, humanizing him and reminding me that this wasn't so simple.

Crap.

"Are you dressed like Ivy?" he asked.

My cheeks flushed as Ivy took me in from top to bottom, her eyebrow quirked just slightly. She had on a wooly sweater and jeans, her long, dark hair pulled into a ponytail and her face clear of makeup.

"*No*, I am not dressed like Ivy," I said bitingly, moving closer to stand beside Dean. His extended arm stopped me.

"It's just the clothes, the dark hair..." started Calder, a slight twitch in his jaw muscles.

"What are you doing here?" I asked, redirecting the conversation to something *actually* important. "Have you come to surrender or to start a fight?" My fists clenched at my sides.

"We have your friends here," said Dean, staring Ivy down.

Ivy twitched. "Raelynn. I know, remember? You *kidnapped* her."

I gave Calder's merfolk friends an angry once-over. "Sorry. Didn't realize kidnapping was so offensive when the *other team* does it."

"This isn't a joke," snapped Ivy, and I could genuinely hear the crackling in the air centered over her right fist, the ice forming to use as a weapon. My own fist raged with heat, glowing orange as fire rose in challenge.

Calder rested a hand on Ivy's shoulder and she *jumped*, positively shuddering and slithering out of his grasp. Trouble in paradise? I supposed that came along with finding out your boyfriend wanted to drown everyone in existence.

"We let her go," I said, "but she came back for the party." I nodded behind me at the soft music, the candle glow through the windows.

Ivy looked back and forth down the street, taking in the Halloween decorations, no doubt. Perhaps she'd been asleep several *days* or she'd otherwise been too worried about coming to surrender to me that she hadn't paid attention to what day it was. "And Lyric's here with her," I added. "Journey and Devam, too."

Ivy relaxed her fist. "Let me see them."

A tittering laugh rang out in the chilly night air as Minnie took a few high-heeled strides forward down the porch steps. "*You* are not in a position to bargain here. I've kept them from witnessing this. That should be enough. Surrender now to our champion and be done with it." She slid her delicate hands onto my shoulders as she kept speaking to my step-sister. "*You*, girl, will be free to go, along with your little friends, once it's done."

One of the mermen, the handsome dark-haired one, launched himself forward at that, and though the redhaired merman and dark-haired mermaid beside him quickly moved to restrain him, he pulled his fist back and it connected with... the palm of Leopold's hand.

Leopold couldn't control the time pause ability very well, not as well as Minnie and Dean, but he'd had enough mastery to use it to cross the yard a few paces.

"Stop!" said Ivy and Leopold narrowed his eyes, squeezing the merman's fist as the merman struggled to launch his other fist at the vampire in front of him, though the fishman's companions were pulling back on that arm.

Minnie lifted a hand and Leopold heeded the signal, flinging the merman's arm away, causing the fiend to stumble backward into the arms of his friends.

"Ember, you need to drop out," said Ivy.

That was the last thing I was expecting right now. "Excuse me?"

Ivy's fist was glowing again as it shook at her side. "Drop out or I'll have no choice but to defeat you."

"*Excuse me?*" I said again. "Ivy, did these evil jerks brainwash you again?"

"I can't drop out," she said quietly. "I won't surrender."

"Of course you can!" I screamed. I must have launched myself toward her because Dean caught me by the elbow, pulling me back. "If the merfolk win, they're going to *drown the world!* Do you not understand that?" My voice grew louder as a raging heat burned up my body to the tip of my tongue, the muscles in my neck tightening.

None of the merfolk even said anything. Two simply righted their aggressive friend while the redhaired girl nudged a pile of yellow leaves with her toe, completely oblivious to what was going on around her. Meanwhile, Calder's lips pressed together in a slight grimace. "They're not even *denying* it!" I shouted, gesturing toward her companions.

"This is your last warning," said Ivy, completely ignoring everything I'd said. "Surrender now or drop out—or I can't guarantee your safety." She turned around and nodded at Calder. He moved back to the truck and the vampires fanned out, forming an unbreakable line around me.

Calder returned with a dimly-lit object in his hands and I recognized it as the orb that Ivy and I had apparently used— my memory of the moment was blank, likely rearranged thanks to Orin's gilded tongue—to enter into our probationary deals to become champions in the first place. It glowed in bright colors: red, blue, and... green?

Minnie gasped beside me. "*No.* They wouldn't dare."

Ivy jutted her chin out. "You know what this means?"

"What?" I demanded to know, but no one answered. Dean offered nothing but a blank look as he stared at the orb in Calder's hands.

"Drop out now," said Ivy, "and—"

"And we'll be back where we started," said Minnie, stepping between us. "Absolutely not." She whipped around to face me. "*Make her* surrender, girl. Defeat her!" Her high-pitched voice was practically shrieking the last few words.

My mouth was dry, all fire boiling within me dwindled down to a flicker. "No," I said. "Not until you tell me what's—"

"Get them!" shrieked Minnie, her lips flattening into a curl around her long, white fangs.

Ruby and Ernesto moved as one, launching themselves at the redhaired mermaid, who finally snapped fully into the moment as she crouched to extend her legs out in an effort to trip them. Leopold was quickly joined by Zelda and Yvonne, all three hissing at the trio of merfolk huddled together as Herbert slid in beside Dean and both vampires headed toward Calder the merman prince himself.

"Wait," I said.

Dean sent me an apologetic look, moving forward in the blink of an eye to the small space between Calder and Ivy.

Ivy dug into her pocket and pulled out a little cannister, spraying it right into Dean's face.

The air smelled strongly of pepper. I sneezed.

It was enough to make Dean crumple back, shielding his eyes.

I didn't know if pepper spray had the exact effect on vampires that it did on humans, but it was liquid nonetheless and vampires' eyes were sensitive. Growling, I felt the heat shoot up inside me again, the venom growing as I raised my hand in the air and launched a fireball forward. It slipped between Minnie and Herbert to land on a pile of leaves in front of Calder's feet, sparking the brittle material and catching fire quickly.

"This was your last chance," shouted Ivy from behind the rapidly-spreading wall of fire. She rubbed the bandages on her neck and I recognized it as the place where I'd bit her, where I'd sunk a small dose of my venom inside her blood. She clearly wasn't one of us—I knew I hadn't used enough venom for that, not that I'd ever turned anyone before—but there was some-thing off about her, something more than the way she was acting. Her skin was even paler, the dark circles under her eyes sunken and more pronounced than I'd ever seen on her before. She shook her head in jerky movements as she and Calder retreated for the truck, the glowing orb under Calder's arm like a football.

My head snapped to the source of a cracking sound to find the redhaired merman crumpled to the ground, his cheek reddening as he spit a little blood out from his lips. His companions looked bruised and scraped, too, though those wounds looked older, likely from our skirmish at the merfolk fortress over the weekend.

The scent of blood on the air broke through both the lingering spice of pepper and the smoky stench of the fire spreading. Yvonne hissed first, with Herbert changing direction to assist her in advancing on the other merfolk, leaving the retreating Ivy and Calder alone.

The dark-haired merman and mermaid got the auburn-haired merman to his feet and then called out to the redhaired mermaid and they were moving on shaky—if determined—feet to the back of Calder's truck. The vampires moved to follow them, but the fire I'd caused had spread, blocking their way. I didn't know if the fire would hurt them the same as it would human flesh, but they hesitated, Zelda screaming and collapsing to her feet as Leopold stared longingly after the retreating merfolk, then down at Zelda, then at the merfolk and then... He swooped in beside Zelda on the ground, taking her in his arms.

"It's okay," I heard him whisper. "Fire is our ally now, Zel baby. Your family is gone. They're at peace," he kept saying as she cried into his chest.

I'd never seen such depth of emotion from either of them.

Yvonne tapped her careful updo gently with one hand. "I don't relish singeing my hair off," she said as Ernesto and Herbert moved to leap over the spreading blaze.

"Put it out!" shrieked Minnie, her high heels getting stuck in the mud. "Forget them—the fire! Our manor!"

That had gotten out of hand fast. And I'd caused it. Unintentionally, I'd caused it.

Numbly, I stepped forward to Dean, offering my support as he still rubbed at his eyes. Behind the crackling, snapping fire, a couple of loud screams rang out in the air, followed by teenage laughter as a truck engine roared to life.

The dark-haired merman pounded on the side of the truck and grinned, his white smile penetrating the darkness. "Good luck putting that out when you're so afraid of water!" The truck took off, its tires squealing against the pavement, a trail of smoke left behind.

"The neighbors are going to call the fire department," said Minnie, letting out a few choice curse words that sounded warped in her baby voice.

"Doll," said Dean through a scratched voice. "You and the bloodbags—you're the only ones who can fight the fire."

Right. I straightened, feeling my fangs retreat as I headed back inside, Rick and Dad and other servants and bloodbag guests already at the door. "Water!" I screamed, and that got more than a few head tilts of confusion. Water was the vampires' enemy. "Put the fire out!" I shouted. They moved into action, which ones *could*, as the ones who had been recently donating blood were groggy and weak on their feet, like my dad. I slid in to stop him from tumbling as Rick and another servant man went for the hose at the side of the house. Of course, even if the vampires hated water, they still needed their plants watered on occasion.

"Hey, Em," said Dad, his voice a little singsong as if he were drunk. "What did I miss?"

Journey and Lyric stumbled into the room, Journey tugging on Lyric's arm to try to keep her back. "What the—? There's a fire in the front yard," said Lyric, her eyes narrowing on me. "And Ivy already left?"

I nodded. "Go help. Before it reaches the manor."

Herbert, Yvonne, Ernesto, and Ruby strode past us, nonplussed, Yvonne still dabbing her hand on her hair.

Leopold and Zelda came in a few paces behind them, Zelda still letting out little hiccups or sobs.

Lyric opened her mouth to ask more, but Journey grabbed her hand and pulled. "Come on." Lyric complied.

I wasn't much help at all. Struggling to keep my dad steady on his feet, I watched blankly as the servants and Lyric and Journey managed to subdue the flames with the hose, the air sizzling with smoke even minutes afterward.

Minnie paced and watched from several feet away, sparing a dark look in my direction as Dean finally joined me, his bright blue eyes red-rimmed and puffed. "Let's get him inside," said Dean, moving to shift my dad's weight onto himself.

"Minnie looks mad," said Dad quietly. "Oh, sweet Minnie. She looks gorgeous even when angry."

Rolling my eyes, I let Dean take him away just as the sound of sirens rang out against the night air, growing louder and louder. Minnie slipped on her more personable face as she carefully stepped around the puddles of water in the yard onto the driveway to meet the firetruck.

She'd work her charm and smooth the whole matter over. I could already picture her blaming a turned-over Jack-o-Lantern or a Halloween prank gotten out of hand.

But I knew once the firefighters were on their way, she'd turn her attention on me and how I'd blundered that pretty epically.

Me, I was still too numb to think it all over.

Ivy was on their side.

Ivy *knew what they were capable of* and she was on the merfolks' side. And they had the orb, which had to offer them some form of advantage.

This war had just gotten serious. And I didn't think there was a way of avoiding one of us getting hurt—or worse— anymore.

CHAPTER FIVE

The day after Halloween was like a switching of the guard at Union High, as even the most devoted of shorts- and T-shirt-wearers finally swapped out summer clothes for a winter wardrobe, putting aside witches and zombies and vampires in preparation for the winter to come—not that October was guaranteed to be warm or November guaranteed to be cold. The weather did what it pleased around here.

And some people never "put the vampires away" just because the spooky season was over.

"Hey, Goodwin, where's your perfect pallid protector?" Joe, my class partner in English, slid in next to me at the table at the library where I had books for my history research paper spread out in front of me.

"Are you showing off your vocab?" I asked. "Nice alliteration."

Joe nudged my shoulder with his fist. "I'm going to assume that's some smart student thing and take it as a compliment."

I flicked my pencil's eraser against my lips. "It was."

"Ah. Anyway." Joe centered his backpack onto his lap. "So you know how there's an essay on *The French Lieutenant's Woman* due today?"

"Yeah..." Even between nearly drowning and almost setting my boyfriend's house on fire, I'd managed to finish it a week early.

"So, like, can you help me with it?"

"It's due"—I checked my phone screen—"in forty minutes."

Joe slapped a piece of ruled paper down in front of him with some of his chicken scratch on it. "I started it."

There were three sentences handwritten on the page, the little tears and rips over the holes on the left side still in disarray from whenever he'd torn the paper out of a notebook.

"Why aren't you typing it?" I asked. "Miss Meyer prefers we use the digital dropbox."

"*Prefers* being the key word there," he said, tapping his pen against his temple and winking at me. "Lend me a hand, partner?"

My mouth opened like a blubbering fish's. I didn't think any help I offered could possibly make any difference now.

I sighed. "Tell me what you have so far."

Joe spent the next five minutes harping on "the French lieutenant" having "a woman," not realizing the lieutenant wasn't even *in* the book, not really. I slapped a hand against my forehead. "Write about how characters come to life when an author is writing a book," I said.

"What?" Joe looked at me like he thought I might have been smoking something.

"Trust me," I said. "Like an author having less control over their characters than they expect."

"You're messing with me," said Joe.

Shrugging, I pulled one of my open textbooks closer. "Or don't. I'm not the one scrambling to finish the assignment."

"Yeah, because you're a genius and everything comes naturally to you," he muttered.

I flushed red at the compliment and didn't even correct him. I did well in school—that did not mean everything came naturally. Or that I even approached valedictorian level, let alone genius. That was more Journey's department.

After a few minutes of silence—other than the scratch of Joe's pen against the paper and someone who kept coughing behind the bookshelf at our backs—I looked up from my book to see Journey and Devam hovering near the library entrance, Journey's brow furrowed, the hand not clutching her tablet and notes animated as Devam kept shrugging and putting slightly more space between them, clutching a singular strap of his backpack over one shoulder.

"Uh-oh," whispered Joe, leaning closer to me. "Trouble in paradise?"

I rapped his hand with my pencil. "Write."

"Ouch," said Joe, shaking his hand out in the air. "Yes, Schoolmistress."

After another few moments, he said, "So how come you wound up dating that new hipster dou—er, guy?"

His initial word choice wasn't lost on me. "Why do you ask?"

Joe had always been one of the few guys at school who talked to me, but he'd never danced with me at a dance or spoken to me about much other than class. I had him pegged pretty early on as one of those people who see you as a tool for getting their homework done.

"Because, like, the whole swim team had this thing going teasing Poole for his raging crush on you."

I dropped my pencil and scoffed. "You're joking." Calder. Calder Poole. And was Joe on the swim team?

"I'm not," said Joe, not looking up from the paper in front of him. "I'm Joe."

"Stop it." I rolled my eyes. "Dad jokes don't become you."

"Noted." He finished writing a sentence with a flourish. "But yeah... Then Poole up and transfers right after you start dating hipster? I don't think it's a coincidence. Guy took it too much to heart." He put both hands over his heart and palpitated them, as if to simulate his heartbeat.

"Just *stop* already!" shouted Journey so loudly, we both heard her from across the library. Several other people looked up from their tables and workstations and the librarian put her finger to her lips to shush her.

But Journey was not deterred. She threw her hand up and retreated farther into the library, not even looking up in my direction, the tears glistening clearly in her eyes. Devam watched her go and then slowly picked up his feet, heading back out to the hallway.

"Definitely trouble," said Joe. "But see, my man doesn't take it so hard. He's got spine."

"How are you so sure it wasn't *his* fault?"

"Didn't say it wasn't." Joe shrugged and went back to writing. "But either way, you don't let it get to you. Play it cool. Rise above."

"Thanks for the advice, Mr. Life Coach." I shook my head and started gathering my books.

Joe was nonplussed. "Poole was *so* into you," he said. "Pretty much made it clear you were off-limits." He looked at me slyly with one eye even as his hand kept writing.

Journey had always said I was a bit dense when it came to boys, but...

"He barely ever talked to me," I said. "And he's dating my step-sister."

"Probably to make you jealous. Playing it cool—on the surface at least."

"If you say so." I thought it over. Nope. I hadn't even had Calder on my radar before this whole vampires-versus-merfolk thing had gone down. He was a junior and we'd had no classes together before he'd transferred. And I'd have *noticed* a cute guy staring at me or something. I had cute-boy radar like that, even if my tongue used to twist into knots at the idea of ever finally dating one.

Now I had *the* cutest boy I'd ever met on my arm. Even if... Even if he and his aunt and the rest of his coven were kind of keeping me at a distance today.

They still hadn't explained what exactly had been up with that orb shining green and why Minnie had reacted that way.

I stacked the books together and it dawned on me—Calder probably *had* been keeping an eye on me because he'd known I lived in the house they were all so obsessed with. Not that it seemed to matter now since Ivy had moved out of it. Maybe it didn't matter as much once someone had already declared herself to be champion. Or her roots were still in our soil, so to speak, with half her family there.

I bet he'd *pretended* to be into me, told other guys to stay away from me, because he'd hoped he might snag me as his merfolk champion someday. But *he'd* chosen Ivy first. Not that I cared. I'd be pretty messed up if my boyfriend had been lying and manipulating me into doing something heinous like Ivy's was.

"Can you look this over?" asked Joe when I didn't have anything more to say to him.

I checked my phone and saw a message from Dean. And there was still the matter of checking in on Journey. "It's almost class time, Joe," I said. "You'll just have to hedge your bets and roll the dice."

"Never pegged you for a gambler, Goodwin." He shot me a wide grin. "But you're all sorts of surprising since you started dating that sallow-skinned hipster."

I looked down at what I was wearing. Yvonne and Zelda had supplied me with clothes from their own closet some weeks back, and while I still wore some of my own, I'd taken to the vampire vintage style. It was kind of cute. Today I had on a pink button-up cashmere pullover and a red pencil skirt, my blonde hair pulled back by a red kerchief I'd tied into a bow.

I smiled broadly. "That's what happens when you're in love," I said. "You get a little wild." I winked and Joe smirked back at me, sliding his paper into a folder and packing up.

I shuffled across the library with my stack of books, looking for Journey. It took me a while to find her in the bathroom, the quiet sniffles echoing out from the door alerting me to her presence. Dropping the books off at a little table outside the bathroom for that purpose, I stepped inside.

"Journey, what happened?" I whispered, looking this way and that for signs of any feet in the other stalls. "You and Devam had a fight?"

"We *always* have fights." She balanced her own stack of tablet-and-notebooks on the sink. "I thought it would be different. Devam is *so* different from my exes. From Avon especially. I thought..." She wiped a tear away. "I thought there was no way his eyes would stray when he had me on his arm. But ever since..." She pinched her lips shut.

"Ever since I introduced you to the vampires." I swallowed, the lump in my throat hard to handle. "Ever since I... bit you."

Journey chuckled darkly and rubbed her neck. The puncture wounds were almost invisible now because Journey, unlike Devam, hadn't gone back for seconds. She'd been at the manor plenty of times, but she hadn't offered her services as a bloodbag. "We've been over this," she said. "I forgive you. You're... going through changes. To put it mildly."

"That still doesn't excuse it," I said, exhaling loudly, my stomach growing heavy. "And the fact is, even if I've kept my *appetites* under control since, I was the one who introduced you to the vampires. I'm why Devam is..."

"An addict? A cheater?"

"Has he *cheated* on you?" I gasped. "With Yvonne?"

Journey shook her head, some tears flapping outward and onto the sink as she did. "I don't think so. Not like you're thinking. But he's *enamored*."

My thoughts flew to my dad, sticking around for weeks after what he'd intended to be a short visit, planning to give up his bachelor life, whatever the cost to the people left behind. I was here, so he saw me, but had he ever even considered saying a goodbye of sorts to Daryl? Dad was self-centered, but usually he had enough wherewithal to not forget a major event he'd promised to attend, like meeting your son's soon-to-be in-laws.

He just didn't promise to go in the first place if he didn't intend to show.

"Do you think he's going to agree to become a vampire when this is all over?" I asked, though my words were a reminder that this was *far* from all over now, even if I'd thought differently just the day before.

"Yes," whispered Journey. She stared up at me. "And Ember, I assume you will be, too, but I don't think I—"

"I don't know," I said, clearing my throat. "I don't know if I am, that is. Going to become a vampire."

"You think Dean will be with you if you *age?*" She said the last word like it was something dirty, her shoulders scrunching upward.

"I think he would. He wants me to go to college and all that, so..." I swallowed. Then there was the fact that if I wanted a family, I didn't think Dean could have one. There was adoption, but exposing a child to a coven of vampires? I shook my head. "But we're talking about Devam. What do his parents think he's been up to?"

"That he's always with me." She turned to the mirror and fluffed at her hair. She'd taken her braids out the other day. Wetting her hands, she rubbed them under her puffy eyes. "They stopped by my dad and grandma's diner the other day and mentioned how sick they must be getting of their son, and Daddy had no idea how to respond to that."

"He didn't give you 'the talk'?"

"Please," she said, taking a paper towel and wiping her hands on it. "He knows I'm safe and I'm on birth control. But I *wish* that was what we were actually up to. Devam can't think of anything but the Horne manor." Gripping the edge of the sink in front of her, she sighed.

Right. Journey was already doing things like that—not with Devam yet, but she had before. Dean and I... Well, he hadn't *asked* and I hadn't pushed and besides, I wasn't sure I was ready.

Too much. Too much was always flying through my head.

Whether or not I was ready for intimacy. A future with Dean. Fishfolk out there aiming to *kill* me. I kicked at the metal garbage can and sent it flying over.

Journey let out a bark of laughter. "What did the garbage can do to you?"

Exhaling out a deep breath to calm the fire and venom soaring within me, I bent over to pick it up and started grabbing the discarded contents. "It looked at me the wrong way," I joked. "Seriously, though, Journey. I'm sorry. I'm sorry I dragged you and Devam into this."

Journey dropped the last of the paper towels back into the bin. "I get it. You felt alone. I'm glad now I know what's at stake." She chuckled dryly, and I didn't point out I hadn't *meant* for her to know. It had just happened because of my inability to keep my fangs in my gums where they belonged around human beings. "Why am I even dwelling on this when there are fin-flapping would-be conquerors of the freaking *world* out there lurking in the shadows?" She started washing her hands. "Perspective," she repeated to herself a few times in a sort of mantra.

I joined her in washing my hands and nodded. Perspective, indeed.

We left the bathroom together and she waited for me as I checked out the books I needed for history. Hitting the hallway just as the bell rang, we shuffled to our lockers to swap one set of books and notebooks for another.

"Hey, doll," Dean said in his deep voice as I shut my locker door. I hadn't even seen him approach. "You still on for a shift at Horne Moving Co. after school?"

My mom thought I had a part-time job working for Dean's family at the headquarters of their moving company. Truth was, I'd been there a few times, but the most I'd done to help out was unfold and tape some boxes together one evening while Dean and his coven had fed on a couple of bloodbags. I'd needed a task to distract myself from the itch burning inside me at the idea of joining them.

"Sure," I said, almost pointing out that since we'd started dating, he'd insisted on driving me everywhere, so with my car still at home, I had little choice in the matter. "But remember I'm supposed to get Autumn from her school. It's a Dad day for her and Easton is in a meeting in Chicago."

Dean nodded, leaned one shoulder against the row of lockers, and pulled out his coin. "No problem, kiddo. Won't take more than a few minutes. Bang, boom, done."

Journey, who'd gone suddenly quiet at Dean's presence, wiggled her fingers at me, her eyes practically glued to the floor as she shuffled down the hall.

"See you," I said back, but she was already well on her way. Dean turned to look over his shoulder as if noticing her for the first time. "I'm not so sure she's got the *temperament* for being one of our *frequent guests*," he said quietly.

"Good," I pointed out. "I asked you not to turn Journey and Devam, remember?"

Dean flinched and slid his coin back into his pocket, sliding an arm around me and guiding me down the hall as if sheltering me from the other students around us, though few even bothered to look our way. We were old news in school now. "Like I said, we've got a deal going. Don't worry your pretty little head about that."

"You ever going to explain it?" I asked, bristling a little at his dismissive tone. My breaths were slow and even, my energy being zapped as we walked. "Why you can't turn anyone until after we win?"

"Not a matter of *can't*. Just a matter of keeping the referee happy."

The so-called "deal." Orin. Why did he care so much about it then? It wasn't like the Hornes would turn an entire city over to their side. They weren't like the merfolk. They just wanted to be free to live their lives.

Dean maneuvered us into a little gap between lockers in front of a darkened classroom. Gripping both of my shoulders, he put a cold, gentle finger to my chin, lifting it up so I was forced to stare into his sunglasses.

Even with the eyewear between us, my toes tingled.

"Hey, doll," he said. "Don't let a little setback get to you, all right? No one's mad at you about the fire. And as for the rest of it..." He shrugged. "We're handling it."

"How?" I whispered. "Why did Minnie freak out over the orb?"

Dean grimaced. "We're checking in with the faery about that right now."

Something felt off. They were too distracted, despite the fact that Ivy had just declared the war still on, that her goal was still victory. "I don't get why Ivy decided to side with them. Did me biting her hurt her feelings *that* much? Enough to make her side with the ones trying to *end the world?*"

Dean opened his mouth and then shut it. "I doubt that had anything to do with it." His face shifted this way and that, as if eyeing the exits. "Besides, it was worth a shot, seeing if the bit of venom within her would turn her to our side."

"Well, it backfired," I spat. The bell overhead rang again and it was quiet—too quiet—in these hallways.

I started to move, but Dean caught me by the wrist. "Don't worry about it," he said. "My aunt can write you a pass."

I gently removed myself from his grasp. "It's fine. I want to get to class." Hugging my tablet to my chest, I stared at him, looking at his vintage-suited self from head to toe. "I still have school to worry about. Because... Because we're going to win and there's going to be a school and a future and everything." I nodded at him, biting my lip and ripping a dry patch so that a trickle of blood oozed out. For a second, the fire surged within me and I felt my fangs protrude as my tongue lapped up the iron it sensed.

Dean smirked. "That's the spirit, hepcat." He smacked my butt and I stumbled in surprise, my eyebrows practically shooting off my face as my fangs retracted at the unexpected-ness of the smack. "Go and get it done."

I wandered down the hallway, checking over my shoulder every few seconds, feeling slightly giddy at the intimate contact we'd just had.

Even if, rather than a boyfriend just being cute, part of me felt it was something ripped out of an episode of *Mad Men*.

CHAPTER SIX

I didn't know if Autumn would recognize Dean's car—a sleek, red, shiny thing that slightly reeked money—so I stood outside of it watching the kids trail out of the elementary school, heading to buses and cars and crossing guards. The sun was bright and though I was keeping my fangs well in check, I'd borrowed a pair of cats-eye sunglasses from Zelda that I was making use of now. After this weekend, the sun would set practically an hour or two after school let out, but the sun was out in full force today, almost as if fighting against its fate, offering up a last hurrah for the year.

Dean wasn't taking the sun well. He waited inside the car, the visor down as far as it would go, one elbow on the door of the car, his fist supporting his chin. He'd been grumpy since school had ended when he'd stormed out of the principal's office to meet me. Minnie and Ruby, the vampire replacement school nurse, had both stared after him and shook their heads.

"What was that about?" I'd asked him.

He'd said nothing, sliding an arm behind my back and leading me to his car.

The short ride to the elementary school had been tense, and I wondered if he was concerned at all about Ivy coming to intercept us and get her sister.

But Autumn spotted me, her long, brown hair pulled back in a wild, messy ponytail, her backpack too big for her small frame, her sneakers lighting up with every step.

She stopped halfway to join a group of girls gathered in a circle, her expression cheerful as she broke into laughter along with them.

Dean honked the car horn behind me and made me jump. Half the people around us looked our way.

"Chill," I said, though I wasn't sure he could hear me through the closed doors. "I'll get her."

I didn't have to. Autumn had turned at the sound of the horn and gave one of her little friends a hug. She skipped over to meet me, the mittens on a string flopping out of either sleeve of her coat as she moved.

"Where's your hat?" I asked.

"You're not wearing one," she said as she pulled up beside me.

"That's true." I dug my hands into my woolen coat's pockets and shivered. "I wish I were, though."

"It'd mess up your pretty hair."

"Well, thank you for saying that." I ruffled her own hair. "But I'd rather have messy hair than cold ears."

"Use your kerchief," she said, taking hold of the backseat door handle.

"I could." I got inside the front of the car. "But nothing beats a wooly hat."

"Hello, Mr. Ember's boyfriend," said Autumn as she buckled in.

Dean seemed to be forcing a smile on his face as he nodded at the rearview mirror. "Kiddo."

"His name is Dean," I said. "You know that."

"I didn't say it wasn't." With a loud *zip*, Autumn dug into her backpack and pulled out her phone.

"Short stuff can call me what she likes," said Dean, but there wasn't the usual overcurrent of mirth in his voice.

"*Short stuff* is going to remember that," said Autumn with a little giggle.

After a number of starts and stops, Dean finally managed to maneuver the car out of the elementary school loading zone and took us back onto the main road. Autumn's school was closer to our house than mine, so it would only be a few minutes until we made it back. We spent half of the ride in silence, a weird sort of tension hanging off Dean that I didn't have the courage or ability to slice through. There was an incessant but quiet little popping sound coming from Autumn, likely from some riveting game on her phone.

"Have you talked to Ivy?" asked Autumn after a bit.

That name sent a jolt to my heart after last night's debacle, but I kept my cool. I had her sister in the car with the vampire prince. There was no way she was trying anything. "Not since the weekend," I lied.

"Dad was *mad* about that leak." There was something mischievous in the way she said it.

That had been the least of my problems over the weekend, but it hadn't taken much to figure out "the basement stairs leak" had had something to do with Ivy's powers.

"Do you know anything about it?" I asked, feeling her out for anything she might have witnessed that she wouldn't have been able to explain.

"No." Her phone went off with a giant video-game-synthesizer boom. She let out a curse word quietly under her breath.

"*Autumn*," I said.

"Oh, let short stuff's tongue fly," said Dean. "Not like there are any tattletales in this here vehicle, now are there?"

"You talk weird," said Autumn. "*Grandpa.*" She giggled at that and started her game up again.

We finally pulled into the driveway and Autumn was unbuckled and out of the car before Dean even shut off the engine.

I moved to follow her, watching as she fished her keys out of the front of her backpack and unlocked the front door. Dean grabbed me by the wrist before I successfully exited.

"Can I have a word?" asked Dean.

Even with his cold touch, I felt overheated. I sat back in the seat and closed the car door, though it didn't fully shut. "What is it? I need to stay with Autumn until Mom gets home. Since *someone* isn't spending any time at her dad's anymore. Though it wasn't like she was ever home when she did."

"Forget Ivy for a minute," said Dean.

That sent a tingle all over my skin. "Forget her? I've been trying for weeks. It's *your* war that kind of made that impossible."

"Well, you're about to get a whole heap more of bad news." He hesitated, his mouth opening, the tips of his fangs slightly visible. "There's another champion."

I jolted backward in my seat. "Ivy dropped out?"

"No, she's very much still in play." He tugged at his collar to loosen it. I wondered how uncomfortable he could feel if he didn't even breathe. "So I never thought it would be an issue, but... Apparently, the third party is giving it a go."

"Giving *what* a go?"

He gestured wildly. "This. Fighting for the consummate lands. Wiping out the other species in the game."

"Vampires, merfolk, and..."

"Faeries." Dean went quiet.

"Orin?" I asked. "But he's *alone*."

"No, he's just the only one you've met." He tapped the steering wheel. "Minnie has met many others. They've never cared to make themselves known before all this, not since..." He didn't explain further.

"*That* was what got her so bothered yesterday? Not me setting the yard on fire?" I thought about that again, how Ivy had shown off the orb, how I'd never noticed the green before. "But who? Is Orin the faery prince?"

"He is," said Dean. "And he's older than any of us—older than Minnie."

"He acts like he's twenty at most." I shook my head. "Some people need eternity to mature, apparently."

"Doll, I think you're missing the forest for the trees here." Dean nodded his head toward the house.

"What am I supposed to be looking..." I went quiet before I could ask the question. "The third champion."

"Has to live in this house."

My lips clamped shut. "Autumn?"

He nodded. "Minnie verified it this afternoon. Asked the supposed referee himself. Admitted it without a shred of shame, so they tell me."

"But how can he referee a match between blood and water if he's part of it?"

"That's what *we've* been asking. Some details need to be ironed out. Don't worry your pretty little head about it."

I frowned at him, causing him to scratch his chin absent-mindedly. "Sorry, doll," he said. "I forget you're wearing the pants here as my champion."

"Women have been wearing pants for enough decades that that expression barely even makes sense anymore." I let out a hot breath between my lips. "So... A kid is in this war."

"And that might explain why Ivy won't drop out, even after what you told her."

So it wasn't some vendetta against me for the bite? I ran the tip of my tongue over my incisors, flirting with the idea of bringing my fangs to the fore. "We have to get a child to admit defeat?" I opened the car door again. "That should be easy enough."

A crash rang out in the air, nearly freezing me in place. I looked up to see a *hole* in what would be my mom and Easton's bedroom window.

"What the—?" I started.

A scream punctured the silence. A high-pitched, child-like scream.

"What's going on?" I started running toward the front door of the house, my bookbag forgotten in Dean's car.

"Ember!" said Dean from behind me, but I kept running. Fortunately, Autumn had left it unlocked.

"Autumn?" I called as I took the stairs two at a time.

Mom and Easton's bedroom door was off its hinges, pushed aside by some kind of overgrown plant.

In the middle of the house.

"Autumn, are you in there? What's going on?" Stepping over the vines blooming into white blossoms before my eyes, I moved inside the room.

Autumn stood on top of Mom's double-wide vanity, Artemis, my white-and-black-spotted kitty, strangely shuddering against her chest. His claws dug into her shoulders, his ears flat against his head, his eyes wide. Autumn supported his back with her left arm, her right hand glowing green and pointed right at me.

"Autumn, what are you—?"

Before I could finish my sentence, a figure jumped out from behind the bedroom door beside me, darting right at my little step-sister.

CHAPTER SEVEN

"Watch out!" I screamed, rushing forward, only bringing up my right hand and summoning the heat of fire to my fist as an afterthought. I bumped my shoulder into the man in front of me, pushing him aside.

He skidded, then leapt, landing in a crouched position atop Mom and Easton's bed. Before I could blink and register the fact that I was looking at bookseller/cabin-dweller/referee-turned-faery-prince-combatant Orin, something grabbed me by the throat.

It was choking, squeezing, closing off my breath. I moved to push away at the hands there, only to find they weren't hands at all. They were *vines*. Thin but sturdy, flowers blooming even as they wrapped around and around my neck.

"Ember!" Dean bolted into the room, then appeared at my side in a flash. He took hold of me, probably intending to bring me into one of his time pauses, when Orin's voice broke through the sound of my frantic breaths.

"Champion against champion, mate."

"Buzz off," snapped Dean.

Orin laid a hand on his shoulder. "You help her now, you're interfering with my champion's attack." He was smirking as the edges of my vision were going black.

"I don't care." Dean whapped Orin's hand away.

I shook my head at Dean and pushed at him weakly. I could do this. Get through this and then figure out what was going through Autumn's head.

I focused. Closed my eyes. Ignored the incessant *need* for air and sought the venom in my veins. The venom spread, eating away at the panic, meeting the fire raging within me. My fangs elongated and I inhaled the tinny, delicious scent of blood, before I stopped needing air entirely.

My eyes shot open once more, ignoring the ends of the vines at my throat and grabbing hold of the line of them still connecting to Autumn's hand.

I set them on fire, breaking the connection instantly, causing her to shriek and cut off the vines erupting from her palm at the same time she let go of poor Artemis, who bolted the fastest I'd ever seen his little legs run, caterwauling the whole way.

My throat rumbled as I let out a hiss between my fangs, searching, searching for the source of blood.

Trickling down the back of Autumn's hands in four long, thin slices. Artemis' handiwork, no doubt.

I launched forward and Autumn shirked, screaming.

"Ember!"

The world went still, and Autumn's shriek cut off, even as the horror stayed etched onto her face. She was sitting on the vanity now, one leg extended to try to get down and run away.

I felt Dean's grip on my wrist then, long after he'd apparently reached for me, long after he'd paused time.

My chest heaving, though I had no need for air, I whirled on him, my fangs bared. "What are you doing?"

"You'll regret it," he said softly.

"She *attacked* me!" I shouted. "She tried to *kill* me."

"She's a kid. Your sister."

"*Step*-sister," I muttered. "No better than the other one." I was so over wishing I'd had a sister, a sibling to grow up with. Even if Mom was going to give birth to another one next year.

The reminder shot through my head like a whip. The thought of Autumn *dying* or even her being hurt... It would rip a hole through our family. And someday there would be a new little sibling who shared our DNA and every time I looked at them, I'd think of what I'd done.

The fangs retracted as I took a deep breath, the oxygen hitting my lungs and pushing the venom away, the fire dancing on my palm flickering down to mere embers.

"What's going on here?" I asked, looking to where Orin stood on my mom and Easton's bed, both his hands clutching his curly mop of hair.

The window beside the bed had that rock-sized hole in it that was going to be hard to explain to two parents already miffed about water damage along the basement stairs.

"They set a trap for you," said Dean softly. "Threw a rock out the window to get your attention and everything."

"But I didn't even *know* they were in this until minutes ago!" I hollered. "How is that fair?"

"They probably thought they would act before you had long to get used to it. Orin would have known I'd have told you by now, but..." His face screwed up in concentration and I knew it was getting hard for him to hold the world's time at bay, to keep things from marching on.

"We're not allowed to hurt Orin," I said, a raging boil roaring up inside me. "Even now?"

"He's still the observer," answered Dean through clenched teeth.

"Then I have to talk some sense into Autumn. That jerkwad brought a *kid* into this. She probably thinks it's just a game." I moved forward, dragging Dean with me to stay in the paused time together and then grabbing both of Autumn's wrists. A person had to be in the human chain at the start of the pause to be dragged along into it.

Just as I clutched Autumn's small bony wrists in my right hand, Dean's hold on time slipped and the room roared to life, Autumn's shriek growing even louder at my sudden nearness, at the way my hand clutched her wrists. Dean stood with his back to mine, putting himself between Orin and me as I helped Autumn down to the floor, my facial muscles working overtime as I tried to calm the rage burning inside me. "What were you *thinking*?" I shouted at her. "Were you trying to *kill* me?"

"No, no!" said Autumn, exploding into tears that ran thick rivers down her cheeks. She twisted and turned, her right hand faintly growing green, but that made it harder for me to control the red in my own. The heat started building there where my flesh met hers, causing her to yell at the top of her lungs and stop attempting to shoot out her vines. "Please. Please! I just thought you'd surrender!"

"How could I surrender if you cut off my air supply?" I snapped.

"Hey, love," said Orin from behind me, "you're frightening the poor thing, can't you see? Maybe don't bite her arm off."

"You stay out of this," I barked over my shoulder.

When I turned back to look at the whimpering, sobbing girl I had clutched in my hands, felt her legs give out as she tried to collapse to the floor, my grip the only thing keeping her standing, I sighed and let go. She fell to the floor, rubbing her eyes with her fists. The little strips of blood from Artemis's scratch were coagulating, the scent still in the air but far less potent, particularly as I kept the venom at bay.

"It's okay, love," said Orin, appearing at our side. Dean moved along with him, blocking him from approaching.

"You stay away from her!" I said. "How *dare* you bring a child into this?"

Orin shrugged and slid his hands into his pockets. "Not my ideal age for a champion, but little orange leaf has got a lot of bottle, I'll give her that."

Autumn hiccupped, her sobs growing quieter.

Orin tried to move toward her again, but both Dean and I blocked him this time, my hand slipping into Dean's and him giving me a squeeze.

Orin chuckled. "You know, Ivy wants me to brainwash your mum and dad again and tell them Autumn's moving in full-time with her mum like her. Doesn't trust you not to get into a donnybrook with the kid, and I don't say I blame her."

Autumn stood on shaky feet, and I tried to keep an eye on her every few seconds as I stared down Orin.

"I was taken by surprise," I muttered. "I would never have attacked her first."

"You'll have to if you want to win this thing." Orin took one hand out of his pocket to run it coolly through his curls. "Because I can tell you one thing: the bloom isn't just dropping out."

"And what do the faeries want if they win?"

I squeezed Dean's hand in mine. To let him know I hadn't forgotten that the vampires would vanish if the faeries won. But I had to know—to know I was doing the right thing. Not just for me. For everyone.

Orin winked and put a single finger across his lips. "My lips are sealed."

"Leave him alone!" Autumn's fists started pounding feebly on my back. "He's a faery prince and your *grandpa* is just some old, walking zombie!"

Turning around, I thrust my palms out to meet her fists, and she kept pounding on them like that would do any modicum of damage.

"Autumn," I said, crouching down even as she kept pounding. "Has he hurt you?"

"Who?" she barked, letting up on the mini assault.

"Orin!" I gestured behind me.

"No, of course not," she said, holding her hands tightly across her chest. "He made me a faery princess."

"Did he ever touch you?" I asked. There was the *kiss* in the ceremony...

"Oy," said Orin loudly from behind me. "I'm not some bloody pedo, all right?"

I ignored him and grabbed Autumn by both shoulders. "Has he ever made you uncomfortable?"

"No," said Autumn, slapping my hand away. "He's my friend."

"But he *kissed* you?"

She bit her lip and then rubbed it with the back of her arm.

"Look, I can't help the consummate rules, all right?" started Orin. "I swear it was just a peck and I'd never—"

Dean let out a hiss and bore his fangs, jumping at Orin, who just narrowly twisted out of the vampire's reach, his hands in his pockets the whole time. "That's rich from an eighty-something macking on a teenager."

"That's not the same and you know it." I jumped up and pushed Autumn behind me.

"Oh, spare me the righteous act," said the faery prince, his chin jutting toward me as he let out a little cackle. It reminded me hollowly of the laughter he'd let out in the mermaid fortress as I'd sunk my teeth into Ivy's neck. "This is war," he finally finished.

Dean jumped again, this time as fast as the blink of an eye, his incisors hovering over Orin's neck as he stood behind him.

"Watch it, walking dead," said Orin, guffawing even as a sheen of sweat started to appear on his temple. "Game-losing penalty you're about to get."

Dean hesitated, his head moving back, his lips curling over his fangs.

Part of me wanted to shout at him to just bite the jerk anyway.

The front door opened downstairs, the clunk of Mom's wedge heels on the wooden floor, the slam of the door behind her. Since Easton had moved in, he'd taken most of the garage up with some old motorcycle and his junk, so Mom no longer parked there. "Girls?" came her voice up the stairs. "I brought dinner. Is Dean here? I saw his car. He can stay and join us."

We all stood in silence for a moment.

"Girls?" Mom called again.

"All right then," said Orin, slipping easily from Dean's relaxed grip. "I'll just give you some time to mull it all over, yeah?"

"You stay away from Autumn," I seethed in a hoarse whisper so Mom wouldn't hear.

Orin shrugged and then headed for the broken window, lifting it up and ignoring several more brittle pieces of glass that fell to the carpet below. "This war will never end with that attitude." Sticking one leg out and then the other, he climbed out onto a tree branch that hung near the window, shimmying off like a gymnast until he seemed to vanish amidst the tree trunk and the shield of yellow and orange leaves.

"*Girls?*" Mom repeated, her footsteps taking her up the stairs, her voice a mixture of harried and annoyed, not sure which to feel just yet.

I sighed and as soon as I whirled around, Autumn started crying on cue.

"Ember? Autumn?" asked Mom, more anxious this time as her footsteps took her quickly into the doorway.

Her jaw dropped, her eyes widening as she took in the scene: the cut vines, the knocked-aside door, the broken glass, Autumn's sobbing.

"What in the world happened here?"

CHAPTER EIGHT

"She scared me!" said Autumn, not even missing a beat, embracing my mom and nuzzling her head against Mom's chest before she could do anything more than blink. Absentmindedly, she patted Autumn's back, surveying the damage, her jaw still agape.

It *seemed* like those were genuinely Autumn's feelings. I'd give the kid the benefit of the doubt. But either way, she'd been the cause of it all and I wasn't just going to let her spin a story and divvy up the blame.

Fortunately, Mom had known *me* as a good kid my whole life, so she'd know the likelihood of me being the cause of this kind of damage was just about zero.

"I *scared* her because I flipped out about the state of this room," I said.

Mom's wandering gaze narrowed on me. "You picked her up. You were supposed to be watching her."

Yikes. I'd walked right into that one. "I was only in the car an extra minute longer," I said. "I heard the window break and then—"

"The window is broken too?" Mom gently pushed Autumn off of her to cross the room and examine the open window closer. Carefully lowering the window, she silently surveyed the damage, new pieces of glass clinking and falling off with each iota of movement, causing me to wince over and over.

The only sound for half a minute was Autumn's quiet choking sobs. I glared at her and she shirked, padding her sock feet into the hallway.

"Oh, no, you don't, young lady," said Mom. She darted past Dean and me and caught up with Autumn, getting ahead of her to block her path. "Tell me what happened."

Even *I* jumped back. That was Mom's angry-with-some-manufacturer voice she only whipped out at work. And she sometimes let edges of it seep into her voice whenever she talked about Dad.

Autumn started bawling again. "I want my dad!" she screamed.

"He's not coming home until late. You know that," Mom snapped. "Now explain to me how and why you broke the window and... and..." Her tightened eyebrows softened as she gazed back at the door just slightly off one hinge, at the withering vines littering the floor. "How in the world did you—?"

"You're not my mom!" shrieked Autumn, pushing at Mom and causing her to stumble back toward the stair railing.

My heart seemed to stop, the movement in slow-motion. Then I realized I *had* stopped time. I *had* stopped my heart. Fangs bared, the world still around me, I ran forward, grabbing hold of Mom and gently pushing her back to the safety of the opposite wall.

The world fell back into place, though the venom was still thrumming through my veins.

"Hey!" I shouted at Autumn as she ran for her room. "Don't you *ever* push someone like that, especially near the stairs—especially someone who's pregnant! You could have killed our baby sibling!"

On Autumn's red-splotched face, her puffy eyes went wide at my bared fangs as she turned around and slammed the door.

"Whoa," said Mom, a hand on her chest.

I thought about breathing deep and sending the venom

away. It was getting too easy to turn—I no longer had to be smelling blood or thinking hard about it, as long as anger rushed through my veins.

But maybe that would come in handy, as my speedy maneuver had just proven.

Dean's cold but gentle grip on my shoulders helped me breathe to activate the oxygen in my lungs, to start my body back to life once more as my fangs retracted.

"Thank you, Ember," said Mom. She looked from where I'd stood in the bedroom to where we stood now. "I don't even know how you got here that fast, but thank you."

I stared at the railing, at the drop to the floor below. She could have done a number on Mom.

"I'm okay," said Mom, blowing out a breath and sending a lock of her golden hair fluttering, "but there's no need to scare Autumn like that."

I wasn't buying it. "She *deserves* it after what she pulled."

"But she's just a kid. She didn't mean it."

Mom was taking in deep breaths, probably fighting some imaginary venom of her own. She stared at the weird damage in the bedroom. "First the water on the basement stairs. Now this."

I didn't point out that last weekend, she was worried that something bad might have happened to Journey, as she was best friends with Journey's mom—and that kind of put house damage in perspective. Then again, just because she'd been "found" safe and sound, pretending she'd gone to a walk-in clinic—that her parents would never see charging their insurance—and having forgotten to call them to let them know, didn't mean she hadn't *actually* been in danger. We'd left the whole fishfolk bus-ramming and kidnapping bit out.

Mom growled and headed for the stairs. "There's chicken if you two want any," she said. "I have to call a window repairman *and* Autumn's father." She shook her head as she neared the bottom of the stairs. "I didn't want to be one of those wives who calls her husband constantly while he's at work. Glory used to do that to him." Her voice grew faint as she retreated to the kitchen.

I arched my eyebrows at the dig at Ivy and Autumn's mom, whom I thought Mom got along with well enough. Dean spun me around, the soft muffled echo of Autumn's sobs through her door a painful reminder of what had just happened. I rubbed at my throat.

Dean's soft, icy fingers trailed a thin line across it. "There's no mark," he said. "The healing factor seems to be getting stronger in you."

I'd turned vampire twice in a short amount of time. "Convenient," I said, thinking of the venom like a reset button.

"Just don't get too reliant on it," he said, his fingers shifting softly up toward my lips. He ran a cold thumb across them. "I don't want you putting yourself in danger thinking you can pass the buck and rely on your healing to fix what's broken." Pulling away, he gestured to my parents' bedroom door. "Shall we clean up? Be careful of the glass."

Swallowing, I nodded. My skin felt icy even at the absence of his touch and I traced my lips, imagining the kiss that had never come.

Dean didn't kiss me that often. He rarely initiated it.

He was always attentive, careful, kind... But there was something cold in the air between us, and it wasn't just his body radiating a lack of heat. "I'll get some trash bags," I said, heading down the stairs.

Mom was on the phone. I could tell she hadn't called Easton first, as her clipped, businesswoman tone was insisting it was an emergency repair, that she'd pay the extra fee, though she growled as she agreed to that. I dug through the pantry for some trash bags, my stomach rumbling at the scent of the fried chicken, potatoes, and mac and cheese.

"Thank you, sweetheart," said Mom, putting her hand over her phone screen to direct her attention to me for a moment.

I smiled and she nodded, talking again with the window repair company.

I grabbed several bags because there was a lot of debris, and while I was at it, I figured I ought to get the gardening gloves too so we could pick up the glass. I turned on the basement light, the flickering sound like a signal to send Artemis scurrying from where he'd been seated on the steps down farther into the safety of the basement. My fingers traced the new plaster on the wall. We'd had fans blowing on the gutted wall for a couple of days afterward, the repairmen just finishing up the work yesterday.

The damage those Sheppard girls had done since they'd rammed their way into my life. A part of me longed for the relative peace and quiet of not that long ago, before Mom had started dating Easton, before the crazy rapid marriage. Before vampires and mermaids and faeries.

I found the gloves quickly, grabbing an extra pair for Dean, though I didn't think a cut would do much damage to him. I piled them with the garbage bags on the basement steps and then cooed at Arty until he stepped out from under a shelving unit he'd belly-crawled himself under. Cautiously, he sniffed my extended hand and then rubbed my arm, throwing his body weight against me again and again.

"I've missed spending quiet time with you," I said, rubbing him behind the ears. "Should I see about getting you some of that yummy chicken? Huh?" I'd be sure to remove the breading, of course. Mom usually got some unbreaded for herself regardless.

"Autumn?" Mom's voice carried even down through the open basement. "Your father wants to speak to you."

She must have finished with the window repair company.

"Autumn?"

Autumn probably couldn't hear with her door closed.

I scratched Artemis under the chin and then scooped up the pile of bags and gloves, hopeful he'd follow me into the kitchen. I knew he didn't like to be picked up much, which wasn't endearing Autumn to him. Why had she even involved *my cat* in her little trap against me?

"Ivy!" said Mom, her voice bright and cheery. "It's so nice to see you. Do you want to stay for dinner?"

I froze. Artemis, trailing behind me, stopped just short of entering the kitchen, looking back at me quizzically as if to ask why I wasn't coming along.

"No, thank you." Ivy's voice carried. "Autumn texted me, told me she and Ember had gotten into a fight—"

Mom scoffed. "Autumn caused some damage... *somehow*... upstairs. She and Ember were fighting about that. It's calm now, but if you'd like to talk to her..." Mom paused. "Your father said he'd like to speak to you." She must have been conferring with the phone.

"Not right now," said Ivy, and footsteps thundered up the steps. More than just hers. Several pairs.

She'd brought her little fishfolk army along.

Mom muttered something in a huff into her phone and I signaled for Artemis to stick to the basement steps. He probably didn't understand me so much as he got terrified by the sound of a crowd because he didn't follow me out.

Sweeping past Mom, my hands clutching the bags and the gloves, I took the stairs two at a time, grinding to a halt at the top when I came face-to-face with Calder.

"Ember," he said, his voice strangely upbeat.

Dean chose that moment to launch himself out of my parents' bedroom, but I held up a garbage-bag-filled hand, maneuvering myself to stand between the two princes.

Ivy had her hand on Autumn's door handle, two more of her fishfolk flanking her.

"This house is supposed to be a neutral zone," I snapped, shaking the thin, plastic bags for good measure.

"We're not here for you," said Ivy, her voice icy like her powers.

"Your sister attacked me," I said in a hushed voice.

"Girls?" said Mom, heading up the stairs. "Ivy, Autumn, your father really is insisting he talk to—"

Ivy pounded forward, meeting my mom at the top of the

stairs and snatching the phone from her. "All right," she said. "But let me handle it."

Grimacing my way, she stormed over to Autumn's bedroom and tried to open the door. It was locked. Without even looking to see how much my mom saw, a little bit of ice shot out from her palm through the door handle and it snapped.

Great. Another bit of damage to my childhood home the Sheppard sisters were responsible for.

Ivy stepped in and shut the door behind her.

Mom looked around at everyone. "There's chicken in the kitchen."

"Thank you, Ms. Goodwin-Sheppard," said Dean, taking the bags and a pair of gloves from me. "But we'll clean up the mess. Ember and I have dinner plans after work."

Calder's ear seemed to perk up at that as Mom's jaw dropped. "I nearly forgot!" She stepped around me to take the items from Dean. "You two go ahead. I'll finish here."

"We'll pitch in," offered the Latina mermaid, brushing past Calder, though he grabbed her by the shoulder of her jacket as she tried to get past him.

"We will," he said. "But then we should get going, too." He stared straight at me, his soft green eyes somehow almost as penetrating as Dean's outrageously blue ones. "We also have plans tonight. Big plans."

Well, if that wasn't supposed to be some ominous threat, I didn't know what was.

CHAPTER NINE

D ean didn't actually take me to work—though that was my cover story for any time I wanted to seem busy after school.

Asking Orin to brainwash my parents into not questioning it like Ivy seemed to have had no qualms about doing might have been the easier route, but now that we knew that forest-dwelling sarcastic sociopath's true colors, it was all the better that we'd never tried to make my mom accept anything out of the realm of possibility.

My dad had taken one look at Minnie and fallen so hard, the whole bloodbag and immortal stuff had become incidental. My mom, though—that was my home. She was my rock. Things would never go back to how they'd been before when it had just been the two of us, but I would hold on to that little last piece of normalcy I had. With every last bit of might in me.

The great thing about putting a little extra effort into my daily wear—and raiding vampire ladies' closets for some vintage chic—was that I never felt out of place during surprise romantic outings.

Not that our little suburb was *full* of black-tie dining, but the steak bistro downtown was as close as we got. Though the inside was chic and sleek, there was a faded old advert on the side of the brick that was peeling away in most places, indicating this structure was probably even older than Dean and his World-War-II-era coven.

I clutched my handbag in front of my knees and looked around as Dean spoke in hushed tones to the maître d'. It was a weekday, so it wasn't too crowded, but the bar was fairly full of businesspeople and the area's semi-elite taking advantage of a free sample of wine the bartender handed out.

I wondered if it bothered Dean that he never looked old enough to get such things, even if he was a contemporary of most of these people's grandparents. Then I remembered he found something of a more succulent nature more appetizing than alcohol.

He did drink things other than blood, though. He'd brought me on a few dates and he'd always had something to drink. I'd seen him ingest a cold broth once. I didn't get how he had a terrible allergic reaction to water on his skin, but liquids down his throat didn't seem to bother him.

Next time he was caught underwater, instead of the diving suit, perhaps he could just swallow up the pool's or lake's contents.

"Doll," he said to me, his hands in his pockets as he nodded over his shoulder. The maître d' was waiting to lead us away.

Dean slipped an arm around my waist, guiding me past the diners seated under dimmed lights, which seemed perfectly Dean's style. As if reading my mind, he removed his sunglasses and tucked them into his shirt pocket, the sun already having set outside.

The maître d' led us past the bathrooms and down another shallow hallway to a set of narrow steps leading down. I checked with Dean to see if this surprised him and the corners of his lips curled up in a dazzling, reassuring look. Sighing, I slipped out of his grasp and moved past the maître d', clutching on to the rickety handrail for dear life as I made my way down.

Laughter echoed from the dimly-lit room ahead and I realized the tinny, high-pitched cadence was all too familiar.

Stepping out into the large basement room, I discovered a banquet hall, darker than even the dining room up above, with just the slightest light flickering from multiple candles set throughout the large table. Around the table were rows of bright blue eyes. Minnie was at the head of the table, my dad and one of the other servant bloodbags on either side of her. More bloodbags were peppered throughout the vampires.

The entire coven was here.

And most of the bloodbags. In fact, the only ones who seemed to be missing were Journey, Devam, and Raelynn. Even Union High's old principal, nurse, and janitor were among those seated, and they hadn't been allowed to move in and become bloodbags full-time, due to the fact that they had families at home. Families that no doubt found something off about their loved ones quitting their stable jobs and spending long hours somewhere they never quite explained.

They may as well have moved in. Their lives had already been upended. From what I could tell, there were school board members, too—how else did the owner of a moving company randomly become principal? I was surprised no parents had protested, even if she was supposedly temporary.

"There you are!" said Minnie, cutting herself off mid-laugh. "Please, come join us." She gestured to the opposite end of the table. The seat at the end and one next to it were empty. "I thought I would treat our fine friends to a nice meal, offer up a change of venue." She grinned at the woman beside her. "Not that Erica doesn't whip up plenty to keep our refreshments well-fed. But she deserves a night off, too."

All of the men stood at the table as Dean moved to pull my chair out—the *modern* men, so to speak, straggling a few seconds behind the vintage vampires. Then he helped me out of my coat and hung it on a hook to the side of the room. Once I'd taken a seat and Dean had helped me scooch closer, they all sat back down, Dean sliding in beside me.

Something sat heavily in my stomach, disappointment at it not being just Dean and me. Disappointment that there was no escaping this reminder of blood and water and... bloom and war.

Worry at the unspoken threat in Calder's words, at the fact that no one had been left guarding the manor.

"We ran into some trouble," said Dean, with all the cadence of an old-timey mobster reporting to his boss. He flicked out his cloth napkin and set it on his lap. "At Ember's house."

"Oh?" asked Minnie. My dad seemed somewhat interested in what Dean had to say, though that haziness never quite totally vanished from his eyes.

Dean looked to me as if asking for permission. He took my hand as I grabbed for my napkin and squeezed it, keeping his ice-cold appendage on top of mine on the table.

A thought struck me that with the typical boyfriend, that small gesture would *warm* me, not make me shudder harder. I slipped my hand out and finished unfolding my napkin.

"The champion of bloom attacked," said Dean. "The faery was there to not just witness, but to encourage—even help."

Minnie let out a curse and it would never not seem out of place on her delicate rose-red lips. She brought up a red-painted thumbnail to her lips. "How *dare* they jump into this, and with no warning."

"I think they wanted us to be surprised," I said, clearing my throat. "I certainly was. And Dean had just told me to watch out for her."

Murmurs erupted across the table.

"She's just a kid," I said quietly. "She doesn't know what she's doing."

Minnie's red eyebrow arched. "You're all just children to me," she said quietly. "But children are champions of this war."

More quiet whispers broke out as footfalls echoed from the narrow stairway behind me. I tensed and Dean leaned back, a reassuring smile on his face.

"We took the liberty of ordering," said Minnie, and I relaxed as the scents of pasta and meatballs wafted ahead of the staff with trays. As three of the waitstaff began putting down food and setting out plates, a fourth went from person to person, vampire and bloodbag alike, and poured a thick red wine into their glass, even pouring for Dean without being asked or asking to see his ID.

Perhaps Minnie had an understanding with this staff, though the waitresses with the plates set some in front of the vampires, too.

Waiting until everyone was served, Minnie then raised a glass. "To us," she said. "To safeguarding the world with our champion." She nodded my way, and everyone followed suit, my dad sending me a wink, like he was just some dad encouraging a daughter who'd excelled at varsity sports.

A flickering smile danced over my lips and I nodded back, raising my own glass of water. "Thanks."

We humans ate in silence for a while, and I felt Dean's bright blue gaze boring into me as he sipped occasionally at his wine. For a moment, I could picture us alone together someplace, the lights dim. But it was hard to do with the murmuring whispers all around us.

"Something's on your mind," said Dean as I wiped my mouth and pushed my plate forward, my spaghetti half-finished.

I chuckled. "That's an understatement."

"Don't worry about short stuff and the faery. We'll figure it all out."

"I thought we *had* figured it all out. I thought this was as good as over." My fingers rubbed the glass, condensation spreading, and I realized as I took a sip I was heating the water with my right hand.

"You craving a normal life again?"

Wanting a normal life again would mean leaving Dean behind. I didn't want to discuss such a possibility. I knew first loves didn't usually last, but Dean wasn't exactly the average high school boyfriend.

"I can't," I said instead. "Journey is worried about Devam. And now there's Raelynn. I've dragged my classmates into this." I set the glass down and looked over the table. "Even the Union High staff wouldn't be here if not for me."

"That's most definitely not *your* fault," said Dean. If I wasn't mistaken, his bright blue irises contracted as his pupils dilated. "We'd have done that to the school of whoever lived in that house."

My breath caught in my throat. He'd said it so casually, and I shouldn't have been surprised, but the reminder felt like a punch to the gut. "As soon as you forced some step-sisters on that person," I pointed out.

"We've been over this," Dean said quietly, leaning back in his chair. "We may have *helped* your ma along, but she fell in love on her own. We even brokered a brief truce with the fish-folk to get it done."

"Because actually making it so this champion versus champion thing would happen was far preferable to never letting enough young people move into that house and just staying out of each other's way?" I curled my hand into a fist and rested it on my lap, trying to calm myself, to push the thoughts of warmth and fire down.

"Doll, I know you're upset about what happened today—"

I opened my mouth to speak but was cut off by Minnie clinking a fork against her wine glass.

"Now that you've all had your fill," she said, her high-pitched voice tittering, "may I take this opportunity to make an announcement?" The table went quiet, all eyes fixed on her—except Dean's. He rubbed his glass with both hands, his gaze focused in front of him. "It's been ages since we've fully turned anyone to a vampire," she said. "But I'm pleased to announce that we should be having our first new rebirths soon if all goes to plan." She affixed her gaze on me as she stood, an action that immediately caused all the men at the table to stand, Dean included. "Erica and Rick, I'm proud to say you've been selected to be the first to join our family once this war is at an end." She pointed to the two servants on her one side, my dad's face pale and aghast. He didn't join everyone else in clapping for them. Neither did I. Instead, I grabbed for my glass of water and swallowed it down.

This was only happening *if* I won anyway, right?

Dad didn't seem to think that part mattered, though. "Minnie, darling," he started, but his voice got lost under the happy shrieks from Erica and Rick, who gave each other hugs as everyone cheered for them.

Minnie's face fell and she shook her head. Her tone was sharp and what little I could make out across the room was, "Not your turn."

Dad stared pointedly at me, his jaw clenching.

What was I supposed to do, put a good word in for him? Ridiculous. I couldn't stop him if the vampires won, but I sure wasn't going to *help* him.

The cup shattered in my hand, sending shards of glass and water rushing down onto my lap.

The room went quiet.

"Doll," said Dean, grabbing a napkin and picking up the pieces. "Watch the heat, eh?" He chuckled.

I'd warmed the glass without even noticing. Suckling on my finger, I remembered doing something like it after yesterday's too-similar disaster. I had to get a handle on this, I—

My heart beat cut out. All I could focus on was the coppery tang of the blood on my tongue.

I shot up, sending the remaining bits of glass to the ground. "I'm going to the bathroom."

Dean folded his napkin and placed it onto the table. "Let me come with you. The staff can clean this up."

"No." I gestured to the wet spot running down my clothes. "I just want to use the dryer."

Before he could answer, before I could do anything but take in those glowing blue eyes staring at me from all sides, I ran for the narrow staircase, taking the steps up two at a time, reminding my heart to kick in, to shove the venom away.

If I won this for them, two humans—at least—were going to join the ranks of vampires, and my own dad was pressuring me to get this over with so he could join them, too.

I dashed past a waitress in the confining hallway and then ran for the bathroom, my hand hesitating on the handle to the ladies' room.

If I won, how many more vampires would there be? Dean talked as if their only goal was to stop the merfolk from achieving *theirs*, but what did a world of vampires unimpeded look like? How many people would be enough for them, for their coven?

I knew they just wanted to live their lives, but they had so many volunteers, so many people waiting in the wings, waiting for their turn to become one of them. Waiting on *me*.

Swallowing, the lingering taste of blood dissolving down my throat, I shot out from the alcove leading to the bathrooms, past the other diners and the bar and the maître d', and out the door.

CHAPTER TEN

My sweater was cute, but it offered little resistance against the chilly late autumn air after dark. My frozen fingers grazed my head to grab hold of the kerchief I'd fashioned into a bow, desperate enough to follow Autumn's advice and turn it into a scarf of sorts to protect my numbing ears.

Where was I going? Where could I ever go where they wouldn't find me?

To be truthful, most of me *wanted* Dean to find me, to wrap me into his arms, to tell me I was worrying too much, that everything would be all right.

I shivered again as a gust of wind hit me, at the thought of Dean's icy arms around me.

"Ember."

I stopped mid-stride. I was blocks from the restaurant and had expected Dean to catch up to me much sooner.

Only it wasn't he who'd called out to me.

Calder leaned against a glass wall adorned with what looked like mazes and Sudoku and crossword puzzles. His hands were shoved into his Central High letter jacket pockets, his shoulders hunched forward as a mist of steam escaped from between his lips.

Vampires didn't have steamy breath in the cold. They didn't breathe at all.

I raised my right hand and summoned flame to it, almost on instinct. "What are you doing here?"

"Hey, relax." Calder looked back and forth, but no one else was foolish enough to be going for a stroll downtown in this chilly weather. "Do you want people to post about the fire-throwing girl on some conspiracy website?"

"What do you care?" I snarled. "The world won't exist much longer if you have your way."

He shrugged. "True. But if you have yours, it'll still be around and you'll have to live with the consequences of starring in a viral paranormal video, right?"

I lowered my hand and willed the fire to flicker out just a little, but I kept the glow at bay. The warmth generating from it shot up my body and gave me strength, offering me cozy comfort even in the face of the merman in front of me. "Where's Ivy?"

Calder leaned back against the glass, apparently satisfied I wasn't going to set him aflame. "With her sister."

"At *my* house?"

"Helping her deal with the fallout of everything that went down once their dad gets home." His green eyes narrowed and he looked as if he were examining my throat. "Autumn said she choked you out—"

"She did. And she was lucky I was reminded she's just a kid because her little foray into this world was about to be over almost as soon as it started." I ground my teeth together.

"Yikes," said Calder. "You've got bite."

I peeled back my lips to reveal my incisors, focusing on the venom to let them grow just a little. "Is that a pun?"

"More like a poor choice of words." He tugged at the collar of his jacket and kept staring at me.

"So what *are* you doing here?" I asked. "You said you had plans, like you were *planning* to attack."

Calder gestured behind him, taking in the decal of the

labyrinth above his head. "More like the others want to do a few things before they either crumple to dust as if they'd never existed or—"

"They flood the world and no longer have the creature comforts of we lowly humans at hand," I finished for him.

He didn't respond. I stepped closer to peer inside the window. There were chairs in a little waiting area, an empty desk with more puzzle décor throughout—including an entire shelf of hands-on puzzles. It reminded me of one of those kids' museums where you're allowed to go from exhibit to exhibit touching everything in sight. "So what are you doing standing out here in the cold?"

"Keeping an eye out for bloodsuckers." He winked.

My brows nearly shot off my forehead. I'd never seen him so relaxed, so nonchalant.

"Besides," he continued, "I wasn't really in the mood."

"For what?"

He gestured toward the sign over the door, and I gazed up.

"An escape room?" I asked. "Journey went to one of those in Chicago." My teeth started to chatter and I rubbed my arms to warm up. She'd wanted me to go to one with her before all this. That was right—we'd looked it up and found there was a local one, but between classes and college planning and series binge-watching sessions, we'd just never gotten around to it.

"Where's your jacket?" he asked.

"Back at the restaurant." I jutted my chin down the sidewalk.

"A restaurant... full of bloodsuckers?"

"You honestly don't know that already?"

Calder stuck both hands out as if to protest his innocence. "I honestly didn't. Though that's why I'm on watch." He chewed his lip. "But if you don't believe me that Ivy's not here, and you plan on charging in there—"

"Why *isn't* Ivy here?" I asked. "Aren't you attached at the hip?"

Calder chuckled, but it wasn't a very warm laugh. "No, that's over now. We're partners in this... And that's it."

So whatever sort of relationship they'd had was at least over because Ivy had discovered what he was really up to? I was so glad she couldn't *date* someone who wanted to end the world but had no qualms about being his battle partner. But she hadn't updated her parents about that, as far as I knew. They still referred to Calder as Ivy's "boyfriend," or "young gentleman," as Easton called him on occasion.

"You're freezing," said Calder. "Why don't we go inside?"

"*We?*" I bounced on one leg and then the other, muttering about how I'd have to have lost my wits to follow a merman anyplace.

"Look at it this way. You're the one who poses the most danger to my people at the moment, and if I keep an eye on you, I don't have to worry about it."

"You might have to worry about an entire coven of vampires walking down that sidewalk looking for me any second now."

Calder peered down the direction I'd come. "Is that what you want to do? Wait for the cavalry? Fight in front of a plethora of small businesses?" He smiled as an older man and woman strolled past. They nodded and said "good evening" in tandem. I watched them go, arm-in-arm, the chill in the air not even seeming to bother them, though they'd had the good sense to bundle up.

"Fine," I said without even really thinking about it. I yanked open the door, which clanged with a little bell. "But I don't care what kind of scene I wind up making if you do anything shady. *Capiche?*"

"You're sounding more and more like those gangsters already." Calder shook his head slightly, but the shadow of a smile across his lips as he followed me inside indicated he was actually amused.

"Gangsters?"

"What else would you call them?" Calder leaned on the counter.

I straightened my sweater, tugging it down and then rubbing my hands together as I took in the glorious warmth of this escape room's lobby. "Vintage," I said. "Elegant."

"Right," muttered Calder. "That's why they walk around like they're from another century. Elegance. Not an inability to embrace the changing world around them."

I bit my tongue then, making sure to keep those fangs from protruding and piercing it. Like someone who wanted the freaking world *to end* had a leg to stand on.

I snorted at my own joke. Mermen didn't always *have* a leg to stand on.

Calder's eyes softened, his throat clearing as he turned to the desk and picked up a Rubik's cube.

"Can I help you—oh, did you change your mind?" A woman wearing a black T-shirt walked toward the desk, the name of the escape room business printed over her breast pocket. "Bob told me just now your friends are doing pretty well." As if on cue, a shriek echoed out from down the hallway behind her, followed quickly by peals of laughter and indeterminate mumbling.

Calder tensed and then relaxed, according to the sounds he heard. I realized I had tensed, too, my palm growing warm. Shoving it into my pocket, I took a deep breath, reminding myself that I'd walked in here *willingly* with the enemy.

I still wasn't sure *why*. But with the glass window, I could watch for when Dean finally got off his behind to track me down.

"Can we do a room with just two people?" Calder put down the cube and gestured over his shoulder. At me.

My mouth opened. "Wait a sec—"

"Of course!" The woman leaned over conspiratorially, her light brown braid flapping over her shoulder. "I'm not *supposed* to say this because we want to sell as many tickets as possible, but personally, I have more fun in escape rooms when it's just my boyfriend and me."

"He's not—"

But she totally ignored me and started typing away on a computer in front of her. "So your friends are in the haunted house," she said. "And we've got another group in the hotel room. But that leaves the time travel machine and the abandoned hospital. Buy out the whole room at four tickets and we can start right away." She let out an over-the-top disgruntled breath. "Boss' policy. Otherwise, we can wait ten minutes for the next start time and leave it open—see if anyone else wants to join you." She put a hand up to her lips and whispered. "To tell you the truth, the odds of that in the middle of the week are pretty slim, but we do have to let you know it's a possibility."

"I'll pay for four," said Calder, pulling out his wallet. "Let's get started."

"Wait just a minute." I found myself reaching out to grab his forearm.

He stared at me as I did, his mossy green eyes endless pools that almost seemed to be pleasing. I dropped my hand and squeezed my arms to my chest.

What in the world was I doing?

"Excellent," said the woman. "I'm Betsy, by the way," she said to me.

"Hi," I mumbled.

"I'll be your game master." She grabbed Calder's card. "Which room?"

A bolt of strange desire came over me, like some small part of me that had forgotten who exactly it was I was standing near and what exactly was going on. *Time travel*, I wanted to say. But my throat was dry. Time travel reminded me of the vampires.

"Hospital," said Calder.

An abandoned hospital sounded scary.

"Oo, a personal favorite," said Betsy. After a few more

keystrokes, she handed the card back to Calder and then came around the counter to point to a line of tablets on stands flanking the entrance to the hall. "I just need you two to digitally sign these waivers," she said.

I must have looked terrified as I shuffled over because she laughed at me. "Standard practice, I assure you. In case of injury or damage, we need to establish liability."

"Yeah, *we're* the ones liable, I'm sure," said Calder, though his tone was jovial enough.

Betsy chuckled and headed on down the hallway. "Just let me get a few things set up."

Calder quickly signed a tablet with his finger and I lingered by the counter, checking over my shoulder to the glass door and window behind me. No sign of Dean. I fished in my pocket for my phone and realized with a jolt that I'd left it in my *coat* pocket, and that was back in the restaurant basement.

Calder's lips puckered out as his eyebrows narrowed. "What exactly happened to you? You're damp."

"Nothing," I said, moving to the tablet Calder had vacated. "Just a little accident with a glass."

"Does that happen often to bloodsuckers?"

"It does to bloodsuckers who can shoot fire from their hands." I signed a poor imitation of my signature with my left hand as I held the right above my head. He laughed.

"Noted. Now let's go."

The footsteps echoed as Betsy returned, a tablet in her hands, waving us after her.

Calder slipped his arm through mine and I just about choked as I struggled to ask him what he thought he was doing. I was so distracted by the close contact that I forgot to check one last time over my shoulder to see if Dean had walked by outside yet.

etsy led us into a dark, dark room and pressed something on her tablet that turned on a TV screen on the wall. The white glow illuminated some of the room around us, throwing ghastly shadows on what looked like a doctor's office receptionist desk, complete with a phone, a turned-off computer, a filing cabinet, and a couple of waiting room chairs and plants, fake hospital policies and tips for healthy living posted in platitudes around the walls. It was a doctor's waiting room shrunken down by like a hundredth, and it wasn't until I blinked a few more times that I realized there were spiderwebs between objects, dirt caked on the posters, a burn mark on the back of the receptionist's chair. A rubber spider dangled down from the ceiling and I squealed and jumped, pushing myself against Calder without thinking. Betsy laughed.

"We haven't even started yet," she said. "First, watch the instructional and safety video, and then there's a little welcome video before the clock starts. Sixty minutes until the ghosts of the mistreated patients get you." She cackled, but it sounded so forced. "Good luck," she added, sliding out the door through which we'd entered.

The room bolted shut after she exited.

What am I doing? I strode over to the door and grabbed

hold of the knob. *Have I lost my mind?* Sure enough, the door wouldn't open.

"She locked us in!" I said, clenching my teeth and trying again.

"Yeah, duh," said Calder, stepping up behind me. "Don't you know how these work?"

"They can't just—"

"If you *really* need to get out—"

But a video started playing on the TV, explaining the rules and how we weren't supposed to tug too hard on anything or touch outlets or break holes in the ceiling. Yikes, what had other people done to make these rules that needed to be stated?

I tapped my foot and crossed my arms and then the video explained that if any of us had to leave for any reason, we had to wave our hands and shout for the gamemaster.

I opened my mouth and began to raise my arm when Calder grabbed me by the wrist. My sweater sleeve had dropped away, so it was his skin—rough, calloused, *warm*—on mine. He didn't speak for a second, closing his eyes like he was in a meditative state. Maybe he *was*. Ivy could sort of read minds from what we'd figured out. Calder's eyes popped open, a knowing grin on his face. "Just give it a chance, 'kay? You had to have been running out in the cold for a reason. Would it really be such a big deal to make your bloodsucking prince sweat a little?" He chuckled and I wiggled my arm free. "Like that guy sweats," he said. "Love to see that. He'd probably start steaming."

I wanted to say something, but I clamped my mouth shut. He was having *too much fun* for a potential destroyer of the world.

The video changed with a jolting wrench of music, a clap of thunder, and a ghastly voice. "Fresh blood," it croaked.

Venom started worming its way through my body and I had to take a deep breath to keep it at bay.

True, this was an opportune time to attack, even if Betsy

was watching. There were no pools of water that would save him. Ivy was my target, the only way I could actually *end* this thing—well, now followed by an attack against Autumn—but a grievously-wounded merman prince might throw a wrench in their plans. What was it Minnie had thought to attempt to create long, long ago? A vampire merman? Or a merman vampire?

A cackling howl from the TV snapped me back to the moment. I'd missed most of the introduction video.

"Stop the mad doctor," said the husky voice. "Or she'll stop *you*. In one hour, you'll become one of us."

The video cut out and the room lightened just slightly, enough that we could shuffle around and look for clues. A countdown appeared on the TV screen, seconds vanishing almost immediately.

"I've done a few of these," said Calder, already picking up potted plants and chairs and anything not glued down to take a look beneath.

I tried to grab hold of the phone on the receptionist's desk and struggled to move it. Some things *were* actually glued down. The receiver itself, though, on one of those curly cords, did pick up, and when I put it to my ear, there was a humming dial tone.

"Found something," Calder shouted. I dragged my feet over to him, tugging absentmindedly on one ear, my mind racing to make sense of the fact that I was standing here, playing a game, with my sworn enemy.

I'd lost it. I'd let all these *feelings* overwhelm me—of how this battle was supposed to be over by now, how Ivy was supposed to know better; of how worried Journey was about Devam, how I'd more or less been responsible for them and Raelynn being a part of this world; of Autumn now being involved, of her putting my pregnant mother in danger; of how I couldn't picture the future I'd always thought I'd wanted with a vampire boyfriend on my arm.

Then it hit me. I wasn't even *sure* that was what *he* wanted if he *could* offer it. I was his "beloved," his "champion," and he clearly did his best to show me that, but I... I wasn't so sure...

"Ember?" asked Calder, holding up a little key in his hand, followed by his rapid-fire explanation of some trick a series of old magazines in a rack had revealed to him. "It's Dean, isn't it?" he asked quietly.

"What about Dean?"

"He's... You're... You're worried he doesn't love you." Calder scratched his jaw. There was a thin layer of pale stubble there.

"You read my mind," I snapped, snatching the key from his extended hand before he used it as an excuse to grab hold of me again. "You used your slimy fish powers on me."

"Well, whether I read your mind or not, I'd say you just confirmed my guess."

Grumbling, I started putting the key in every keyhole or lock I could find.

"That's a no-touch sticker," said Calder at one of them, appearing behind me. "Didn't you listen to the video? Some locks are just there to hold in mechanisms." He came up behind me and reached to the side of me to point out the bright red sticker with an *X* on it on top of the lock in my hands.

I could *feel* his warm breath on my ear, *sense* him all around me.

Growling, I smacked his arm away, creating an escape route for myself and swirling on him. "Watch it," I said. "Or it'll be a repeat of Dress Castle. My fire singeing you and bringing the whole place down with water sprinklers activating." My hand glowed slightly and I had to toss the key onto the receptionist desk when it grew too hot.

"I always wondered if you felt at all guilty about that," said Calder. He tugged down his jacket sleeve so he could pick up the key without scalding himself, I supposed. "They had water damage and were closed for weeks. I think they just reopened."

"I didn't do it on purpose. You came out of nowhere—"

"Shh." Calder held a finger to his lips and his eyes rolled upward. "The game master is watching." The sound of a chorus of cheers from somewhere down the hall broke out, reminding me that sound carried in this place, too.

I crossed my arms and paced, pretending to be taking in the room around me.

With a snap, Calder let out a little sound of triumph as a drawer in the filing cabinet opened. He was crouched down as low as he could go, so perfectly positioned for me to kick or punch or *bite* him.

He jumped up with several manila folders in his hand. "So you're not a business-wrecker," he said softly. "Not on purpose. Then calm down and let's play the game." He handed me one of the folders.

I wanted to point out how disingenuous it was for him to *care* about a clothing store getting soaked when he wanted to see all stores in the entire world turned to soggy artifacts beneath a plant-wide ocean, but I sighed instead, slapping the folder on top of the receptionist desk and flipping through the pages. There was too much to read through, but I skimmed, speedreading as best I could. It was a fake patient file, innocuous for the most part until the last few lines. It was an abnormal blood test and every few letters was bolded. "Is this a code?" I asked.

"Same thing here," said Calder, showing me the two open folders in his hand. He nudged me with his arm. "See? You've got a knack for this when you put your mind to it."

I rolled my eyes and stepped aside so he could place all three pieces of paper together. "This is a combination."

"To what?" I asked.

"Look for anything that uses seven letters."

Stomping my feet, I looked around at the locks, peering this way and that. The clock was already down to forty-five minutes, but I couldn't care less if we actually won this thing.

"Wait," I said as Calder approached some of the places I'd already checked. "A phone number. In letter form."

"Phone number?" Calder cocked his head.

"You know, like 1-555-BUY-STUFF. The numbers have three letters a piece that correlate." I grabbed for the folders and twisted them around until I thought they were in the right order, going by the dates of the blood tests.

Picking up the phone and hearing the hum, I punched in the number equivalent of the letters and the hum cut out. It started ringing—though there was something off about it, like it was a prerecorded message—and Calder appeared at my side, shoving his face flush up against mine so he could listen to the call, too.

Yelping, I bent to get away, but he shook his head and grabbed hold of my hand clutching the phone, rearranging my grip on it so we could both hear.

"You were right, detectives," said the voice. "Dr. I.N. Sanity isn't who she appears to be." I laughed at the stupid name pun, like, realistically, who hired a doctor with that name and didn't think twice about it? "Her experiments with patients' samples are revealing the same abnormality... We think she *created* the abnormality by giving them shots of her own special cocktail."

With a loud buzz, a door previously locked—not the one we'd entered through—popped open.

"We think she's still there, even though the government shut this place down months ago. She and her experiments— but be careful! If you don't manage to confine her before the authorities arrive, it'll be too late. For you. For everyone." The phone went dead, the dial tone humming in our ears once more.

I laughed again, trying to make sense of the scenario, but Calder had already hung up the phone for us and taken my hand. "Come on!" he said, nodding toward the countdown clock on the screen. "Dr. I'm-Sanity has to be in here!"

"*In*sanity," I said, giggling. Then with a quake in my stomach, I realized I was laughing. *With the enemy.*

CHAPTER TWELVE

Lights were flickering in the next room we entered, which was adorned to look like a hospital room, complete with a bed on wheels. In this compressed little universe, a receptionist's room led directly to a hospital room, no hallway between it.

If I could accept that this whole scenario was going on, I could accept that.

I'd accepted vampires, mermaids, and faeries. For real.

Calder dropped my hand and went straight for the bed, rifling through it with abandon.

"Slow down," I said. "Someone has to remake the bed."

Calder paused, looking up at me and grinning. "*Someone's* clearly never done an escape room before."

Grinding my teeth, I walked around the room, following his example and picking up anything that responded to my touch.

A clang rang out and I whirled around to find Calder swooping to pick up a metal bed pan that was still echoing hollowly as it came to a rest.

"There's a clue in the poo," said Calder, standing up and digging his hand into the pan.

I yelped and the corner of his mouth twitched.

"It's fake." He held what looked like a glob of dog doo up in his hand.

"I'll leave that to you," I said.

"It's a decoder ring." He dropped the poo back on the bed and took a closer look.

"So a patient ate and pooped out a ring?"

"Maybe to prevent Dr. Insanity from getting it."

Guffawing, I searched around, identified a couple more locks, and left Calder to his nasty ring.

I was shifting some clear, floppy plastic charts around trying to see how they best lined up when Calder spoke, his voice quiet but still audible even over the spooky sound effects and the ticking countdown on the second TV screen that hung on the wall across from the hospital bed.

"Dean doesn't love you. I know that's what's worrying you right now, and... You're right."

The fake medical charts fluttered out of my hand. "Excuse me?"

The turning of the ring in his hand made a little annoying successive tick, like the sound of a mouse scratching on the wall. "He's only ever viewed you as a necessity to his cause."

"And I suppose *you* have nothing but altruistic reasons for seducing Ivy." I huffed as I bent and angrily slapped my hands down to pick up the charts, the venom pounding out from my heart, the thunder of my heart soaring in my ears.

"It's a code for this lock," said Calder, like I cared at all just then.

Tossing the charts back where I'd found them and clenching the edges of the desk, I stared at the platitude poster taped to the plaster in front of me, the thumping growing louder as I realized there was a splatter of brownish-red ink meant to simulate blood dashed across it.

"I tried to be a good boyfriend for Ivy," continued Calder. "Really, I did. I just... My mind was otherwise occupied. I couldn't be everything she needed me to be."

Tried? So she'd had the sense to dump him, confirmed. I

still couldn't respect her, considering she knew what the fish-folk had in mind. "I bet plotting world destruction does make it hard to woo someone."

My eyes darted back to the charts as I took deep breaths, shoving that venom down, down until I had need for it.

Calder let out an audible sigh as something clicked and a drawer opened behind me. He appeared to be rifling through the contents, but I didn't turn. Instead, I shifted those charts around, a pattern becoming visible to my eyes, but my mind in no mood to get back into the distraction.

"You have no idea," he said. He went quiet for a moment. "I don't agree with it... You know. What my mom wants."

That made me turn around. "You don't want to drown the world?"

"I don't." A muscle in his jaw twitched and he looked up from a pile of gauze stained, I hoped, with fake blood to stare directly into my eyes. "And Ember, if I win, it'd be up to *me*, not her. The champion is *my* beloved, not the queen's."

"But you just told me you couldn't be much of a boyfriend. Not much of a beloved, then, is she?" I crossed the room and grabbed hold of the gauze. They didn't smell of blood, so with just a little focus, I wasn't bothered by them. "They make a pattern," I said, winding them this way and that across the bed. "I think they spell something."

"Or add up to letters." Calder strode round to my side of the bed and reached around me again, helping to straighten the gauze. He smelled of musk, of pine, of salt.

"Numbers," he said quietly, pointing to the finished arrangement.

I nodded. "One of the four-code combinations." I turned to indicate a safe in the corner, but that made it so we were face-to-face with *very* little space between us. His lips hovered over my forehead, my fingertips brushing his arm.

"I liked you," he said softly. "I've always liked you. I've had a crush on you since the moment I laid eyes on you."

The noise that came out of my throat was an octave higher

than I thought possible. My mind was whirring—with what Joe had told me just earlier today. That felt like a lifetime ago.

"Poole was so into you," Joe had said. *"Pretty much made it clear you were off-limits."*

Finally, I got my wits about me and shoved him away. "You're just saying that to mess with me." I crouched by the safe and inputted the code. It popped open and I dug my hand inside.

"I'm not," he said. "But I can see why you'd think that."

I unloaded the safe, putting another manila folder, a key, and some photos on top of the nearby desk. Bolting up to my feet, I stared at him. "If that were true, why didn't you choose me?"

"I tried." His breaths were noticeably shallow, his hands fidgeting on the hem of his jacket. "But I turned to mush around you."

Scoffing, I stared at the pile of new things next to the charts. "There's a pattern on the charts," I said, shifting them slightly so he could see.

He walked over and rested a hand atop mine over the charts. "Forget all that," he said. "Look…"

I pulled my hand away.

He didn't stop, though, shifting even slightly closer. "You seemed enamored with that bloodsucker. I didn't think I could compete." He pulled on his jacket hem again. "It's not like Ivy was super into me, but she at least wasn't lost in Dean's hypnotic eyes, you know? I had the chance with Ivy in the woods and I took it." He sighed. "I thought that winning this war was more important than my feelings. I was wrong."

"Well, I'd have to say everyone involved in this disagrees with you there." I stared at the countdown and there was a little chirp as a message appeared scrawled across the bottom of the clock.

"She must have thought we were stuck," said Calder, waving at the screen. "We haven't asked for any clues yet, but some gamemasters offer a little extra help."

I moved closer to the screen for a better look.

Calder stopped me. "I should have picked you," he said. "I should have been braver. I should have fought harder. I shouldn't have listened to my mother pressuring me—"

I ripped myself out of his grasp. "Yeah, I imagine you feel that way. Since Orin told me I have the potential to be the strongest of any of the champions." I straightened up, tugging on my sweater. "Since my *roots* on that property are deeper."

"That's not why." Calder bit his lip.

I rolled my eyes and turned around to read the clue.

We went through the motions after that, the gamemaster throwing us another clue here and there because even when we weren't making progress at all, neither of us cared to speak up and ask for help. Neither of us cared anymore.

And when the clock ran out and we failed to finish the final few puzzles, peppy Betsy walked in and flicked on the lights. "You two were doing so well!" she said, shaking her head. "But Dr. Irene Nan Sanity wins again, adding two new patients to her haunted hospital." She tapped on her tablet. "Your friends won their game. They were waiting outside, but then they said you'd just catch up."

Catch up? Where had they gone?

"What name should I put down for your team?" asked Betsy, all smiles.

I stared at Calder, but he looked down at his feet.

"Lying creep," I said, pushing past Betsy to get back to the hallway.

"Well, that's an... interesting name," said Betsy, but I was already down the hall and out into the waiting room. No one was there.

"Ember, wait," said Calder, but his voice was quiet, hesitant.

I stepped outside and barreled down the sidewalk toward the restaurant, not looking back.

CHAPTER THIRTEEN

I didn't get too many blocks before a car screeched around the corner, Dean's shining blue eyes piercing through the windshield right at me. The car ground to a jerky halt and he got out, leaving his car in the middle of the one-way street.

"Where have you been?" he snapped, but instead of heading for me, he opened the passenger's side door. I peered in to find Herbert and Ernesto in the backseat, my coat and purse between them.

I shivered.

"Get in, doll," said Dean, but his voice didn't carry its usual sweetness.

Sighing, I did as bidden and Dean shut the door, moving around to climb back into the driver's seat just as another vehicle appeared behind us and tapped its horn.

Dean signaled in the mirror his apology and started us moving, heading away from downtown. As we passed the escape room, I turned my head just slightly, hoping not to be noticed, and peered through the maze and puzzle stickers to see inside. Calder wasn't anywhere to be found and Betsy and some other employees seemed to be closing up for the night.

"Oh, *there's* a fine-looking snack." Leopold's lips smacked so loudly, I could hear it from the front seat. I turned to find him leering at Betsy, stretched up on her toes to bring some shades down over the windows, as we turned the corner.

"Can you stop doing that?" I demanded. "Stop looking at every person as a dripping bloodbag?"

"Touchy," said Leopold, leaning back in his seat. "Dames." He shook his head.

I wanted to sock him.

"Where were you?" Dean's voice had an edge to it. "You were gone for ages and Ruby went to check on you in the bathroom, but you were nowhere to be found, and then we tried you on the Ameche, but your phone was in there." He gestured over his shoulder, and it took me a second to translate his old-timey slang. "Call Minnie, tell her we found her and"—he gave me a onceover, taking his eyes off the road—"she appears unscathed."

"I just wanted to be alone," I said. "For a little bit."

"Like I said," said Leopold. "*Dames.*"

Dean shook his head and Ernesto made the call, the car near-silent except for his one-sided conversation.

Ernesto tapped Dean's shoulder. "She said they ran into some trouble when they got home. Flipping fishfolk trying to install a sprinkler system on *our own front lawn.*"

I gasped, but it turned into a hiccup and I laughed at the bizarre turn the trap had taken. They hadn't run to the vampire manor to ransack the place? To burn it to the ground and finish the job I'd inadvertently started? No, instead they were watering their lawn, to take them by surprise?

"Never mind, she said they were pest deterrents—motion-activated." Ernesto nodded into the phone and chuckled. "They ran for their cars as soon as they pulled up. The deterrents were hooked up to the hose, but they hadn't figured out we'd shut off the water line to the outside in the basement. Talk about strictly from dixie."

I wondered how the merfolk had gotten to the vampire manor so quickly, thought that maybe it had all been a ruse, that Calder's friends hadn't been in one of the escape rooms at all, but then I realized there were more than just those teens. There were plenty of fishfolk adults, though they usually seemed content to leave all the responsibility to their children.

"*If I win, it'd be up to* me," Calder had said.

"Ember?" asked Dean, his voice more quiet. "Is there something you want to talk about?"

Leopold let out a little amused grunt, and I wanted to share my feelings less than ever. "No," I replied.

"Something seems wrong," said Dean.

Leopold grabbed hold of the back of my seat and leaned forward, sniffing me, though I knew he had no need of inhaling. "She doesn't smell like she's on the rag."

"Gross," I said, waving my hand above my head and whapping it against the car ceiling. "Get away from me!"

"PMS then," he said, leaning back in his chair again.

"*Dean!*" I glared at him.

Chewing his lip, Dean pulled over at a gas station just outside of downtown. "Give Herbert a call and hitch a ride with him," he said, leaning over his shoulder to glare at Leopold in the backseat. "You, too, Ernesto. I need some alone time with the lady."

"Are you kidding me?" barked Leopold, a fiery flash in his bright blue eyes. Ernesto at least had the decency to already be climbing out, his fingers dancing over his phone screen.

"I'm not," Dean said.

Leopold made a little gesture like cracking a whip, complete with sound effect, and climbed out.

Gripping the armrest, I fought the urge to let my venom pour through my veins. It wasn't like that jerkwad was going to be that scared of my fangs, like those trick-or-treaters had been.

"Sorry about that," said Dean, backing the car up and heading down the road.

We sat in silence and I realized with a shiver that naturally, the vampires hadn't bothered turning on the car's heater. I moved to do that, and just as I turned the dial, Dean's own hand came to rest on mine. "Do you want to talk now?" he asked.

And what would I tell him? I'd run off because I'd been overwhelmed at all the literal bloodlust going through my head? That I'd met the enemy—well, *one* of the enemies—and had actually had a halfway decent time with him when he hadn't been lying out of his rear end and trying to manipulate me?

That the enemy prince had hit one of my biggest worries right on the head?

"No," I said again.

Dean clutched the steering wheel with both hands. "I'll take you home."

At first I felt relief, wanting nothing more than to climb into my soft, warm bed. Then I realized with a start that home had been the scene of the disaster earlier today. "Autumn might attack me."

"I'll sneak around back and climb up the terrace. Watch over you while you sleep."

I thought of Edward and Bella and how romantic Edward's admission of doing the same thing had seemed to be when I'd read the book as a kid. Dean was outright *telling* me he was going to do it, and his reasons were so different.

I massaged my temple. I shouldn't have wanted him to watch me sleep because he was obsessed with me. But some deep part of me *did*, the part that had grown up reading books like that and wishing, hoping to be loved that way one day.

"I'll be fine," I said, waving my hand in the air at him.

"I'm not letting you stay there alone until we figure this out."

"Are you worried because you actually care what happens to me or are you worried because if another champion kills me, you and your coven are as good as dead?"

"What a thing to say," said Dean.

"You didn't answer the question."

"Ember, of course I'm worried about you." His blue eyes flicked toward me.

"But...?"

"But what?"

"But you're also worried about keeping vampires safe."

"Shouldn't I be?"

I sighed as we headed down my street. "You don't understand."

"No, I don't, apparently." Dean parked in front of my house. The lights were all off except for a lamp Mom kept on in her and Easton's room when she read before bed. It looked like their window had been fixed already.

"Look," I said, getting out and then opening the backdoor to grab my coat and purse. "Just stick around here if you care so much about making sure I live to see another morning. But don't hang out in my room like that while I sleep. It's creepy."

Shutting the doors behind me, I turned toward the house, wiping the tears I hoped he hadn't seen me shed away.

———

"Ember, this is your third order of cheese curds and as your friend, I have to tell you, enough is enough." Journey slid in across from me in the booth in her dad and grandma's diner that I'd taken root in the last few hours after school. "I'll have to take your keys away."

"Ha ha," I said, snatching the basket she'd placed down in front of me and cradling it like *my precious*. "Now you sound like my boyfriend."

Journey cocked her head. "Okay, now you're shedding some light on the reason why you followed me here after school to drown yourself in fried, hot cheese instead of entangling your limbs with your debonair gentleman's like you usually do these days."

I glared at her and popped what was probably my thirtieth cheese curd into my mouth. "He's so... *old-fashioned*," I said, wiping my hands on a napkin from the dispenser my mom had furnished for the place. It was a little kitschy, a little vintage to suit the décor. "I've barely driven since we started dating." I gestured outside to my car. "I walked outside the house this morning and he's already opening the passenger side of his door and I jiggled my keys at him and got into mine. I'm surprised the thing still ran."

"Good for you. And he was okay with that?"

"He still trailed me to school," I said, popping another one in my mouth and washing it down with soda. "And then tried to convince me to go work"—I put the word in air quotes—"at his aunt's moving company after school when he knows and I know that's all a bunch of bull."

"Yikes. Since when are you so saucy?" Journey was on shift, but there was only one other customer in the place just then, so she leaned back in her booth and stole a few of my cheese curds, downing them in one bite. "I get what you mean about needing some space, but can you blame him for being overprotective? Considering what you told me happened yesterday?"

Yesterday. Ages ago.

I hadn't told her about Calder. I hadn't told anyone. But I'd filled her in about the news about Autumn and the little psycho's attempted murder.

"It was supposed to be over by now," I said quietly.

"And then what?" asked Journey, almost as quietly. "Have you decided what comes after?"

I shrugged. "College at least. I don't need to work at Horne Moving Company and spend all my free time lazing about the manor, sucking..." I hunched over as the only other customer passed by to get to the bathroom.

"Do you think they'll even stay here once they win? I mean, they could go *anywhere*."

"I wonder." I swirled my straw in my glass, clinking the ice against the sides. "There isn't a normal future for Dean and me, is there?"

"Does it matter?" Journey let out a great, deep sigh and

cradled her cheeks with both hands, her elbows sliding forward on the table. "How often do high school romances last anyway?" I knew she was thinking more about Devam than Dean and me.

"But with *vampires*, you'd think..."

"You're thinking of Edward and Bella, aren't you?" she asked, a flickering smile on her face. "Or Damon and Elena?"

"Well, can you blame me?" I shoved the glass away. "The only instructional manuals I have to deal with vampire boyfriends painted a bit of a rosier picture."

"Oh, stop," said Journey, nudging me across the table. "Dean is a perfect gentleman and you know it."

He was, but that didn't mean he *loved* me.

My phone buzzed and I checked the screen. It was Dean asking me to check in.

I'm fine, I typed. *Hanging with Journey.* I shoved the phone back into my purse.

"Baby!" shouted Journey's dad from behind the counter. "You know you're on the clock, right, and I don't pay employees to goof off with friends? Come clean the grill!"

Journey rolled her eyes and stood. "Maybe if he paid employees more than the bare minimum, he'd actually *have* some to yell at besides me."

I sat alone for a bit, the other customer walking past and throwing down some cash to pay his bill before leaving the place. As his black pickup drove away, the spot he'd vacated left a choice view of Orin's bookstore down the road. There were no cars there, and I knew Orin only kept it open on a whim. I wondered if he'd even be so easy to find now that he'd dragged a little kid into this.

I wondered if there was any way to convince him to get Autumn to drop out of the battle with that orb—was he the one who had it? No, the merfolk did last I knew.

Did I ask Calder to give it to me, with the aim of getting Autumn to drop out? Wasn't that Ivy's aim as well?

But then... There would be no victor in this battle, and this war would just go on and on and on until the next time there were three kids in that house.

Mom was pregnant, but would she really have another after that?

I grabbed my purse and fumbled through it for some money. I couldn't believe I'd been considering calling *Calder* for anything, even if it was all *business*-related, so to speak.

Quickly shouting goodbye toward the back of the restaurant, I headed outside and drove my car slowly down the road to The Hollow Tree.

CHAPTER FOURTEEN

I didn't expect the door to the used bookstore to actually open. So I didn't know what I'd expected then. For this to be a dead end, to go home, to go back to the arms of my overprotective vampire who kept me at arm's length.

But it did open, the jingle of the overhead bell ringing out in the silence.

A furry cat opened one eye from the top of a bookshelf bathed in the last sunbeam of the day, her tail flicking up dust mites in the air.

"Blimey." Orin strolled out from the backroom behind the counter, a pair of glasses on his face that he pulled off and tucked into his shirt pocket. "You're not who I was expecting."

"And who, exactly, *were* you expecting?"

"Well, that doesn't matter right now, does it?"

"We need to talk."

He gestured between an aisle of books toward the pair of reading sofas in the back. "Shall we? You can never be too comfortable when discussing important matters, I always say."

Clutching my purse in front of me, I shuffled after him, the prattling he did about the place being in need of a good dusting, but how it was hard to find good help these days, mostly going over my head as I retreated toward the back and took a seat across from him. I kept my legs crossed tightly at the ankle, the purse on my lap, leaning forward so I was ready to jump at the drop of a hat. Orin leaned back in the chair and practically melted into it.

"So, what are you on about?" he asked.

"The orb," I said. "Do the merfolk still have it?"

"Hmm," said Orin, stroking his chin. "I didn't expect you to be ready to drop out at this juncture."

"It's not for me." The words tumbled from my lips quickly —*too* quickly.

"Are you sure about that?" Orin's eyebrow arched. There were traces of green even amongst the dark hair there. Amongst his eyelashes, too, the closer I looked at him. He smirked. "I know I'm handsome, but don't let my beauty distract you."

My gaze darted to my feet. "I want Autumn to drop out."

"And you think she would, given the opportunity?"

My mouth opened and closed, then opened again. "See, this is why it's not *fair* that you're a prince in this conflict. You can't be a third-party *observer* and then—"

"Also be a third combatant?" He leaned forward, threading his fingers together. "Oh, but I can, little girl. Do you think I was doing this referee thing for a laugh? You don't get owt for nowt. There's no one who can stop me."

Something cold washed over me, and it wasn't just in my head. A literal breeze seemed to move through the dusty bookstore, ruffling my hair.

That didn't seem fair, either. The vampire and merman princes each had powers—I assumed Calder did—but they didn't extend to fire and ice. Why did Orin have mind control abilities as well as some sort of apparent slight mastery of the wind?

He was right. No one could stop him. And here I was, willingly walking right into the lion's den.

I stood quickly.

"Now, hold on a minute," said Orin, leaning back and clutching the armrests. "I didn't say I *didn't* have the orb."

"So you do?"

"I didn't say I didn't have it. I didn't say I did."

Taking a deep breath, I tried to stop myself from throttling him. "If you had it, would you let your champion drop out?"

He shrugged. "*She* would have no interest in dropping out, yeah? And I have no interest in forcing anyone to change their mind, even if I *could.*" He tapped the side of his temple.

"You didn't use any of those powers to convince Autumn to be your champion?"

"Please." Orin looked affronted and fanned himself lazily with one hand. "You think I could cheat the consummate lands out of a proper, willing champion like that? Not worth the risk. Besides, kids are easy to manipulate, especially creative ones—no magic needed."

Pinching my lips to bite back a reply, I turned on my heel and started walking toward the door.

"Maybe *you* want the orb to use for yourself," he shouted after me. "You know, you wouldn't be the first vampire mermaid."

I halted. "What?" I spun on my heel.

Orin was rubbing his chin, staring off into space. "Or would it be a mermaid vampire? Oh, you know what, you *would* be the first vampire mermaid. But a vampire mer*man* on the other hand..."

"I don't know what you're talking about!"

"Don't you? Not entertaining thoughts about swapping spit with the other side? Getting a little of both worlds?"

"*No!*" My voice was so loud, the little bookstore cat jumped from her perch and trotted off toward the backroom.

"You're scaring Feilia," said Orin, shaking his head. "Girl does me a favor and keeps other little pests out of this place, all right? Don't be disturbing her."

"I couldn't care less about your pest problem right now."

My toes tapped impatiently on the hard floor. "Why would you even call me a vampire mermaid? It was..." I bit my tongue. He knew too much as it was, and he wasn't someone to turn to for help. He was enemy number two. Or maybe even number one.

"It was Ivy you tried to turn into one, yeah?" Orin got up and shuffled closer, sticking both hands into his oversized cardigan pockets. "But you didn't get enough venom into her body." Pointing at his neck, he whirled one finger around it as he neared. "But it's in there. It's swirling in there, like a little niggling feeling at the back of her mind." He grinned. "So at least you didn't make a dog's dinner out of it."

I took a careful step back, my back running up against the bookshelf.

"But, see, maybe you're wishing you could be bitten by a fish and have some sort of saltwater running through *your* veins, nagging at you that maybe the grass is greener on the other side. But it's not so simple as that, is it? Not that you know of. *You* would have to be convinced to come over of your complete and total volition."

"I don't know where you're getting *that* idea..." My heart thundered. Calder's little trick. He was *trying* to get me to fall for him. As if I could fall for someone who wanted to flood the world! Unless... Unless he wasn't lying about him deciding not to do that if he were to win.

But no. I wasn't stupid enough to trust him.

"So you're saying you know something about merfolk strategy?" I asked. "And you're telling me this because...?"

"I'm not telling you anything you don't already know." He brushed past me, heading toward the cashier's counter. "Just spelling things out is all. And before any of you rotting undead or slimy seafood nutters get any ideas, the faefolk have no interest in producing any sort of hybrid."

Hybrids. Maybe there was more point to a vampire mermaid than making it so Ivy would want to surrender and not fight her own kind. Maybe—now that we knew there were three parties in this fight—two had to join against one.

At least until the third was out of the running.

But Dean and Minnie... They'd never go for it. Would they?

The bell over the door jangled and my purse slid right off my arm as I whipped toward the sound. It wasn't a threat or a vampire boyfriend attempting to wrangle me back to the manor. It *was* a familiar face, though.

"Evening, love," said Orin. He bopped up from beneath the counter, a thick hardcover in hand, like he'd anticipated her walking in. He *had* said I hadn't been whom he'd expected.

"Hi," said Raelynn quietly, wriggling her fingers at me and rushing toward the counter.

It was nice to see her out and about after the mess on Halloween. Even if it was still in proximity to the world of champions and princes and betrayal and all that good stuff.

"Do you have it?" she asked Orin.

"I do, but this is my only copy. Who said I had to sell it to you?" Orin looked all serious and Raelynn shirked back, clearly dejected. "Relax, love. Only pulling your leg, all right?"

Orin started chuckling and punched a price into the register. Of course this dusty place wouldn't have an electronic scanner.

I was curious to see what Raelynn might have bought, but that was the least important thing I had to consider just then. Pestering Orin had clearly gotten me nowhere. My phone buzzed and I fished it out of my pocket. Dean was asking where I was and if I'd join him for dinner.

No, I typed into the phone. *Kind of full. Besides, I haven't eaten at home in ages, so I'm going to today. Autumn's at her mom's.*

Dean started typing a reply and then hesitated. As I was staring at it waiting to see what he might say—if he would fight for me to spend more time with him, if he would tell me how this afternoon apart, our first full one since getting together, would be too much for him—Raelynn appeared directly in front of me.

"Are you headed to the Hornes'?" she asked, causing me to

nearly jump out of my skin. Her eyes were bulging, little lines of red throughout the whites.

I took a closer look at the paper bag in her hand, but I couldn't see what kind of book she'd bought.

"No," I said, clearing my throat. "I've got other plans today."

"Oh," said Raelynn. Her face scrunched together as if working up the courage to say something. "I... I broke up with my girlfriend." That explained the bloodshot eyes.

"Oh?" I said, slipping my phone into my purse. This felt rather out of the blue. We knew each other, but we weren't super close. But even so, I could lend an ear for a minute if that was what she wanted. I knew I'd want one if I ever broke up with Dean. My throat went dry. "I'm sorry to hear." I remembered her girlfriend—*Ivy*'s friend—at the Halloween party. She certainly hadn't seemed happy to be there.

To be honest, even before I'd had any reason to spend time with Lyric, I'd been kind of annoyed by her. She just rubbed me the wrong way. And besides, Raelynn was a good student. She could do better than a girl who seemed to care more about clothes and sports than grades.

"She didn't understand," said Raelynn quietly. She grabbed my hand and squeezed it. "Please. You have to go with me. Okay?" Her smile looked rather strained. Like she was an alien attempting to grin for the first time in her life.

The lump in my throat felt like it was going to jump out of me for a second. She'd only been bitten *once*, Dean had assured me. It had been the only way to guarantee she'd be cool with the experience and not run straight to the cops as soon as she was let go.

But she'd only been exposed to the coven at all because Minnie had ordered *my dad* and several of the others to take her as some sort of reassurance against Ivy. Since they'd taken Journey to lure me into a trap, I hadn't felt *too* bad about it at first. Now, staring at the eager, inflamed eyes of this girl in front of me, it was time for the guilt and shame to come knocking.

"Listen, Raelynn—" I started.

"You can call me 'Rae,'" she said, her face brightening. "We're friends, right? You'll go with me to the Hornes'." There was still the *tiredness* weighing heavily on those puffy eyes, though, that told me that *something was very wrong here*. Post-breakup jitters didn't quite account for her eagerness to go to Dean's.

"Rae, you don't want to hang out with..." I lowered my voice to whisper, even though only Orin was within earshot. "*Vampires.*"

"I do!" said Raelynn loudly, as if talking about "mythical" creatures publicly was a very normal thing to do. She rifled through her paper bag and drew out what she'd come here to purchase. It was a book about vampire mythology, and it looked quite old, like it had been written long, long before the internet was available to answer all of the questions an aspiring vampire might need and then some.

But I could see Journey searching down some old book like it was the *original* authority on the matter, like holding it in your hand instead of reading it transcribed online because of public domain would lend more weight to its importance. I often got the feeling, too. It *did* seem to score brownie points with teachers.

But scoring brownie points was not something Raelynn needed to concern herself with in this endeavor.

"All of that doesn't even apply to the Hornes," I said, shaking my head. Some distance away, Orin let out a little tittering chuckle before disappearing into the backroom.

"I know," said Raelynn, dropping the book back into the bag. "They can go out in sunlight, for starters. And I don't know if garlic does anything to them. And I've *seen* their reflections. And do they feel the compulsion to count items like stones or sticks that scatter in front of them?"

That was a new one to me. "What? I... I don't know. Come

on," I said, speaking in a hushed voice and nodding toward the door. "Don't trust this bookseller, okay?"

"Is he part of it?" asked Raelynn, a fire lighting up her eyes. "Is he a bloodbag or something?" She giggled. It seemed so weird to hear those words coming out of her mouth.

I held the door open for her, not budging until she stepped through.

"I wanted to ask you if they need to be invited to enter private premises," said Raelynn, rattling off her objective like a reporter for the school newspaper.

The door jangled as it shut behind her. "I don't know," I admitted. I thought back to the first time I'd met Dean—well, he'd been hired to move furniture and boxes into my house, so presumably someone had invited him and his fellow vampires inside. But it wasn't like anyone invited him to school or restaurants or stores—or was it only households? I shook my head. This girl was getting me thinking about the wrong things.

"They're not at all what I expected," said Raelynn, pulling her book out and flipping through it.

The comment stung hard. Not that I'd expected them to *sparkle*—not really—but the girl kind of had a point. "I know. Kind of disappointing really." A flittering smile danced across my lips.

"Oh, no, not at all!" said Raelynn, looking up from the book. "I didn't mean that. If anything, they're even more fascinating. What's with the obsession with old-timey stuff—but not, like, Gothic or Victorian era stuff like you'd expect?"

Shrugging, I walked down the couple of steps to the gravel parking lot. "Dean told me most of them turned in the 1940s, during and after World War II. They just sort of... stuck with how they liked things back then."

"Yet they still use modern phones and, like, that record player they use? It's a retro model. Totally made in the last decade. There are optional phone hookups for streaming music, too."

"When exactly did you have time to check out the *record player*?" I asked, genuinely amused. I leaned against the hood of my car.

"Last weekend," she said. The weekend she'd been... *kidnapped*. I knew that making her a little enamored with the experience would be necessary to prevent her from going to the cops with exactly what had happened, but I was definitely beginning to see the vampires had worked a *little* too hard to convince her it was all a great thing. Perhaps she'd gotten too much venom in her bite.

Shuffling my toes in the gravel, I stared down at the specks of white dotting my dark shoes. "Raelynn..."

A car drove by on the road and drew my attention.

When I turned around, Raelynn had dropped her bag and opened the door to her car next to mine.

"Sorry," she said, turning back around. In her hand she had some sort of... Taser?

"Wait, what are you—?"

She Tased me, and my eyes were still swimming as she dragged me into her car.

CHAPTER FIFTEEN

"You have to understand," said Raelynn. "I had plans. Big plans. My mom was the first woman in her family to go to college, and I *had* to keep that up, you know? She became an accountant, but I was going to go bigger. Become a lawyer."

My arm felt like it was on fire, like I'd been struck by lightning there—and it certainly wasn't the fire I could summon. I felt dizzy. Nauseous. I started retching and slammed a hand against the dashboard to steady myself, vaguely reminding myself I didn't recognize this vehicle interior.

"You doing okay?" asked Raelynn from beside me. She was driving. We were moving. Going somewhere.

"*No*," I managed. My jaw hurt. My bones hurt. "You *attacked* me."

"I wasn't sure if you would come along if I asked," she said, as if that explained everything.

"What are we—Where are we...?" I couldn't form the words properly. "I could have *died*," I said instead.

"You're young and healthy... I think?" Her voice sounded *so* reassuring. "My dad's a cop; I took it from him. I asked him once, and he said they try to guess whether or not a suspect can handle it before they use it."

"Suspect...?" I said. "You *Tased* me," I babbled. The world was spinning. Nothing came out of my throat when I heaved, though.

"You're *fine*," she spat out. "And it was a stun gun, not a Taser."

Oh, *sorry*.

"Look, okay, so I went to the Hornes' place this morning." She was prattling again. "*Before* school. Like, if my mom ever hears that I skipped, she would *flip* and get my *abuelita* on the phone from Puerto Rico to rip me a new one."

I didn't *care* about that. I didn't *care* about any of this.

"But I just thought... Maybe a little bloodletting before I went? To give me a boost of energy?"

"What are you saying?" I asked. We stopped suddenly and the seatbelt I didn't remember putting on dug tightly across my chest.

"So they were, like, *okay*, but only if you do us a favor and keep an eye on Ember today? Because she *wants some space*." Raelynn said that like it was unreasonable and glanced my way, her face fuzzy. "Principal Horne said it like that. And I get it. I mean, well, I didn't *always* get it. I thought couples should spend all the time together that they could, but then this happened and I get what Lyric used to mean when she said I was being clingy. She is *so* clingy right now. Or she *was* until I sent her packing." She nodded as she faced forward, gripping the steering wheel. "Hey, do you need some air? You look dizzy."

The window beside me rolled down, and I leaned into it, the cold, cold air like a balm to my face.

"Anyway." Raelynn rambled on and we turned suddenly, my face pushing forward into the breeze. "But... so they're worried about you, I guess? I don't get exactly what's going on, but Devam was there, too, and he explained that you're fighting Ivy Sheppard? Like *literally* fighting her? Oh my goodness, I forgot she's *your* *step-sister* now, isn't she? What's up with that? Do you guys literally punch each other?"

This was the most I'd ever heard the girl speak and we

weren't total strangers or anything. She and Journey got along well, and we'd done some group class projects together.

"Anyway, so they asked if I could make sure you went to their place tonight somehow," she continued. "I mean, they didn't exactly *say*, 'Steal your dad's stun gun and then knock her out and drag her there if need be,' but they made it clear I had to bring you if I wanted to go, so here we are."

"Here we are where?" I asked, my mind slowly but surely gaining some clarity.

Raelynn gestured around her. "You. Me. On the way to some vampires." She laughed manically. "I can't tell you, though, like, I *still* should really get some homework done tonight because just in case this doesn't work out, I need to go to college, obviously. And my parents need to *think* I plan to go to college."

"If what doesn't...?" I shook my head, the cold air from the window suddenly making me shiver. "Raelynn, are you hoping to become a vampire?"

I couldn't say why I hadn't figured it out earlier. Case in point, me being kidnapped and dragged to a vampire manor.

Like what had been done to her. Touché, universe. Touché.

"Well, don't you?" she asked.

I thought about what was best to say, then went for the truth. "No."

"You don't want to be a vampire?" Raelynn asked the question like she thought I'd passed up the chance to inherit a billion dollars.

"I don't," I said aloud, and I realized I meant it.

What did I want? I wanted to be with my vampire boyfriend. But did that mean I'd have to become a vampire to do it? I ran my tongue across my incisors, then felt one growing slightly as I focused on the smell of *blood*, the feel of it in my nostrils. Did I have to become a vampire completely? Would I always be able to switch back and forth like this, even if I won this fight?

I ran a hand over my forehead and there was something

sticky and crusty along my hairline on one side. I looked down and saw my fingertips dotted in blood. "Did I hit my head...?"

Raelynn winced, air sucking through her teeth. "I might have bumped it when I was dragging you in here, but you're fine."

"Raelynn, are you *hearing* yourself?" I asked. "You're not even *thinking* straight."

My heart thundered, the feel of the venom *thriving* in my bloodstream pushing the heart beat to slow, to cease, my heart trying valiantly to stop it. Feeling nauseous again, I leaned forward, but the smell of my own blood danced in my nostrils and my fangs extended, my throat hissing as my eyes clenched against the light of the setting sun.

"What's happening to you?" shrieked Raelynn. "That is *not* a side effect of a stun gun." She slammed on the brakes, the seatbelt digging against me again, but it didn't hurt this time. Then she quickly pulled the car off somewhere—I didn't know. I couldn't think. I couldn't see. I didn't have sunglasses with me and keeping my eyes open sent sizzling fire to the membranes of my eyeballs.

Raelynn stopped again and put the car in park, unclicking her seatbelt. "I'll call an ambulance—no, maybe I should call the Hornes."

It sounded like she was fumbling with her phone. "I'll let them know where we are—"

The *thrum* of the beat of her heart, the lifeblood in her veins. I could hear it. My eyes closed, my throat parched, I could *sense* it even without her bleeding out.

Unbuckling my seatbelt, I launched at her, my fangs bared, sensing more than seeing where to bite—where to sink my teeth into the flesh along her neck.

———

The warm, inviting taste of the liquid lingered on my tongue, on my lips. The sun had set and at some point, I'd opened my eyes, but I wasn't seeing anything, wasn't looking at what I was *seeing*, not really. This was all a dream. All there was was the sucking of my lips against the increasing coldness of the flesh beneath it, the pull of the blood in my throat. The venom burned as it left through my teeth into her skin—it burned as I felt it come back, back into my throat through the blood I drank.

"Ember, doll, that's enough," said someone nearby. Quietly. Softly.

A gentle tug on my shoulder. A cold hand approaching my lips, cradling my fangs and *plucking* them from my snack. From my treat.

I hissed at the threat, baring my fangs at it. But it offered me no such quenching. No blood.

Dean. He maneuvered carefully, guiding me out of the car and cradling me in his arms. Voices echoed in the darkness and more shadows moved in to take my place in the car.

Dean rocked me and soothed me, uttering nothing but *shh* as if I were making noises, as if I needed to be *calmed*.

I didn't need to be calmed. I needed blood. More blood. More fire in my throat.

Only I... I couldn't sense any nearby. I looked around. Where were we? There were the woods to our left and gravel beneath our feet. I realized we were at one of the little off-shoot parking areas where people could wander off into the woods for hiking or biking or whatever it was that called them to those trees.

The trees were half-bare by now, the ground littered in their fallen leaves, their orange and yellow and red death throes.

"She turned," said an airy voice. Zelda, I thought.

Leopold swore and Ernesto said a prayer quickly beneath his teeth. I giggled. A vampire saying a *prayer*.

"Minnie isn't going to like this." Herbert. "That girl has family. People who'd miss her."

"And what about the deal?" asked Leopold. His voice was always sharp and harsh.

Deal? Miss her...? I felt unsteady on my feet, the tree trunks swaying around me. *Miss who?*

With a wrenching bout of clarity, my fangs retreated, taking the venom with it, my heart thumping madly to life. My legs gave out and Dean's arms were all that held me aloft.

"Hey, ladies and gents and all you good people," said an upbeat, cheery voice with a touch of a cockney accent. "Nice and chilly night, eh?"

Orin strolled down the road and past us toward the path leading into the woods, his hands in his pockets and a book tucked under his arm. He paused when he stared into the open door of Raelynn's car. "Oof," he said, his face twisting as if in pain. "That's going to be hard to explain away, isn't it?" He shuffled closer to the car. "Is she *dead?*" He asked the question with all the curiosity of a child wondering if there were cookies in their mom's grocery bag.

I felt sick. I vomited right on Dean's shirt and he didn't even flinch, instead patting my back.

"She's not dead," snapped another familiar voice. Ruby. The "nurse."

My heart soared. She knew something about health. She could save her.

"Ember used far, far too much venom. She's one of us now," said Ruby instead. "It'll just take her a little while to wake up."

I vomited again.

"Hmm," said Orin, leaning back. "Undead is still dead, love, I'm afraid. This is some serious business."

"We haven't turned a single person since this war began," added Leopold, stomping toward the faery-observer-turned-enemy-prince. "We've upheld our part of the deal for decades."

"Yeah, and now you haven't," said Orin. He *tsked.* "Turning an innocent. She had no idea what she was getting into."

"This girl definitely wanted to join us," said Zelda, her voice airy and soft.

"Just a taste of venom and you upend her whole life. Such a pity." Orin's curls bounced as he shook his head.

"We haven't broken any rules," said Dean beside me. It was the first time he'd spoken up in a while. "*We* haven't *killed* any humans at all, really. It was our champion."

My breath caught in my throat and I struggled for air, struggled and struggled. I fell with such a heaviness that not even Dean could keep me standing, and he settled for sliding down to the pavement with me.

Orin pursed his lips. "Relying on a technicality then, eh? Okay, well, I feel generous." He trotted over to me and looked down, then shook his head, as if he were witnessing a dirty mongrel hit by a car die on the side of the road. "Such a pity. But tomorrow's a new day. Best clean yourself up." He pulled a handkerchief from his pocket and pointed to his jaw and down his throat. "Got something on your face, love." Chuckling, he started walking backward toward the woods. "I'm going to leave this mess to *you lot*... Should be fun." His eyebrows wriggled before he vanished behind the trees, never once turning around to watch where he was going.

Sobbing, I dry-heaved, pressing the handkerchief to my mouth. It came back dyed in blood. Dried blood. Not my blood.

"Well, we did lament that Minnie seemed to be choosing *old* blood to join the coven first," said Herbert unhelpfully. "It'll be nice to have a girl our age, right?"

Their age?

I stared out in the darkness, up at the sea of bright blue eyes blinking back at me.

They hadn't been *our* age in decades. But they, like Raelynn, would never be anything but young. Ever again.

I fainted.

CHAPTER SIXTEEN

I should have stayed in bed beneath my comforter for all the good going through the motions was doing me. But Dean insisted I try. And I was tired of resisting.

That meant I let him watch over me at night, too, without my mom knowing. It wasn't romantic. He was more like a bodyguard.

And in my state, I was in no mood to put up a fight should Ivy or Autumn come knocking.

I'd barely seen Ivy—not that I would at school or home these days. Autumn was still supposed to live with us half the week, so she came back, but she seemed kowtowed whenever she peeked in on me and found Dean standing there, framed in the dim glow of the Christmas lights hanging over my bed year-round. She didn't even tell Mom what she'd seen. She'd gotten off with a grounding after last week's shenanigans that hadn't seemed to affect her. The girl liked playing with her toys without anyone else regardless.

Now I was back at school for the second day this week, staring blankly at some of the student council members who were decorating a dingy wall between lockers with turkey and cornucopia cut-outs. I was seated outside the principal's office, where Dean had instructed me to sit in view of two of his "aunts." The human secretary never questioned why I was just sitting there after I told her I was waiting for someone, but she did keep looking at me askance as she answered phone calls, typed on her computer, and dealt with the various students straggling in.

School was over for the day, but I couldn't recite any of my lessons if someone had paid me to.

"Hey, Goodwin."

Joe was standing in front of the secretary with a few tardy slips in his hand, the woman already taking them from him and typing into her computer. "Seeing if I can get some of these excused on account of swim practice making me late all the time."

"Perhaps if you *know* you need extra time, Mr. Cruz, you would allow yourself said extra time," said the secretary. "None of your teammates have problems getting to class on time."

"None of my teammates have this head of hair," he said, fluffing at his dark coif.

The secretary muttered something under her breath and kept typing. "I'm afraid you've exceeded the allowable number of tardies, Mr. Cruz. That requires an in-school suspension to make up the time."

"Gimme a break!" he shouted, almost making going-through-the-motions me jump. "I'm only five minutes late."

"Per day." The woman handed the slips back to him. "Now it's time to pay the piper. Tomorrow, report to Room 35C at 8 A.M. *sharp* or face the prospect of a second in-school suspension. Good day."

Joe groaned and snatched the stack of papers back, but instead of shuffling to the door, he meandered over to the line of chairs beside me. "Other than my mom having a fit," he said quietly as he sat down, "I actually couldn't care less. A day off from classes and a chance to catch up with schoolwork? Yes, please."

"It's a *punishment*," I said quietly.

"Maybe for a goody two-shoes like you."

I didn't feel like a "goody two-shoes" anymore.

He leaned back in the chair, dropping his backpack to his feet, getting comfortable. I would have wondered why if my brain cared to wonder anything anymore.

"Speaking of the smart club, you know Kelly, right?"

For a second, my numb mind sorted through the Kellys in our grade, but then I hit on it: Raelynn Kelly. The person making everyone chatter these days.

Joe didn't wait for me to acknowledge anything he'd said. "People say she, like, contracted some disease in that bus accident she and the Model U.N. team were in a couple of weekends ago. And I'm, like, how do you get a *disease* from an accident? But it has to do with her blood and stuff. Maybe she bled too much."

It had to do with her blood all right.

"And she was acting really weird all last week. She dumped her girlfriend, and I mean, who dumps Lyric Penham? That girl is *hot*, lean and tall and athletic, just how I like 'em. No offense." He nudged my arm with his elbow, as if I'd take any. "Hot is hot regardless." He winked. "Anyway, I know you're good friends with Journey, so I wondered if she said anything to you about it."

It took me a second of silence to respond, the click of the secretary's keys on her keyboard filling the space between us. "About what?"

Joe scoffed. "The accident! Kelly being all weird afterward and stuff." He leaned forward and whispered. "The freaky blood disease that's hospitalized her in some specialty clinic upstate."

I wasn't sure how *that* much had leaked to the general school population. That was how Minnie had decided we'd handle it. Not by making her disappear from her friends' and family's lives, but by making it seem like she'd come down with some rare disease treated only by the clinic owned by a man she'd quickly seduced over the weekend in time to become a bloodbag. It wasn't upstate—that much had been exaggerated by whatever gossip machine was at work—and the plan had counted on the *enthusiastic* participation of Raelynn herself. The call to her parents that she was spending the weekend at a friend's. The call to them a few days later to meet her at the doctor's clinic. The newly-developed light sensitivity, the poor blood circulation to explain her coldness to the touch.

Her inpatient hospitalization consisted of Raelynn scrambling to get to the clinic every time her mom or dad or a friend signed up for visiting hours ahead of time. Blood diseases carried increased risk of infection, so visiting hours had to be carefully controlled, they'd said.

Meanwhile, Raelynn was spending most of her time at Horne manor learning all about how to properly quench her thirst without overdoing it.

Like I had.

When I'd killed her.

A girl stepped out of the nurse's office, dark circles under her eyes and her hand on her stomach. I didn't need either of that, though, to smell the scent of iron in the air and know she was in the middle of that time of the month. Ruby stepped out the open door after her and sent a look my way. "Do you need something, young man?" she asked.

Joe straightened bolt-upright at the purr of the seductress' husky voice. "No, ma'am." His heart was beating so wildly, it was echoing in my venom-filled ears. I had to cover them both and focus on letting my mind go blank to get it to calm down.

Ruby stepped toward me. "What about you?"

"I'm fine," I snapped.

Ruby pursed her lips and went back inside the nurse's office, leaving the door open.

"Oh, hey, so remember when I was telling you about Poole last week and his thing for you?" Joe asked out of nowhere. His heart had slowed somewhat and I lowered my hands from my ears.

"I ran into him over the weekend," he continued, digging his phone out of his back pocket and scrolling through it. "I told him you were still attached to the hip to pasty boy, and *he* told me he and your step-sister were 'just friends' now." He air quoted the "just friends" with one hand. "Anyway, he was all, like, weirdly insistent on shaking my hand and held it an unnaturally long time as he sort of tuned out, which was weird and something I definitely took note of, but you know, Central guys are a little weird. Must be something in the water. I've learned that at swim meets—oh, he quit the swim team at Central! I couldn't believe it."

Joe was talking so quickly, my sluggish mind couldn't keep up. But I zeroed in on one thing he'd said—the abnormally long handshake, the glazed-over eyes. When Journey and I had asked Ivy to read our minds—we'd just *guessed* she could do something like that because she'd known about my dad joining the vampires, and it was either that or astute spy work, though the latter had seemed totally possible at first—she'd grabbed me and her eyes had gone kind of foggy. She'd also told us mindreading didn't "work" a specific way, totally confirming it did work *some* way.

Merfolk could probably read minds, but they had to hold you to do it. I would totally give myself some points for figuring that out, but I didn't care anymore.

But so Calder had read Joe's mind. For some reason.

Joe was still talking. "He actually asked me for your number!" That made me snap to attention. "And I was like, dude, first off, give up. Secondly, why can't you ask your just-friend-ex or whatever for her number?"

"You *have* my number?" I asked, feeling dizzy.

Joe clutched a hand to his heart. "I'm hurt, Goodwin. You gave it to me for a class project, remember?"

"No..." It wasn't like he ever texted me. Huh. Maybe he had for a project over a year ago we'd done together.

"Anyway, don't worry, I didn't give it to him," said Joe. "Dude was acting too weird. 'I can't get it from Ivy. She'll know what I'm up to.'" He mocked Calder's voice in a way that didn't sound like Calder at all. "So I was like, 'Yeah, I guess so. Anyway, nice seeing you.'"

Ivy would know what he was up to? What *was* he up to?

"Hey, Ember," said Journey.

I looked up to see her lingering in the doorway. Her smile was faltering, though she tried to put on a brave face. She knew what had happened, had been at the manor for much of the aftermath. "Dean's back from..." *The clinic*, she probably wanted to say, but her eyes darted to Joe. Dean had been part of the team smoothing over the issues concerning Raelynn's family getting used to Raelynn's new "blood disease." I'd asked him to help out, to make me feel better about the whole thing. And maybe just a small part of me also wanted some breathing room from him once in a while, even if it was only allowed in the proximity of two of his aunts.

"Hey, Slowe," said Joe, running a hand through his precious hair. He turned on the charm for my best friend.

"I gotta go," I said, standing and shuffling over toward Journey.

"You forgot your bag," said Joe, bringing it over to me and joining us as we stepped through the hallways. I took it from him without a word, the weight of it so burdensome in my hand. Journey and I walked quietly, somberly. Joe didn't seem to notice, prattling all the way.

"I've got to go," he said at last, shifting his backpack up his shoulder and giving us a salute. "Tell Kelly to get well soon if you see her."

"Is he talking about Raelynn?" asked Journey softly. She stared at the floor.

"Yeah." I looked at the scuff marks and the grime along with her.

"Devam is... *angry*," she said after a minute.

We hadn't really talked about her problems in days. Mine had definitely eclipsed them.

"He's not in any danger of turning," I said. "What

happened with Raelynn and me was a freak accident, complicated by the fact that she—"

"No, I mean, he *wanted* to turn. He outright told me. He's mad Raelynn turned first when he's 'been a bloodbag' longer." Her voice went especially quiet on those last few words, though the hallways were largely empty.

I realized then that that was what Journey had been afraid of all along. Devam getting too *hooked* on the quenchings, getting too caught up in this world of vampires—wanting to leave reality behind, to forge a new reality.

One he'd never have even known about if I hadn't stupidly invited them to Dean's house at Homecoming—or if I hadn't lost control of my *thirst* then.

My heart was thundering once more, the warmth spreading from my hand, meeting up with the chill of the venom moving throughout my body.

"Em?" Journey's hand on my shoulder snapped me back to the moment.

"I'm sorry," I whispered, pushing all thoughts of venom and fire away.

"I don't know what to do anymore," said Journey. "He wants me to turn with him. Said they've proven with Raelynn they can do it now, even if you have families who'd miss you—"

"Three teens coming down with the same rare blood disease would be an epidemic," I said. "Might draw national press Minnie wouldn't like."

"Fudge the press," said Journey. "*I* don't want to become a vampire!"

"Of course. I didn't think you did, not after everything you've seen—"

"Yeah, and that's half of it. Devam is just in la-la land, always spending time at that manor—"

"Like my dad."

"Like your dad." She nodded. "But your dad at least has, um, *done* some things to help in this fight. I've *been smack-dab in the middle of it.* Devam doesn't know anything of the danger. And I feel like..." Journey bit her lip.

"You feel like what?" I prompted.

"I just feel like somehow this guy has become my responsibility, like I'm his last tether back to the real world, to who he used to be. I mean, he sometimes hangs out with all his old friends, but mostly only on *my* urging, only with me. And it's, like, I really liked him—I *like* him—but we were only dating a short while before..." She couldn't bring herself to say more.

"I ruined the good thing you had going," I said.

"You didn't ruin it," she said, shaking her head, though it seemed her heart wasn't fully in the denial. "Maybe it's just in his blood. This kind of *addictive* personality. If it wasn't venom, it'd be alcohol or drugs or driving recklessly or..."

My phone buzzed and I dug it out of the front flap of my backpack. "Dean's probably wondering where I am. Are you headed to the manor with us today?"

"I have to," she said, sighing audibly. "Devam already left as soon as school ended. I'm telling you, if Minnie didn't *kick him out* for trying to show up on school days, he'd never leave. Or he'd head to the moving company office or wherever he could be near vampires all day." Her eyes darted down the hallway to the open janitorial closet and I knew she was looking for Herbert, who sometimes showed up as the school janitor. The ridiculously handsome school janitor with sunglasses that made all the heads turn.

Glancing on the phone, I realized it wasn't Dean. *Don't ask me how I got your number*, wrote an unknown number. *But I need to talk to you. I know what you did. I can guess how you must feel.*

I have a way to undo it. The only possible way to make Raelynn Kelly a human being again.

It was signed "C."

CHAPTER SEVENTEEN

"**S**he's doing great." Dean gripped the steering wheel and were it not for the paleness of his skin, his knuckles would probably be turning white. "She's fine, Ember. You need to tell yourself that. Embrace who you are. Embrace what happened."

Embrace the fact that I'd killed someone? Sure. That would be *so* easy.

My mind kept turning over the message from "C," who no doubt had used his mindreading powers to get my number from Joe, though I doubt Joe knew it offhand. It didn't matter. I didn't really care at all about merfolk manipulations or whatever it was they could do. My life had been strangely merfolk-free these past few days. Like the battle had been put on hold while I'd tried to sort my mess out.

Then again, it could be a trap. What could the merman prince who wanted to *flood the world* do to make a vampire un-undead?

"Ember?" asked Journey from behind me in Dean's backseat. "You okay?" She sounded nearly as glum as I felt.

I shook my head and said nothing, gripping my phone in my jacket pocket. I'd deleted the message, but I'd put the number in my contacts under "You Know Who." Some small part of me couldn't entirely throw out the idea of a solution to what I'd done.

"We're here," said Dean, putting his car in park in front of his manor and shutting off the engine. I hadn't even been observing where we'd been going.

"I thought we were going to the office first," I said. "Don't you have a move tomorrow to get ready for?"

"The other guys are handling it." Dean reached over and squeezed my hand in my lap. The hand not guiltily stroking the phone in my pocket. "I thought it might be good for you to... spend some time with her."

"With the girl I ate to death? Sure." I ripped my hand from Dean's and unbuckled my seatbelt, getting out of the car without waiting for him to open it. He scrambled to catch up, stopping to open the door for Journey in the back before dashing up to meet me at the front porch. Based on his speed, it was clear he'd paused time to catch up to me.

"You didn't *eat* anyone," he said, fishing in his pocket and pulling out that infernal coin he played with along with his ornate front-door key.

"Correction: I drank her."

Dean didn't say anything as he opened the door and waited for both Journey and me to head on through. It was quiet for once, no antiquated music permeating the air, no soft shuffle of shoes dancing in the parlor or dining room. There was scuffling, though, the sounds of pots and pans clanking from the kitchen.

"Erica," called Dean, heading back that way. "What's for dinner for the bloodbags—er, the champion and her friends?"

I didn't hear a response. I was no bloodbag—no one had ever bitten me, I'd just been granted these on-and-off venom powers by accepting the role of champion—but I was hardly any better. I was worse, actually.

"Ember?" Dad peeked out from the divan near the crackling sitting room fireplace as I stepped into the dining room. He had on a nice vintage suit like Minnie liked her servant bloodbags to wear, but unlike a few of the others, whom I saw heading to and from the kitchen to set the long table in the dining room, he was just... lying there.

Dad never stayed in one job for long. He also never stayed in one state for long. It had been harder for two exes to track him down for child support that way. But since I'd turned eighteen, he hadn't even had to worry about that, unless somehow my brother or I could sue him for back payment. But I knew for a fact we'd never see a penny.

"You know, the vampires all work," I snapped, not feeling charitable at all. Journey stiffened behind me as she put her backpack down on top of one of the couches. "At the moving company—at school. And the bloodbags at least work as servants here. If you're hoping that immortality will mean an eternity of laziness, think again."

"About that," said Dad, standing and not at all seeming that chastened. How had he ever wooed my mom? I'd never understand. And "opposites attract" just never made sense to me. "So... Everyone tells me *you* turned that girl."

"I'll go look for Devam," said Journey quietly beside me, though it was hard to hear her over the tap of my toe on the hard floor. "Unless you need me?"

I shook my head and let her leave. Then I spoke. "And?"

"And I was wondering if... You could change me?" He pointed to his neck where multiple scabs had formed, making him look like some kind of addict who shot injections into his neck. I supposed he was.

"Minnie explained that it wasn't your turn." I had no doubt if I won this battle, his turn would come. I wouldn't even care. I just wondered if it'd be up to me to tell Daryl or if Dad would at least take enough responsibility to find some excuse to tell him goodbye.

"I doubt it was that little girl's turn, either," he said. *Little girl.* He still saw people my age as little kids.

"I didn't turn her on purpose." I stomped over to the fireplace and warmed my hands with it. The warmth sent a tingle to my palm, the red starting to glow there.

"But now you know you *can* turn people," he said. "If you're looking for more practice…" He pointed to his neck.

I whirled on him. "Dad, have you even let Daryl know why you didn't show for his dinner date with his future in-laws? Did you even remember you have another kid?"

Dad tugged on his collar and shoved both hands into his pockets. "Sure. I sent him a text saying I was sorry. I had business—"

"Like he'd believe *that*."

"Since when are you so close with your brother?"

"And whose fault is it if I'm not?" I growled.

"Probably your mother's."

I let out a loud, aggravated scream, stopping just short of stomping my foot. "I can't believe you. You can't be *that* bad of a father."

"All right, all right, I get it. Blame me for everything." He "washed his hands" of me in a pantomime.

"I don't *blame you* for everything," I said. "I don't even see you enough to blame you for anything. I didn't even think about you much before all this. Now it seems every time I turn around, you're there, asking for something from me—"

"I asked for *one* favor. But you know what? Forget it. Like mother, like daughter." Dad turned on his heel and disappeared into the kitchen, to where he probably was supposed to be doing something or other to feed the bloodbags and take care of the house.

Dean exited the kitchen at the same time and looked over his shoulder as Dad passed, then looked back to me as if to ask what had gotten under *his* skin. Me, of course. I ruined everything lately.

"Ember—" started Dean, but I was already headed toward the front door. I hadn't even bothered to take my coat off.

When I got there, though, I froze. Beyond the frosty glass

of the front door window, there was a figure whose hand was hovering over the doorbell. She froze.

Ivy froze.

Dean reached for the door handle.

"What are you doing?" I seethed from between clenched teeth. "Are you going to invite our *enemy* into your house?"

Dean looked at me askance. "I thought we agreed she wasn't the enemy—the Sheppard girls aren't the enemies. They've just been caught up in this."

Through the frost of the door, I could see Ivy lift both hands up. "I'm not hiding anything," she said. "We need to talk."

Dean opened the door and I snarled, getting my fist warmed up because she was *always* the one who started it. Well, almost always.

Ivy stepped inside, her hands up the whole time.

"What are you doing here?" I sneered. "Unless you're here to surrender, you couldn't be stupid enough to come alone."

"Well, I might point out you're *stupid* enough to let me in." She lowered her hands slowly and sent an arching brow Dean's way.

I glared at him. That was basically what *I* had just said.

"Kidding," said Ivy, clearing her throat. "I really do just want to talk." Her hands rested at her sides now. That didn't mean they couldn't turn lethal at any moment, though.

"Where's your prince?" asked Dean, fishing his coin out of his pocket and letting it roll between his thumb and forefinger.

"Never mind him," said Ivy, the muscles of her jaw clenching. "Is... Is what I think about Raelynn true?" She shifted slightly to peek over my shoulder, as if she'd find her hiding behind me.

My palm sweated and the echo of the wild beat of my heart thrummed in my ears. "What do you think happened to her?"

"Lyric's hysterical," said Ivy.

"Oh, you have time for your Union friends?" The glow of my palm was hard to miss, and her eyes darted toward it.

Her own palm started glowing blue.

Dean stepped between us, putting a hand on my shoulder. "If you're not here to surrender," he said to Ivy, "I'm going to have to ask you to leave."

"Why?" Ivy gestured to her neck, which was no longer bandaged. You had to look close, but there was the faded scar tissue of two fang marks. *My* fang marks. "Didn't you want me to be one of you? Don't I belong here like the other teenagers you manipulate into becoming addicts?"

She brushed past Dean and me, and the move was so unexpected, neither of us swooped in to stop her.

"Raelynn?" she called out, heading into the living room.

The girl was brave, I'd give her that.

Dean and I trailed after her, and Journey came out to see what was happening.

"At least *you* don't look like a bloodsucker," said Ivy, her fist clenching as it gave off its blue aura.

"What are you doing here?" asked Journey, shirking back a step. Merfolk *had* taken her hostage, after all.

"Looking for Raelynn." Ivy swept toward her and Journey moved to block her path. Ivy's eyes narrowed. "So she is here."

"She's visiting with family right now, but she'll be joining us shortly," said Dean. "You don't want to be here when my family returns—" He tried to grab for her arm as he might have grabbed mine.

She yanked her appendage out of his reach. "They can't hurt me," she said. She whirled on me. "Only she can. Right? If you want to win this thing?"

I cared less and less about *winning* anything. I just wanted this all to be over. I just wanted what I'd done to Raelynn to not have happened at all... As if that were possible.

I have a way to undo it, Calder had told me.

Ivy jutted her chin out, exposing her neck toward me. "So bite me! That's what you do, isn't it? Bite people? Kill them?"

"I..." The fire in my fist was dying out, the flickering glow there more like the last dying embers of a blaze. Dying embers...

"That's not what she was trying to do to you," said Dean, his hands stuffed in his pockets. His bright blue eyes were so piercing, they caught even Ivy off-guard, her muscles releasing some of their tension as she met his gaze head-on.

"I was trying to create a... vampire mermaid," I said. I looked to Dean for confirmation I should proceed and he nodded stiffly.

Ivy laughed. "What? Why?"

Journey nodded at me over Ivy's head and retreated into the back of the house.

"To get you on our side," said Dean, and he stepped closer to her. She didn't flinch.

"So you *were* trying to kill me," she said, zeroing in on me.

"Becoming a vampire isn't the same as dying," said Dean quietly.

"Yes, it is," said Ivy.

I stumbled on my legs, suddenly weak by the thousandth reminder of what I'd done. I leaned on the mantel for support, Dean so focused on Ivy in front of him that he didn't sweep in to steady me.

"With the two powers combined, we'd stand a chance against the fae—" started Dean.

"You didn't even know the faefolk were a part of this when you tried to bite me," said Ivy. "Did you?"

I hadn't. I looked to Dean. He shrugged. "It wasn't about that initially. It was about..."

"Uniting us," I said, standing tall as best I could. My throat felt dry. *Thirsty.* "Putting an end to this war, the champions, the whole thing."

"The last time you bloodsuckers tried something like that, you wound up killing the merfolk king," said Ivy.

"That's not what happened," said Dean softly. "Not exactly."

"Oh, yeah? Then what *did* happen?" Ivy asked.

Dean leaned forward and *whispered* something to her.

To Ivy. Something I couldn't hear.

"No," said Ivy, shoving him back. "You're lying to me."

"I'm not." Dean tugged at the knot of his tie at his neck, as if he could ever feel choked.

"What are you talking about?" I demanded to know. My knees felt wobbly again.

Ivy's posture perked up. "Oh, is it a secret? Is that why you whispered it to me? Well, I'm not your secret-keeper." She strode closer to me. "He just told me he was that merman king's brother and that *Minnie* tried the venom on both of them." She scoffed and looked him up from head to toe. "That would make him Calder's great-great-uncle. I can..." Her voice went shaky, her fingers dancing across her throat. "I was going to say I couldn't see the resemblance, but I... I actually kind of see it..."

But most of what she'd said felt hollow. Her words were like a kick to the gut.

"No!" I shouted. This was ridiculous. He was lying to her or... He wouldn't have kept something from me. There was no reason to keep such a thing from me.

"Relax, doll," said Dean, heading my way. "I don't like to talk about it around here. No one knows it but Minnie and—"

"And *Ivy?*" I asked. "You chose to tell *Ivy* before me?"

"So it's true?" Ivy frowned. Then she shook her head. "Look. I don't even *care* if it is. Merfolk and vampires can all go jump off a cliff for all I care. I need to see Raelynn."

Dean took her hand in his and she seemed so taken aback, she let it happen, though she jumped. His skin was cold. I knew that.

I should have been the only one to know that.

"It didn't work on me," he said. "I became full vampire. I can't... I can't swim ever again. Not like I used to." There was something like hurt in Dean's eyes. I hadn't seen them glisten the entire time I'd known him. "But a champion biting a champion—two women who can change from one form to another at will, perhaps you could retain the ability to do both—"

"That's not what you told me," I said curtly, my hand aflame now. "You're pinning your hopes on *her*? You told me if she got some venom, she would surrender."

"I... Ember." Dean stuck out the tip of his tongue, one pure-white fang protruding with the movement. "Of course I want the vampires to win, but—"

"I don't even understand what your goal is anymore!" I shouted. "Or maybe I just never understood—"

A shriek from the back of the house interrupted me, followed by the clatter of dishes to the floor.

Dean bolted toward the kitchen, and I followed, the flame flickering stronger in my hand. I didn't even notice Ivy on my tail until she pulled up next to me in the kitchen.

Erica, the chef, lay crumpled on the ground, blood pouring from two holes in her neck.

The scent wafted across the room and hit me like a sledge-hammer, the venom spreading with abandon.

It wasn't she who had screamed, though. Journey was at the back door, her trembling hand covering her mouth.

"What happened?" I asked, heading toward her as Dean checked Erica for signs of life.

"She's fine," he said, putting his lips over the holes on her neck for a moment. Pulling back, he wiped the blood from his mouth with the back of his hand. He'd rather casually helped himself to a snack while she'd just been lying there... I was too shocked to comment. "Someone bit her without warning and she convulsed, hit her head on the counter." He pushed gently on a wound on her head, too. "Ruby can fix her up just fine."

"It was Devam..." said Journey quietly from behind me. She looked over her shoulder at the door behind her, but there was no one there. "He turned."

"Oh, you're home early." Yvonne strolled into the kitchen, licking blood off her pale-white hands. "So I might have gotten a little carried away with the boytoy—"

Journey screamed and launched herself at the vampire vixen.

CHAPTER EIGHTEEN

Ivy was the next to move after that, bolting toward the front door.

For a second, I hesitated. I didn't know which direction to go.

Dean stood and put himself between Yvonne and Journey, protecting Journey more than he was Yvonne. The vampire seductress' fangs were out, and she hissed as my best friend blubbered and pounded her fists against Dean's chest.

I hadn't bit Devam myself, but I as good as sealed his fate when I'd brought him to this place. I couldn't help him now. The scent of iron in the air, the *blood*, was overpowering.

Ivy was the enemy. Ivy was the special one Dean wanted to end this war, not me. I didn't get to be special. I didn't get to be loved. I wanted this all to be over already.

"Ivy!" I shouted, running after her. She was at the door now. I let my venom rip, my fangs pop out, and focused, focused on pausing the moment to bring me closer to her.

It worked. Not for long, but for long enough. I joined her at the door just as she opened it, her face frozen in an expression of shock as she stepped out into the early evening.

Minnie, Raelynn, Leopold, Zelda, and Ruby were walking up the steps right in front of us.

Time flickered back to life and I took advantage of the moment to bite Ivy right then and there on the neck, adding new holes to her other side.

The blood felt so *warm*, so *refreshing* as it wormed its way down my throat.

Minnie's high-pitched tittering laughter didn't feel real in my mind as I heard it.

"Ember! Ember, wait!" Dean was at my side, tugging at me.

"Don't stop her!" shrieked Minnie. "I don't know what's responsible for this turn of events, but—"

Ivy went limp before me and Dean split us apart, catching her in his arms. He carried her like a princess before me as I took in the tangy scent of blood through my nostrils and wanted to *quench* and *quench* some more.

"Ohmygosh, that smells *so* divine," said Raelynn and she launched herself forward at Ivy, at the blood trickling down her neck.

"Wait!" shouted virtually everyone—Raelynn could not be the one to deal the finishing blow.

I snapped back to the moment, my fangs retreating, the air flowing back into my lungs.

One moment, Dean was there, and the next he was gone.

I found him at the end of the driveway, heading toward his car.

The door of a nondescript car nearby opened and tall, lanky Lyric stepped out. "What's going on?" she asked. Had she driven here with my step-sister? And Ivy had convinced her to wait in the car? "Ivy?" She ran toward where Dean was putting Ivy *in his car*.

Fire and fury soared through me.

"Bae?" asked Raelynn.

Lyric froze as she turned toward us. "Rae?"

Before she could do anything more than stare, though, a rustling through the grass drew my attention and Devam—looking pale and sickly—ran straight forward, his fangs bared.

"*What* is going on here?" Minnie demanded, stepping

forward. In a flash, she was there beside Devam, tackling him to the ground in one move like an expert martial artist. Only Lyric fell with him—whether from shock or because he'd succeeded in biting her, I didn't know.

But there was no fresh tang of blood in the air.

In the chaos, Dean's car drove away.

He drove away. He'd taken Ivy away when I'd needed him more than anything. My jaw worked and dried blood cracked on my chin.

"You lot are never dull," said a familiar voice. Orin popped out from around the side of the house, wriggling his fingers in the air. "Thought I might find something interesting to observe here today. Glad I wasn't wrong."

"Orin?" asked Raelynn, and she licked her lips. "What are you doing here? You smell..." She took a big whiff of the air. "*Great.*"

Orin chuckled, his shiny white teeth on display. "Just try it, love. But thank you for the compliment."

"Who turned this child?" asked Minnie from the lawn. She yanked Devam by the arm and dragged him toward the porch. "Have you any idea what you've done?" she asked, heaving him up to me.

"It wasn't me!" I said, my throat suddenly going dry.

"Well, well, well," said Orin. "What excuse do you have for me now? Your champion says she wasn't the one who changed him."

"But she..." Minnie's face scrunched up. "This boy wouldn't have been here if not for the champion."

Orin's eyebrow wiggled. "A stretch, but... I'm a sucker for *creativity*. Can't wait to see what kind of excuse you come up with next time. A few more vampires 'round here, and I'll start to really *feel* my loneliness, you know? Maybe time to ring up the relatives, all right?"

Minnie closed her eyes and seemed to be refocusing herself. "Inside," she snapped, and everyone picked up their feet to move. "All of you." She shoved Devam forward, then gestured over her shoulder. "Leo, get the girl."

Raelynn squealed. "If she *understands*, she can join us," she said. "We can be together. Forever."

"You watch what you say," said Minnie, rounding on Raelynn, all pretense of politeness gone. "You children have made such a mess of things..." She pinched her temples, as if vampires could ever get headaches, and walked inside.

Journey rushed passed me into the house—she must have left out the back door after Devam. She didn't say anything, but the look she shot me as she passed was enough to chill my blood, to splash a dose of reality against my face.

Leopold and Ernesto carried Lyric in between them. I didn't smell blood, but just the fact that she was here...

"Wait," I said as they were halfway up the steps. "Put her back in her car. I'll drive her home."

"We don't answer to you, dame," said Leopold, a sleazy smile on his face.

"Sorry, kid," added Ernesto and they kept trudging up the steps. Zelda got the door for them, and inside they brought Lyric, adding another Union High student to their number.

This was getting out of control.

"So why do you think the vampire queen just up and let her prince take off with your mortal enemy, eh?" asked Orin. I'd almost forgotten he was there. "What kind of rumpy pumpy do you think they might be up to?"

"Did you know?" I asked, turning on my heel.

"You'll have to be *a bit* more specific." He scratched the back of his head.

"That Dean was..." My voice went quiet, but everyone else was inside. "Calder's uncle?"

"Great-great-uncle?" Orin nodded. "Sure. What of it?"

"Well, doesn't that change things?"

"How, exactly? Last I knew the vampire merman union didn't succeed. Killed one bloke, turned another full-bloodsucker."

"Does Calder know?" I asked quietly.

Orin stepped closer, leaning against the railing leading up the porch. "And why does that matter to you?" There was a light dancing in his eyes and I didn't think it was mere metaphor.

"Where's Autumn?" I asked.

"With her mum last I knew," he said. He shrugged. "Didn't really feel like corralling the munchkin into this mess. I'm more of a wait-and-let-your-enemies-destroy-themselves type. Unless there's a *real good* opening to take advantage of."

"I noticed."

Autumn was still oblivious when it came to exactly what she was a part of now. Dean had run off *with Ivy* instead of taking care of me. He was so cold, so... practiced. And he'd had decades to practice before he'd gotten hold of me.

What did Dean have to offer me? A future as a vampire by his side? Being pampered when he felt like it, but always with those cold, dead eyes? I was no beloved of his. I was just a champion.

The merfolk couldn't be allowed to destroy the world. But Calder said that wasn't what *he* planned to do, and it was up to him if they won, wasn't it? Not his mother? I mean, I knew it was probably a trap, but he'd said there was some way to bring Raelynn back to life. And it had to help Devam now, too. And Lyric, before she got caught up in this mess.

"Well," said Orin, taking a few steps back. "I best be off and make sure a prince doesn't lure an unsuspecting champion away from her kind and put a stake in her back. Or a fish hook."

I didn't ask if he meant Dean and Ivy or Calder and me.

———

I refilled my mug with hot water for the third time since I'd arrived at the café nestled at the front of the big discount store just outside of town. After all that, I'd walked home, thinking, then once I'd made a decision, I'd driven here. Using Mom's discount card, I got a drink for free. I didn't think I could stomach much else. The jasmine tea was potent as it hit the back of my throat, but I needed to feel it, so I took another drink, not bothering to blow on it first, and I nearly choked on it, my lips sore, my tongue burnt. I took a seat facing the door and kept waiting.

He shuffled over from the front door, not even bothering to blend in with his gaudy purple-and-gold Central jacket. His ears and cheeks were red from the bitter wind outside, and I was reminded how *alive* he was.

"Sorry I'm late," he said, pulling out the chair across from me and speaking in a hushed voice. He slid a backpack off his shoulder and put it on the ground beside his feet. "I had to make sure I wouldn't raise any suspicions."

"And do you know where your champion is tonight?" I asked, dispensing with the pleasantries.

"She was with her friend."

"Yeah, the same friend who lost a girlfriend to the vampires this week," I pointed out. "You didn't think it dangerous to let her go anywhere with that friend alone?"

"What are you saying?" Calder folded his fingers across the table. There was a hint of nervousness to his voice, but he seemed rather calm and collected considering.

"She marched right up to the Hornes' front door." I took another sip of my drink. It had cooled enough that it didn't irritate my already on-fire tongue.

"Is she...?" He shook his head. "If she'd died or surrendered, I wouldn't be here."

"First off, thanks for that." I put my mug back down. "For assuming I'd kill her." Okay, to be fair, I might have gotten close enough on occasion.

He opened his mouth to speak, but I held a hand up to stop him.

"Secondly, would it all be over by then? Now that there are three champions? What happens if one up and surrenders?"

"I had to ask my mom," he said, chewing on the inside of one cheek. "She does think it's over for us if our champion is killed by another champion or surrenders. Even if there are still two species going at it."

I shrugged. "Okay then. I guess we'll see," I said, sounding more confident than I felt. Considering the bond between Ivy and Autumn was stronger than the bond between me and either of them, I knew which of us had the biggest target on her back.

My phone buzzed with a message, but I took it off the table without even looking at it, sliding it into my purse.

"That sure of yourself, are you?" asked Calder. "And what if the merfolk team up with the faefolk against the vampires?"

A woman three tables over glanced our way as she bit into her cafeteria salmon and I leaned forward, lowering my voice.

"If that were the case, you'd be more worried about protecting your champion. And less worried about finding a nice public setting for you to entrap your enemy." I sat back. "Why meet here?" There was something about it that had bothered me the moment I'd walked in, but I couldn't put my finger on what exactly.

"Outside of town, public place—I figured you'd be more likely to show up." He rested his forearm over the back of the empty chair beside him. "It's not a trap."

"Right." I glared before downing the rest of my tea.

"If you think it is, why did you show?" Calder clamped his lips together, holding back a smirk.

I was about to get right to the meat of the matter. But I had something else I wanted to get off my chest first. "I... didn't know you existed before all this."

His face took on a tinge of red as his smirk fell. "I'm not surprised."

I tucked a strand of hair behind my ear. "Granted, I've never had a lot of friends"—before he could respond to that, I lifted my hand—"no, it was fine. I was happy with the friends I had." I looked him straight on. "But I was always looking for a boyfriend. Believe me, I would have noticed a cute guy who supposedly liked me. Even if he was an underclassman."

"Thanks? I guess?" Amusement sparkled in Calder's eyes once more.

"So why did Joe tell me you told the whole swim team you were into me?"

"Cruz? Yikes, talk about breaking the bro code." His eyes narrowed. "Has he been hitting on you?"

"No!" I shook my head, then cocked it. "I don't think."

Calder shrugged and stared down at the little flip-book of ads in the middle of the table. "I've kept an eye on you since the day I started at Union High."

"Because you knew I lived in that house you're all so obsessed with." I let out a hot breath.

Calder flipped through the ad carousel. "That wasn't why."

"I can't imagine other motivations for keeping an eye on me."

"You're beautiful. Smart. Sweet. Funny, if I was able to hear you talking to your best friend."

"That sounds like stalking..." Strangely, my insides weren't revolting at the idea of having this catalog model of the fine abs who had no business being this naturally tan in late fall watching my every move.

I needed help. In more ways than one.

"I wasn't lying when I told you I had a crush on you," he said. "And that I panicked and went with Ivy because I had an opportunity." He swallowed visibly. "And because I thought that bloodsucking prince had swooped in and swept you off your feet in two seconds flat."

I changed tracks, though my heart was thundering. My brain told it to calm down, to put aside all that dumb hot-guy-radar stuff I used to joke about. "Do you know who he is?"

Calder laughed, looking up from the ads touting the benefits of ordering a Thanksgiving dinner from the store. "Yeah. Kind of hard not to notice the complete lack of melanin, the sunglasses, the mobster act—"

"I mean, do you know who he used to be?" I squeezed my hand in my lap, the revelation and how it had been revealed still hurting.

"Should I care? Someone who should be dead." His voice got quiet on the last word.

"Your great-great-uncle," I said. "At least that's what he told Ivy tonight."

"What?" His wide grin quickly fell. "You're serious. Well, he's lying."

"Orin said he wasn't."

"Yeah, well, we all know to trust *that* sprite, don't we?" Calder stared away at the area where a few milling people were ordering food, though due to the late hour, the place was hardly packed.

"They said that Minnie tried to make a vampire merman twice. Your great-grandfather and... his brother, I supposed it would be."

"It was *Minnie*?" he said, snapping back to attention and putting air quotes around her name. "That bloodsucking temptress queen of theirs?"

"Who did you think it was?" I played with my mug, shifting it back and forth in my hands, feeling the last of the warmth seep out of the glass. "Minnie is *old*. I don't know how old, but way older than the rest of the coven."

Calder let out a chuckle, but it wasn't pleasant. "She killed my great-grandfather. My mom wasn't born yet, obviously, but her father told her..." He went quiet. "Well, I guess that doesn't mean he told her everything. *He* wasn't born yet. His mom was pregnant with him when the king was murdered." He went strangely, eerily quiet.

"So you believe me?"

"I don't think *you're* lying," was all he said in response.

"Would it make a difference?" I asked. "If Dean were..." I looked up to find the woman who'd been seated closest to us picking up her tray, walking away, leaving us quite alone in this little niche of the dining area. "If Dean were once a merman prince?"

"Dead is dead," Calder said, though his jaw clenched when he was finished speaking, the little flip-book of ads seemingly demanding all his attention.

I didn't say anything for a while as the woman returned, grabbed her bags, and left.

"My dad died saving me," he said out of the blue.

"What?" That was *not* how I'd expected this conversation to go.

"When I was six." He let out a deep breath and took another, deeper one, as if steeling himself. "I swam too far, went out to the lake—Lake Michigan, I mean. My parents were chasing me, screaming at me to slow down."

I let him speak, my throat suddenly dry.

"I got sucked into a current from a tour boat." Calder wiped his nose with a finger, not looking up from the ad-carousel. "Dad managed to push through to get me, to push me back to my mom's waiting arms, and then—"

"You don't have to tell me this," I said, reaching a hand out and covering one of his. It was warm, sturdy.

"His fins got caught in the boat's blades," he said, swallowing. "He bled out... Right along the coast of Chicago."

"I'm-I'm sorry," I said. Holy cow, that was *awful*. I shuddered just imagining it.

"Mom blames me. She always has. She focuses more on the bloodsucker who killed her grandfather because it's an outside enemy, someone who isn't her flesh and blood to blame."

"But Dean might be just that," I said quietly.

One of his shoulders bobbed up and down. "For a while, I got it. Her desire to see the world flood. To see it end. The tour boat didn't even know what it hit. I mean, they couldn't, but... It just went on its way." His voice went quieter. "I can still hear the tour guide just prattling on, making a joke about choppy waters."

"Calder, I'm really sorry." Clearing my throat, I pulled back and stared into my empty mug. "I am. And if we weren't at each other's throats, I might... I might be a good friend to you."

"I don't want you to be my friend," he said, and I looked up to find his mossy eyes piercing right into mine. Something warm and fuzzy spread out from my core to the very tips of my toes. In my head, I thought for sure he'd say, "I want you to be my girlfriend."

But instead, he said, "I want you to be my champion."

CHAPTER NINETEEN

"How on Earth do you propose *that* could happen?" I laughed so hard, a few people over by the cashier looked our way and I let the dark, hollow laughter die.

Calder lifted the backpack he'd brought in up onto the table. Unzipping it, he showed me he still had the orb that had caused such a fuss. It glowed red, blue, and green.

So Orin had lied about having it. Figured.

"Renounce being champion of blood," said Calder, "and I'll get Ivy to renounce being champion of water—then you can declare yourself the champion of water."

"And she'll declare herself the champion of blood?"

Calder shrugged and zipped the backpack up once more. "If she doesn't, the war can't begin in earnest again."

"It's proceeding *in earnest* right now and we never get anywhere." I clutched the empty mug tightly. It was retaining less and less of its warmth. Dean was somewhere out there with Ivy, maybe getting her ready for some plan, maybe convincing her to surrender, and I was sitting here with the enemy without anyone being the wiser.

Anyone except Orin, maybe.

Then again, maybe since Dean *trusted* Ivy so much that he'd reveal his secrets to her, maybe that wasn't what they were doing at all.

"How would that benefit me again?" I asked quietly. "I'd just be trusting you that if I win for you, you wouldn't flood the world."

"No, I'd bring back the dead."

That had me choking on nothing at all. "You're serious."

"Not *all* the dead," he said, running a trembling hand through his hair. "I'd undo our mistakes—yours and mine."

Nausea tickled in my throat. Mistakes like biting Raelynn until she turned. And Devam. He would have to be part of the deal. Not that I would tell Calder about Devam just yet. "That's your plan? For making Raelynn human again?" I shook my head. "It won't work."

"It will," he said, sliding the backpack back to the ground.

"It won't. You're not thinking this through." My face grew tight. "First of all, what about all your lectures about how 'dead is dead' and they've had their time—"

"A teenager turned in the past few days *on accident* doesn't count."

"And your father?" I asked, shirking back slightly when I saw his face. "How would he even come back? He doesn't have a body walking around. He's *gone* by now, I'm sure—"

"Yes," snapped Calder. "But if winning control of the consummate lands can call upon nature to flood the entire world, I think it can find a way to bring somebody back."

I shook my head. "No."

"No what?"

"No, I won't agree to that, even if it's somehow possible."

Calder's eyebrows scrunched together, his voice quiet but harsh. "You walk around with dead people all the time! But this is unacceptable to you?" He pinched his lips. "Fine, fine, I get it. But what if I only turn Raelynn back?"

"That wouldn't be enough for me." Sighing, I shoved my chair back and stood before he could demand I explain more.

"I could wish that all vampires turned human once more," he said softly.

That would save Devam, too. And Journey and Lyric if they got changed somehow before I could stop it...

"Your prince would become human," he said, his throat scratchy. He cleared it. "You could have a normal future together. Marriage. Kids. If you wanted that."

The emotions roaring through me at that moment *did* include a little dance inside at the prospect of my *human* boyfriend, of a future that wasn't so weird and confusing and overwhelming. As if Dean would want to be with me after I went to the other side.

But that wasn't even the most important thing rolling through my mind. The others from Union High... human again. My mistake undone.

No more vampires would mean no more war. I hoped. By then they'd be defeated, and... "What about the rule that says the species defeated disappear if they lose?" I asked. "Which would mean *two* species now."

"That's undoable with the wish," Calder said, clutching his hands together on top of the table. "We can wish for *anything*, Ember."

"And you really would ignore what your mom wants you to wish for, and also what *you* just told me you wanted to wish for, bringing your dad back, for this?" Picking up my mug, I shook my head. "I'm sorry. I can't trust that."

"Think about it," he said quietly. "I have the orb. I'm your only way out of this no matter what. Unless you really do plan on beating your step-sisters into submission for an undead herd of zombies."

And he'd have me do the same for a bunch of fin-flapping half-humans. I turned around without a word and made it halfway to the dish drop-off when a squeal startled me and almost made me drop the mug.

"What are you doing here?" asked a familiar enthusiastic high-pitched voice, followed by the clomp of feet.

I turned to find Autumn rushing my way, a navy wooly coat over her neon green leggings and a white-and-pink knitted hat on her head. Two long strings dangled off it and flapped back and forth with every movement. Several paces behind her was her mom, heaving slightly as she clearly pushed herself to keep up with the kid, her own windbreaker open over an employee uniform for... this very store. Right. That was why the idea of meeting Calder here had felt a little... off.

I turned back to find Calder, to see what he thought of this development, but he wasn't at the table. I caught sight of his backpack exiting out the cafeteria area and into the store, Glory—Ivy and Autumn's mom—not seeming to notice as he passed by her, his head hanging low.

I kept backing up until I reached the dish drop-off and put my mug down on a tray behind me, never turning my back on the little monster.

"Sorry," said Glory as she finally caught up. "For some reason, Autumn really had a hankering for the meatballs. And I was out of them at home." Her lips made a thin line. "Even though I picked some up a couple of weeks ago."

"Mom gets us an employee discount," said Autumn, coyly joining her hands behind her back as she stared up at me.

Glory looked all around. "Is, um, Easton and Noelle...?"

"No." I'd barely spoken to Mom or Easton lately. They'd clearly noticed something was off about me but had let well enough alone since I wasn't about to talk about it. "I came alone." I stared down at Autumn. If Orin was trailing Dean and Ivy, then Autumn could be his little avatar to report back on what was happening here. How he always seemed to know where blood and water clashed, I couldn't say.

"Do you want to join us for dinner?" asked Glory. Her voice wavered somewhat as she fumbled with a zipper hanging off her oversized purse.

"No, thanks, I just finished," I lied. The prospect of eating with these two—with everything going on—just set my stomach in knots.

My phone buzzed again and I used checking it as an excuse. "I need to get going, thanks." I offered Glory a faltering smile, keeping an eye on Autumn as I stepped away.

Autumn watched me like a little serial killer, a too-big smile on her face. Once I made it to the store door, I actually looked at the messages I'd been ignoring.

Mom checking in to see if I wanted dinner. Mom asking I at least tell her what I was doing. Mom starting in on a lecture about whether I was eighteen or not already, I was still living in her home—

Journey asking why I'd up and vanished on her. She didn't have anything else to say. I knew she had other things to focus on just then.

Dean saying he was sorry for taking off like that. He was sorry for keeping that truth from me. But I needed to meet him at Standing Springs park right now. That was dated almost an hour ago now.

And a voice mail from Calder.

"If the bloodbags win, they won't wish to undo their immortality," he said. *"In fact, they want the freedom to turn more people. It's only been this conflict that has been keeping them in check, the deal with the faeries to turn no one new since your house was built—not without permission. If they win, they can do as they please with abandon. They won't even have to bite anyone. They could just wish it and everyone in the world would turn."*

Scoffing, I slipped the phone into my purse. If they wished *everyone* to turn, there'd be no more blood to quench their thirst with. True, they didn't *need* blood, despite what all the stories claimed, but they certainly didn't seem the type to go without a great pleasure in life for no reason.

Calder was nuts if he thought I would ever stoop to trusting him not to drown me and everyone I cared about.

When I got to my car in the parking lot, I found a little growth of green flowering vines wrapped around the driver's side door handle.

I took my key fob and whacked at the growth, my fingers

shaking as it fell to the cold ground. At last I finally got the door open, staring back at the store as I climbed inside.

The vines was Autumn sending me a message that she was watching me, I supposed. I could attack her right now. Lure her to the bathroom or to the parking lot, where there were fewer witnesses, and demand she drop out of this thing.

Even if that meant I couldn't win this thing. That no one could.

Calder had the orb... Maybe I could *trick* him, make him think I needed it to drop out with the promise of becoming his champion.

I just had to find him.

I tried starting the car. It chugged. I tried again. Something clanked from under the hood.

My blood beginning to boil once more, I hit the button to pop the hood and got out, staring down at my car's innards a moment later. There were vines woven through the entire mess of mechanics, seeping in and out around my engine.

That little—

———

"I don't even get how this happened," said the tow truck guy, ripping at some of the vines and throwing them down to the ground. "Did you drive through a jungle on the way here?" He looked over the top and both sides of the car, as if looking for more evidence that I'd made a trek through vines.

Then he crouched down. "It's almost like someone got at the car from underneath." His muffled voice echoed out into the chilly night. "Or the car has been here for ages and a growth of vines just up and grew through the undercarriage."

"Can you fix it?" I asked, not interested in his theories as to how this happened. I knew how.

Bouncing on one foot and then the other, I watched as my mom's car pulled up beside us and took an empty space a few spots away. I'd responded to her text at least, with a "help, need tow" line of my own.

To Journey, I'd just said I was sorry.

To Dean, I'd said only that I wasn't coming.

He wouldn't know where to find me. And I'd like to see him try something on Ivy if he wanted any hope of winning this at all.

"I think. I don't know. I have to get it back to the shop." The guy stood back up again and closed the hood. "It's a miracle this thing ran at all."

Only it hadn't, not since the growth of vines had appeared. But I'd let the guy assume the car had stayed stagnant, not running in some messy overgrowth of a yard, until it had driven me to the vine-less concrete of this store's parking lot. It was more palatable than the real explanation.

Both Mom and Easton popped out of her car and I groaned. Double the fun. Then I grew irritated with myself for thinking that. Just a few months ago, Mom and I had been really close. I wouldn't have even bothered going to a store like this without her, not unless I was with Journey or with Journey and her mom, and even then, her mom would probably have invited my mom along.

"What's wrong with the car?" Mom asked, tugging on her coat collar as she approached. She had the right to be panicked. She'd bought it for me and still paid all of the bills associated with it.

"Some kind of plant growth situation," said the tow guy, walking back toward his truck. "I'll take it into the shop and call you with an estimate tomorrow."

"Plant growth?" asked Mom, taken aback. "What kind of plant growth?"

But Easton had already popped the hood once more and taken a look inside. He whistled. "How did *that* happen?"

Your little demon spawn, I wanted to say.

Mom strode over and jumped back when she looked down. "What on Earth...?"

"I've got some paperwork for the owner to sign," said the tow truck guy. He held a pen out toward me, then toward my mom. My mom dove in and took it from him, launching into a conversation I could only assume the purpose of was to negotiate as good a deal as possible. "I'm a member of AAA," she said. "And I know how to shop around if I don't like a quote." That was almost a threat.

The tow truck guy chuckled. "If the engine is shot, no quote in the world could make a difference. Be cheaper to buy a gently used vehicle, frankly."

The blood seemed to drain from Mom's face.

"Daddy!" The pounding of familiar feet echoed out across the pavement.

"Hey, kiddo!" Easton said, preparing to catch Autumn in his arms. She jumped right up into his embrace and Easton grunted, seemingly for show, but the way his face turned down just slightly, it probably wasn't entirely exaggerated. "You're getting big."

"Hi," said Glory as she approached. "Car trouble?"

Understatement of the year, thank you. Sighing, I stared at Autumn, hoping I was injecting plenty of venom into the look.

"Autumn said she saw something leaking out of the bottom of this car when we came in." Glory chuckled. "I had to drag her out from looking under it and everything. I guess she was right, though. I didn't realize it was *your* car, Ember."

Something leaking, my shivering tush.

"Ember was in the café," said Autumn as her dad put her back down on her feet. Mom was grunting and mumbling to the tow truck guy, who took the paperwork from her.

"Do you have everything out of the car you need, miss?" he asked me.

I nodded, tapping my purse.

"Okay, then, everyone please step back and I'll get it hooked up."

We all shuffled over toward Mom's car.

"You didn't tell me you'd seen Autumn and Glory," said Easton to me. He stared over my shoulder. "Ivy with you?"

I chuckled, and it wasn't a pleasant sound. "She's with my boyfriend."

The heads of all three parents turned toward me, any sign of mirth or anger dropped.

"Honey, is that why you've been so weird lately?" Mom asked, stepping in to put an arm around my shoulder.

"Ivy?" asked Glory. "Ivy has Calder—"

"What kind of sick little jerk would do that to my daughters?" said Easton, and I felt a twinge of guilt at the plural there.

"Chill," I said, pushing Mom's arm off me. "It's not like that." *It's not.* "They just had some stuff to do... It's been a long day. Can we go home?"

"Sure," said Mom, holding the back door of her car open for me. *She* was the pregnant one. I should have been doing nice things for *her*.

"Bye, Ember!" said Autumn, peeking around her dad's leg. Her hand was glowing just a little bit green as she waved at me. "Sorry about the car!"

She giggled as Mom shut the door and I sunk into my seat, a raging headache pounding my head so hard, I just about zonked out on the ride home.

CHAPTER TWENTY

"Ember, we're home," said Mom loudly, the quiet murmuring of her conversation with Easton that had acted as background noise to my in-and-out slumber cutting out along with the sound of Mom's car's engine.

Easton got out first. "I'll warm up dinner again." He cleared his throat and wriggled his fingers at me before heading inside.

"Do you want to talk about it?" Mom said after a moment.

"About what?"

"About... what's got your goat."

Where to start? "I don't know what you want me to say."

"Let's start with what you were doing at a store by yourself so late in the evening. I didn't see you with any bags. Did you buy anything?"

"Really?" I snorted. "I didn't know window-shopping was a crime. Especially considering I *am* eighteen."

"Fine, forget the car disaster, though *I'm* going to find that very hard to forget since cars aren't cheap, you know." As if *I* had done anything to break my car. Look to the little monster who'd trashed your house! Which Ivy also had done, via water dribbling down the basement stairs.

Did Mom even begin to have a clue how much *easier* life

had been before she'd had to go and get married and ruin everything?

I took a deep breath, the warmth overtaking my hand so bad, I had to sit on it, lest Mom see every time she kept flipping around to look me in the eye.

"Are you having boyfriend troubles?" Mom asked.

"Step-sister troubles," I said truthfully. "But you don't *care* about any of that, do you?"

Mom's lips flattened into a thin line. "Did Ivy steal your boyfriend?"

"Stop talking about Dean!" I said. It wasn't just the heat now. The venom was thumping through my body, my heartbeat out of control as it tried to fend it off.

The thump of Mom's pulse was thundering in my ears.

Quench. Blood. Thirst.

"Then what *do* you mean by any of this?" Something like a cloud drifted over Mom's eyes. "I... I want to ask if something happened at Homecoming, but I thought... Nothing happened, right?"

I had Orin's handiwork to thank for Mom stopping herself from probing that idea further. Opening the door, I felt a blast of the chilly air hit me full in the face.

"Ember, we're not done talking—" Mom started.

"You didn't even ask me if I wanted a bigger family," I said quietly.

Mom's hand went to her stomach. "You always used to tell me you wanted a sister."

"Yeah, like when I was *five*." I threw my hands up in the air. "You couldn't wait a year until I was at college and out of the house? Away from all this?"

Mom shrunk back as if I'd slapped her. "Ember, my life was on hold for a long time after your father and I divorced—"

"That's not my fault."

"I didn't say it was."

"Why couldn't you have at least dated for longer?" I asked. I stared at her hand on her stomach. "It couldn't have been the baby. Easton seemed surprised at the wedding ceremony."

It was the first time I'd even really mentioned the baby in over a week. So much had happened since then, the knowledge that Mom was brewing a little Goodwin-and-Sheppard mixture was faded background noise.

"I love him. It's as simple as that." Mom shifted back around, her coat crinkling loudly in the quiet of the car. "I know you're at that age when you *think* you understand that, and believe me, I thought the same when I was your age. When I was younger even."

I fanned myself, allowing the cool air to whap against my face, even as Mom shivered in the seat in front of me. "Parents never think teenagers know what romance really is. Got it."

"This isn't one of your TV soap operas or books, Ember," said Mom, her voice raising in pitch somewhat. "I'm serious. If this boy is playing around with your step-sister, with anyone, he doesn't deserve you. He doesn't even deserve your tears."

Again, back to Dean.

"But you and Ivy are always going to have a connection." Mom patted her stomach again, even though nothing was close to showing yet. "She may do something that hurts you, but you need to have it in you to forgive her."

"Sure," I said, stepping out of the car. "Can we go inside now?"

Mom's long, audible sigh rung out against the night air as we made our way to the front door and inside the blessed warm cushion of the furnace-manufactured hot air. The feeling of being chilled from outside while burning up inside had been at war within me, the relief offered by the furnace suddenly too stifling as I ripped my coat off in the hallway and jammed it, one sleeve inside out, onto the coatrack.

Mom was slower to take her coat off, more careful with hanging it up. I was already on the third stair headed to the second floor.

"I'm sorry I didn't discuss it more with you," she said.

"That I didn't ask how you felt about... About our family expanding."

I turned to face her. Mom and I had never fought before all this.

For a second, I could squint and pretend the hand on her stomach meant nothing in particular, the humming from Easton in the kitchen as the microwave beeped maybe just Journey's mom getting things ready for a girls' night in.

"But you're not a child," said Mom, tossing her hair back. "You're not an adult—but you're not someone I should have to coddle, either. If you'd had objections to my marrying, that doesn't mean I wouldn't have done it."

And the whole illusion shattered again.

"I didn't care that you got married," I snapped. "I didn't even mind the idea of letting some *strangers* move into our house. I just didn't realize his two brats would be such a thorn in my side." Stomping up the stairs, I didn't even bother to acknowledge Mom's stuttering attempts to get me to come back and talk to her.

Talk to her about what?

I slammed the door to my bedroom behind me and tossed my purse onto my desk. The automatic timers on the white Christmas lights over my bed clicked on, bathing the dark room in a soft, warm glow.

"Where in the name of canned heifer have you been?"

The shadowy figure at the end of my bed almost made me scream. I had to clamp my hand tightly against my lips to stop the sound from trickling out.

The last thing I needed was Mom or Easton to head up here after my illuminating *talk* and find *him* seated in the dark atop the comforter Grandma had quilted for me when I'd upgraded my bed from twin to full.

Dean's blue eyes were hard to miss now that I knew to expect him.

The fire within me quickly surged back through my veins, and I waved a hand in the air before sitting next to him and crossing my arms tightly across my chest. "My car is busted. Thanks to the little weaselly champion of bloom."

"She was at the manor?" he asked.

Right. He'd left me there. *He'd left me there.* Without a ride, I might add. What did he think I'd done, gone back for my car and then driven right back to his place?

"What do you care?" I asked. "You left me to deal with everything on my own. While you took our *enemy* to the park and expected me to trail after you like some puppy. You *drove me*, remember?"

Dean shuffled both hands together between his knees, and I wondered if that was actually doing anything to "warm him" or if that was simply some leftover memory from the time when he could *feel*. Cold. Empathy. Anything.

"I just wanted to try to get her to surrender, one more time." His bright blue eyes flicked toward me. "Only I *needed* you there to accept her surrender. No point if you weren't."

"Oh, was that the plan?" I crossed one leg over the other and tossed a strand of my hair over my shoulder. "Because it looked like to me that she was the only thing you cared about in the midst of that chaos, that all you could focus on was getting your sassy, popular brunette to safety."

"Are you *jealous*, doll?"

"Don't flatter yourself," I said, picking a piece of lint off the front of my sweater. "You may be ancient, but I'm just a teen. I'm too young to know what real love is." It wasn't lost on me that I was parroting my mother.

It wasn't lost on me that the words felt like broken bits of glass as they exited past my lips. That my stomach squeezed in on itself as my chest constricted tightly.

"I thought *you* wanted this ended without bloodshed," he said quietly. "I thought Ivy surrendering is something *you* would have wanted."

"That was before the first casualty," I said bitterly.

Dean's ice-cold hand reached for mine and I shuddered, pulling away. He sighed and clasped his hands together in front of him. "You couldn't help yourself with Raelynn. That wasn't your fault."

"I beg to differ."

"It was a stressful situation—"

"That *you* and *your family* created because, what, you couldn't stand to give me a little space to breathe?" I thrust my chest out. "Never mind. Forgot you don't remember what it's like to need air. To breathe."

He didn't have a response to that.

"And what about Devam?" I asked. "I didn't bite him myself, but I..." I chewed on my lip. "You can't understand, Dean. What it's like to betray your friends—"

"I wasn't lying when I said I was a merman prince. Once."

I hadn't even thought about that specifically. That if he was the brother of a merman king, then he would have once been a merman prince.

Like Calder.

Like his great-great-nephew.

"And you betrayed your people?" I clenched a piece of Grandma's quilt tightly in my fist. "Why?" I asked, quieter.

"I don't know," said Dean. "Truthfully, I don't."

The heat searing my palm fizzled somewhat and I let go of the blanket to find it singed just slightly in a palm-shaped imprint. The black wasn't too noticeable amidst the blue. Not unless you knew to look for it.

"There was a war going on," Dean started. "A *big* war. A war amongst humans."

I bit down on my tongue to stop myself from saying I wasn't stupid enough not to have heard about World War II.

"Cary and I... We thought about enlisting. At first, our pop was still king, and he refused, assured us we'd fail our medicals by *sweetening* the pockets of the army doctor sent around to conduct such things. Pop had big money from the construction business, see.

"I was too young yet to enlist. But I was going to, the moment I turned eighteen. Find me a different army doctor, one a few towns over Pop couldn't reach and..." Dean stared at his feet. "Cary didn't understand. He was married by then—a sweet mermaid gal who'd crushed on him since we were kids—and she was going to have his baby. He was only twenty, still young enough for the war, but he didn't care. He didn't want to leave them."

"But you wanted him to?" I asked, remembering Grandma's stories about how hard it had been on her mom to wait on pins and needles for news about her then-fiancé. My great-grandpa had driven tanks in the war. Busted down walls holding in horrors. My throat went tight.

It felt so strange to be speaking to someone who lived in a time when this had all been reality, not a sad, cautionary story in a history book. My great-grandpa had been dead before I'd been born, my great-grandma the merest memory of a wrinkly old woman who had no clue who anyone was surrounded by other old people and nurses and smelling of antiseptic.

Dean was here. Handsome, youthful. Dead. I couldn't forget dead. But here.

"I didn't want him to have to go," Dean said quietly. "I understood. Besides, he was heir to the throne, so to speak. If you count lording it over a few dozen merfolk and owning a construction company a throne."

He was quiet for a bit longer. "But me? No one would miss me if worse came to worst. I wanted to *feel* something. Wanted to do my part."

I nodded. I'd felt that way once, only I hadn't been serious. I'd loved goofing off and hanging out with Journey too much to actually want something major to upset the delicate balance that had been my cozy life. And this was why. All of this, this insanity, was why.

"Pop died in a construction accident not too long after Cary tied the knot." Something like anger danced over Dean's cool blue eyes. "Cary was king then. Such decisions were up to him. For a little while, he told me sure, as soon as I turned eighteen, I could... Well, I never turned eighteen." He stared at me and I felt strange, knowing in some senses I was "older" than him. In only the most vague, intangible of senses.

"Before that, though, there was all this pressure. From our ma, from the rest—'enough with this living one day to the next,' they tell us. Remember the war? The real war? Ma especially was hard on Cary about that. Even though there hadn't been a vampire sighted in..." He shook his head. "I suppose I don't rightly know. A thousand years at least."

"Until there was?"

"Until Minnie approached Cary all quiet-like one day at the office." He smirked. "Well, it's hard for Minnie not to turn heads. No one was prepared for her. No one really *expected* a vampire to show up."

"Where did she come from?"

"I don't know. Still don't. Minnie doesn't like to talk about it." He frowned. "But from what the faery has said, I think he and she have known each other a long time. *A long time.*"

Well, I couldn't count on Orin to share anyone's secrets. Even if he did, I wouldn't trust him. Even if he was telling the truth, I would question the reason *why* he'd shared it with me.

"She seduced my brother," said Dean quietly and I stiffened. "In more ways than one."

Yikes. "And you...?"

"She never did that with me," said Dean. He offered me a faltering smile. "She made me her prince, her 'nephew,' but never her lover. Said Cary was made of sturdier stock. That I was just a kid."

"There weren't that many years between you."

Dean shrugged. "I wasn't jealous of that, believe me. I saw the hurt on his wife's face. She didn't know exactly what was going on, but she knew something was. Knew *someone* was coming between them. She pressed me for more information and I... I let slip too much. Cary erupted at me one night that Janie had found out and lectured him about embracing the water, our noble bloodline, and how he'd betrayed them all by spending time with some human floozy... And he told her. It wasn't a human. It was a vampire."

The air hung icily with that word. The venom thrummed somewhere in the core of my heart.

"He told me so many things, I couldn't keep track. Minnie wanted peace, an end to the war before it even started again. Vampires and merfolk in one—some kind of hybrid creature." His face grew sour at the words, even though *he'd* pressed the idea on me, too. "How there was another, more ancient enemy." He chuckled. "That would be the faefolk, always content to stay on the sidelines, so we thought." Dean reached into his pocket and pulled his coin out, fumbling with it between his fingers. "And then he told me... I wouldn't be able to enlist. He'd stop it like Pop would have. Punishment for telling Janie before his... transformation... was complete."

"He was already getting venom?" I asked.

"He was by then. He was driven mad by it. By her. By..." Dean squeezed his lips tightly. "He didn't care that Janie was pregnant with his child. That he was a king. That our kind had wanted to *rule* this world, to make it a merfolk paradise, since the beginning of time." He sent me a sideways glance. "That kind of stuff had just been myth, you see. None of us actually wanted that. So I thought. Ma and Janie—they seemed to want it. To clutch on to anything that might tempt Cary away from the ultimate temptress. A purpose. A new life embracing the water over the land once and for all. Never forgetting our roots and that our time on this Earth was just temporary." Dean stared down at his hand, which he flexed in front of him, the other clutching his coin tightly. "Temporary." He laughed dryly.

As he started to fiddle with that coin again, I put my hand on top of his to stop the movement. He let me take it from him without comment, and I turned it in the glow of the lights over my bed. It was an old half-dollar. Only the few I'd seen had had a president on it, but this had a woman in a flowing gown, seeming to clutch to the bounty and harvest around her. This one was dated 1942.

"Cary asked Minnie to finish the job," Dean continued. "To make him her first new vampire in a fresh new world. To make a vampire merman a reality. She obliged, bringing him just to the cusp of fully turning, and then... He got wet."

"He got wet?"

"Water and vampires don't mix." Dean looked crestfallen. "He could still turn into a merman, but he sunk. He sunk to the bottom of the lake. By the time some of the others found him, saw that red, steamy trail leading up to the surface, they realized he'd been caught halfway between human and merman somehow." Dean wriggled his fingers at his neck. "That he hadn't grown gills. That he hadn't been able to breathe underwater."

"He died," I said quietly.

"The first merman to drown." He chuckled darkly. "There's got to be some kind of poetry there."

My throat was dry. "But how did you...?"

"I was angry. At Cary for leaving us, for falling for that woman—for trusting me with his secret, for introducing her to me, but also for getting mad that I'd told on him, for saying he'd never let me enlist. Stupid, I know. A stupid thing to focus on in that moment. Though Janie was still pregnant with the heir, Ma wanted me to step in as king until the child was of age... That wasn't what I wanted. At all. I was going to enlist. I was going to put the whole terrible mess behind me. The memory of my brother. My father's wishes. All of it.

"Minnie came to me. One night I was sitting there alone in Standing Springs Park. She apologized for what had happened to my brother, assured me it hurt her as much as it hurt me." He traced the back of his hand with his fingers. "She didn't have to work that hard to seduce me to her cause. I asked her what she thought had gone wrong with Cary's transformation and if she thought she could fix it."

He snatched the coin back from me and stared at it. "'Not

enough venom,' she told me. 'So make sure I get enough,' I told her." He slipped the coin back into his pocket. "Turned right then and there. Hard and fast and vicious-like—my skillset attesting to it, I think. Pausing time is easier for me because of it. The others, they turn slowly." He chewed on his bottom lip. "Though I wonder about that new girl..."

"You couldn't turn back into a merman again, though?" I asked.

"Nope. Well, I didn't dare even try. One foot in that water and..." He gestured with both hands over his head like an explosion had gone off.

"I was dead to my family. Dead to the world—no way I was enlisting like that regardless." He shrugged one shoulder. "Besides, I had a new purpose. New freedom. Of sorts."

So he'd told me now. Everything I'd wanted to know. Everything I wished he hadn't kept from me. But I just wished it hadn't all come out like this when... "What did you do with Ivy?" I asked suddenly.

"She got away," was all he said, and he turned to shine his bright blue eyes on the window, on the forest bathed in moonlight behind us. "Turned into a mermaid and dove right into the water. I guess she didn't get enough venom for it to affect her the same way..."

I wondered if she'd had enough venom to affect her in any capacity.

If I should have injected more. Harder. Faster. More viciously.

With a hiss, my fangs popped out of my mouth as the venom shot through my system.

Dean didn't even flinch. He just sighed.

That was enough for the fangs to vanish entirely.

CHAPTER TWENTY-ONE

"I'm making an appointment with your doctor," said Mom, her toe tapping impatiently, her arms crossed so tightly over her chest, she was practically giving herself the Heimlich.

"Mom, I'm *fine*," I said, pulling the comforter higher over my head.

"If you were fine, you wouldn't be missing so much school."

"I'm not falling behind with anything." I remembered to sniffle then. "Journey gives me all the homework." As if. She wasn't even talking to me. Not that I could blame her after what had happened to Devam.

"Ember Amelia Goodwin, I can't call you in sick for a third day in a row without a doctor's note." Mom sat on my bedside, reaching a hand for my forehead. The scent of iron beneath her thin skin pulsated through her veins, and I *thirsted* for just a little bite, my incisors growing longer.

"Yikes!" shouted Mom, pulling her hand back. "You're ice cold."

Grinding my cheek against my pillow, I told myself to *stop*. Focus on deep breaths. Focus on *breathing* at all. Get that heart jumpstarted once more.

The air between my open lips grew warmer as I counted slowly, breathing again in rhythm.

Mom's hand rested on my forehead once more. "Maybe it was my hand. But you are kind of clammy. No fever, though." She rubbed my upper arm. "Ember, why don't you want to see the doctor?"

"Because I'll be fine soon." I wasn't sure I would be, actually. Dean had tips for coping for life as a newly-turned vampire for the likes of Raelynn and Devam, but I wasn't a newly-turned vampire. I was a part-time one. It was just that it was looking to be less and less part-time.

"There's that thing going around at your school," said Mom quietly. That *thing* was Raelynn and Devam coming down with a "weird disease" that made them cold to the touch and several shades paler. Thanks to Minnie's help and a bloodbag of a "specialist" doctor, though, the parts about them no longer having heartbeats or functioning lungs were conveniently left out of the story their parents were being told. "I don't want to risk it," Mom continued. "Let's make sure you're okay."

"Fine," I said, burying my head into my comforter. I could keep the vampire part of me at bay long enough to pass a basic inspection, right?

In a place teaming with bodies and samples of blood? Maybe not.

"All right. I'll text you with the details and see if I can leave work early to take you." Mom stood. I'd almost forgotten I no longer had a car since I hadn't had cause to need it over the past few days.

"Sure," I mumbled, knowing perfectly well I was acting like the stereotypical sullen teenager I'd sworn I'd never be.

I hadn't factored vampires and mermaids and elemental powers into the mix when I'd made that little vow, though.

Mom lingered at the door. "I'm not sure if you should go with the Slowes this weekend. Not until we're sure you're feeling better."

The Slowes this weekend? I peeked an eye out from under my comforter, waiting for Mom to elaborate.

The puzzlement must have been clear on my face. "To

Chicago? Phil has that conference he's going to for the restaurant and Lacey thought it'd be fun to take you and Journey and her nephew to the city for a couple of days."

It was vaguely ringing a bell. I'd agreed to it over the summer when life had seemed so much simpler. When I hadn't been indirectly responsible for my best friend's boyfriend becoming the walking undead.

"Yeah," I said. "We'll see." I doubted Journey would be going with her parents herself at this point, let alone would want *me* to tag along.

"Is your father still in town?"

I stiffened. Like I needed her seeing what he'd devolved into. "I don't know. You don't need to tell him about this. It's nothing—you'll see. I just feel a little… lacking. In energy."

"It could be mono." Mom sighed. "But that's not why I asked. I only called him when you went to the hospital because I figured it was something *important*. I never bothered telling him when you had smaller illnesses before."

I poked my head out from underneath the comforter again. "Then why did you ask?"

"Daryl called me—at the office. He didn't have my personal number, he said, but he wanted to know where your dad went after he came here to visit you. Apparently, he's ghosted his son. Not that that's surprising." She twisted her lips. "What's surprising is the young man managed to keep successfully in contact with him in the first place."

I really didn't want to get into all of this just yet. "Daryl already asked me," I said. "I told him if I saw Dad, I'd let him know he's looking for him." I had. And Dad hadn't cared. He was probably a bite or two away from joining the walking undead at this point, so long as Orin didn't care about this "deal."

"Hmm." Mom flicked off the light switch. "So he never said goodbye to you?"

"No." That was true enough.

"Figures." Her hand lingered on the door knob. "Get some

rest. And check your phone. I'll have Yvonne make the appointment and I'll text you with the details."

"Okay," I mumbled. Mom shut the door behind her and a few minutes later, the door downstairs opened and shut, breaking through the house's delicate silence.

"Do you think Yvonne will schedule you an appointment with our own Doctor Gibbons?" Dean pushed aside the ruffled white bed skirt and crawled out from the space underneath my bed.

"It might seem too strange," I said, my words muffled through the comforter. "I can hold it together long enough to get an all-clear from my physician."

Staring at Dean as he futzed with straightening his suit, I found it hard picturing the debonair gentleman on his stomach just waiting out the morning routine of the house, but that was what he'd been up to the past few days. Ever since I'd tried biting *him*—as if he'd had any blood for me to ingest.

It had just been the stress. Becoming overwhelmed with it all. The *pounding* in my head, the blackening in my vision, was happening too frequently now. It was why I'd insisted on staying home the past few days from school, why Dean had taken up his post under my bed. That and keeping an eye on whatever Autumn might be up to, though she was at her mom's now.

Along with my other enemy. Who'd swum away from *my* prince's efforts at rescuing her, who'd thrown his generosity aside.

"I'm your only way out of this no matter what."

Did she even know what *her* prince had been up to, meeting me on the sly, offering to help me?

My eyes flicked guiltily to Dean. I hadn't told *him* about those meetings.

"Well, she'll figure something out." Dean pulled his phone out of his pocket, a rare piece of modern technology the vampires allowed into their midst, making his fashion choices seem more like dress-up for a themed party than a genuine way of life. Dean had never spent *this* much time with me before, especially not with so much going on. But he had a big "family." More than enough to handle the chaos caused by two new vampires created in spite of Minnie's agreement with Orin to halt all full transformations until after the battle was over.

Sighing, I kicked off the comforter and padded in my slipper socks to the closet. I wasn't actually *sick*. Not like I couldn't move around and do anything. I hadn't spent the last few days cooped up in bed.

My closet was half a stranger to me now, filled with cute ModCloth-style outfits, only these were vintage things straight from the original decade itself, gifted to me by Dean's "aunts." They made me feel amazing every time I put them on. For a second, I contemplated putting something vintage on, doing the whole makeup job to give myself the smoky eye look, but a cozy pink sweatshirt falling off its hanger called out to me. My own clothes were pushed way in the back, and it took some shifting round to access the ratty old thing.

"I'll give you a moment to change," said Dean, stepping into the hallway and closing the door behind him.

Without comment, I swapped my pajamas for the sweatshirt and jeans. Then, rather than telling Dean I was "presentable," as he called it, I sat there on the foot of my bed, one ankle under my other thigh, just thinking.

Thinking about everything.

Thinking about how I didn't have the heart to keep going with this.

Then again, if this frequent transformation kept up, soon enough my heart would be as good as stone.

Out of habit more than anything, I pulled my phone out of its charger on my nightstand and checked my messages.

Journey still hadn't responded to any of my every-few-hours texts. But she'd read them. It was like she'd known I'd *know* she'd read them and that made the silence all the more powerful.

There was an unread message for *me*, though. From C.

You doing okay? I heard about what happened with your car. There was a break and then another message. *We need to end this already, get that little girl out of the running. Have you thought about what I said?*

My heart thumped at the thought of Calder just then. Why? Why did it care that he was pretending to be concerned about how I was, reminding me to fall for his trap, to believe his lies? And how had he found out about the car? Oh, that was easy enough to figure out. Orin could hardly keep his mouth shut after a "victory" of sorts.

But, I mean, Dean had a car and there was such a thing as walking and buses and ride shares. Autumn's act of vandalism seemed like a petty—if expensive and utterly irritating— prank. Or maybe the bright idea of an actual child living in fantasy land trying to slow her enemy down.

Checking to verify the door was still shut, I typed back. *I still don't know if I can trust you.*

Calder saw the message and started typing almost immediately. *I understand. What can I do to show you I mean it?*

Nothing, I started typing, but then I deleted it.

A knock came from the door, followed by Dean's predictable, "Are you decent?"

"Yeah," I said, pushing aside the messages and placing the phone back on the charger on my nightstand.

"So," said Dean as he reentered the room, sliding his phone back into his pocket and leaving his hand in there, "Minnie's been talking to Miss Slowe. Now that Devam has been 'admitted' to Dr. Gibbons' hospital for all intents and purposes and his parents placated as much as can be expected, she's focusing on getting Miss Slowe and Raelynn's girlfriend into the fold."

"No," I said sharply, jumping to my feet. "No more teens turned into vampires."

Dean held out a wary hand. "Now slow down. You didn't let me finish."

I glared at him. He had the decency to shirk back.

"We don't mean as vampires," he continued. "Besides, now

that there are two teenagers from Union High struck with this 'mysterious disease,' we're getting dangerously close to CDC and government interference. We want them as members of the household, so to speak." So bloodbags.

"No," I said again. "You saw what happened with Devam and Raelynn when they were just supposed to stay bloodbags. They got addicted."

"Some of the bloodbags do," said Dean. "Others seem just fine with the little high they get from each quenching."

"Dean, I don't want more of my social circle to become the walking dead."

The vampire in the room looked as if I'd slapped him.

I realized too late I'd insulted him. But it was the truth.

"I don't want anyone to be like me," he said quietly. "Not if they're not sure."

Were you *sure?* I wanted to ask.

"But my family comes first," he said.

"Which family? The vampire or the merfolk one?"

It was like I'd dealt him another blow.

"I told you that in confidence."

I gestured around us. "And? No one's here to overhear us."

"I just don't want you to get into the habit of speaking about it. You and Minnie and..."

"*Ivy*," I finished for him.

"Right. Well, you're the only ones who know."

"And what happens if someone else finds out?" I asked. "You're the *prince*, aren't you? Don't they have to do what you say?"

It dawned on me. He was the vampire prince—the supernatural being without the ability to produce heirs the conventional way—because he *had been* a prince. A merfolk prince.

"How can you...?" I massaged my temple. "How can you want to see your people eradicated?"

"Because they're not my people." Dean leaned against the post at the foot of my bed. "Because they want something I don't agree with, whether I'm already dead or not: Eradicating the living."

"And your vampire family wouldn't understand that? That you wouldn't betray them?" A lump in my throat formed at the word *betray*. My phone buzzed from the charger on the night-stand, but I ignored it.

"I'd rather not chance it," snapped Dean. Something sharp pierced through his glowing blue irises.

"Yeah, because they won't be suspicious at all when you run off with the champion of water like you did that night." My fists clenched at my sides. "What did you even tell them you did with her?"

"The truth," he said. "She *can* be convinced to surrender. It's the sister, I think. The little girl being a part of this that's making Ivy stay in the game... She won't want to win, but she's got to pretend around the merfolk that she does."

The revelation made a sudden snapping *sense*, explaining why Ivy would be so cold as to continue to fight as the merfolk champion even after what we'd told her. I thought maybe she hadn't believed us despite everything she'd seen, or that maybe... It had all been for love.

"That doesn't change the fact that you told her before you told me!" I shouted, my blood growing warmer, pushing through my veins. A small, tiny part of me knew I was being irrational, but it was drowned out by the anger at everything— at what I'd done, at what my path had led to, at the Sheppard sisters standing in my way, at my stupid dad sticking round only because of Minnie, at Dean continuously acting without me, trying to shelter me, seeing *Ivy* as more of an equal than me.

My phone was ringing now, which meant it was most likely Mom since she was one of the few who seemed to hit *call* rather than *message*. Taking a deep breath, I answered. "Yes?"

"Ah, good, you're still awake," said Mom. Talk radio blath-ered on in the background and Mom took a break from speaking to sip what I could easily guess was her morning coffee. "I called Yvonne right away and she got you in to see Dr. Patel in an hour. So I'm waiting to come into the office and am coming back to get you."

"Okay," I said glumly. So my regular physician. I supposed Yvonne assumed I could keep my stuff together to pass a quick examination with a regular doctor.

I wasn't a full-time vampire. Yet. If I ever would be.

I promised her I'd be waiting to get in the car as soon as she pulled into the driveway.

"Doll," said Dean quietly, "you have to consider what's at stake. There's no room for jealousy—"

"I'm not *jealous*," I said, though part of me knew that was a lie.

That was precisely what I was, and I didn't like the feeling. I hadn't ever thought I'd be a part of this kind of *drama*. I was supposed to be above that. Dateless, focused on studies... Watching dramas unfold on screen with my best friend.

"You could have fooled me," said Dean, his husky voice not sending shivers down my spine like it once had—but shooting heat up from my core to my head.

Holding back my trembling fist, I wondered at the feeling of wanting to sock him.

Dean stepped back. *He must have read my mind—he is part-merman.* That idea went through my mind partly as a joke, but that was another thing! Whether he still had those powers himself or not, he should have known how the merfolk mindreading thing worked, and he hadn't said a word. He hadn't pretended to discover the way it worked through some other means if keeping his secret was so important to him. He hadn't warned me to stay on my guard, to not let merfolk touch me. He'd acted as if he hadn't been sure about the merfolk trick at all.

Like he'd been secretly giving Ivy a leg up on the competition—on me.

I wasn't an idiot. He'd *always* looked at her with kind of... a fascination. Back when we'd first met him, when he'd been moving us in, back at school before the trek into the woods.

Oh, sweet skies... I *had* been an idiot.

"I'll hang back and meet you at the doctor's," he said, stiffening. "Your mom won't see me following you—"

"*No*," I barked, taking my phone and shoving it into the purse I'd stored under the nightstand.

"No?"

"I'm going to the doctor's with my mom." I slipped the crossbody purse over my head. "Like a normal teen. No vampires allowed."

"But the scent of blood—"

"I'll manage," I said, heading for the door. "It's a clinic, not a surgery center."

"After the stunt that little punk pulled on you, you have to be careful. Doll—"

I swirled on him at the top of the stairs. "Don't *doll* me."

A car horn rung out from out front and my feet picked up, heading down the stairs before Dean could follow me.

I forgot about the time pause, though.

With a whoosh, Dean appeared at the bottom of the stairs, one hand on the banister and the other on the wall, blocking my way.

"Don't be foolish," he said, his bright blue eyes pleading as they stared up at me.

"Tell me you love me," I said quietly. "And not just that you *need* me."

His gaze darted tellingly down before his mouth opened again. "I... Doll, you're real swell. Of course I love you."

It sounded so shallow, so forced.

How could I have been so unaware?

My teeth trembled in my mouth, a sudden wave of nausea assaulting my throat, and I pushed past his arm, daring him to stop me.

He clearly thought about it, but he didn't.

I bit my lip, focusing on the pain to try to keep the tears

from falling. The iron tang of my own blood hit my tongue and I flinched as I stepped into the outdoors, overcast sky or not.

The bright light was like fire burning my eyes.

"Ember, you can't handle this alone—" He hovered just out of sight of the driveway, a few steps back.

"Leave me alone!" I shouted. "Just for a day—give me some space!"

Before he could answer, I stepped out, my rage shoving aside my lust for blood and making it so I was fully human again.

CHAPTER TWENTY-TWO

One part mindful breathing. Two parts rage. One gigantic part hurt. Those factors were key to keeping my mind off the slight odor of blood in the air, the teaming scent of living beings whose blood ran actively through their veins.

I wanted to be alone. Away from here. Away from Mom. From everyone. This was the kind of thing I needed to tell Journey, but even though she was a part of this crazy supernatural world—and that was my fault, too—she wasn't speaking to me. For good reason.

Instead, I texted the only person I could. The only person who knew and was at least pretending to care just then.

I wouldn't fall for any of his traps, but hey, if he thought I was having second thoughts about being the champion of blood, that would serve my purposes regardless. He'd feel more confident, make his move, and then... And *then* I'd tell the vampires what I'd been up to.

Only after I was *sure* he was lying about being able to save Raelynn and Devam.

I know you don't want to hear this, but a small part of me can't blame him, wrote "C." *I tried to love my champion and I couldn't force what wasn't there.*

"Ember, do you know what shots Bradview wants you to do?" Mom turned from me back to the receptionist. "My daughter's already in an early acceptance program," she said, a smile lighting up her face. "Doesn't have to spend her senior year scrambling to figure out what's next."

Ha to the ha. If she only knew.

"I don't know," I said, focusing on my text conversation. Calder of all people was supposed to be buttering up to me right now. If he wanted to gain my trust, you'd think he'd be nothing *but* sympathetic. But no. He was sympathetic to the guy who'd pretended to love me. Because I was *that* unlovable.

Mom turned back to the receptionist and continued scheduling my physical for the summer to get my shots and health sign-off for school. I'd managed to keep my cool during the examination when Dr. Patel had given me a birth control shot, blaming my illness on period problems. She couldn't find any other cause for it other than "hormones." Sure, whatever, as long as it got Mom off my back.

That time of the month was becoming too much for me anyway, the scent alone sending snapping jolts to my brain these days—I wouldn't have wanted to experience another period in the state I was in.

Never thought you'd sympathize with him, but okay, I wrote, knowing how drama queen I probably seemed. I started writing "like uncle, like nephew" but deleted it.

That's not what I mean, he wrote back. *Ember, I meant it when I said I've always had a thing for you. When I got paired up with Ivy instead, I panicked and... Dean had clearly gotten your attention. I thought it was Ivy or no one.*

A real flattering way to start a relationship, I wrote.

Mom said something to the receptionist, then turned and grabbed my arm. "Ember, come on. Peel your eyes off that phone for one minute and let's go. We can stop on the way home and get lunch."

Grumbling, I slipped the phone back into my purse,

itching to pick it up when it shook with the notification of a reply.

"How are you feeling?" Mom asked as we made our way through the parking lot. The air wasn't frigid just yet, but the cold breeze buffering up against us reminded me that winter was on its way. "Remember the list of side effects to watch out for?"

"Yes, Mom," I said, sighing. I did feel a little dizzy, but who could say from what exactly?

We got into the car and I slipped my hand into my purse to cradle my phone as soon as I'd put on the seatbelt.

"Okay," said Mom. "If you feel sicker, let me know. If you feel okay over the next few days, then you should be fine to go this weekend."

Right. The trip to Chicago with the Slowes. I shifted my phone screen just right so I could take a look at it inside the purse without having to pull it out and clue Mom in on what I was doing.

It's not, Calder had written. *I should never have gone with Ivy. I should have fought for you. I'm sorry.*

I snorted and had to parlay that into my conversation with Mom. "Sorry," I said. "I need a tissue." I dug around in the purse and pulled one out. "I'm not sure if they still want me to go—"

"Nonsense. Lacey was just talking to me about it. I told her I'd let her know what the doctor said first."

I wouldn't have wanted to flood the world, thank you, I texted to Calder.

"I don't think *Journey* wants me to go." As the words left my mouth, Mom stomped on the brakes a little too hard.

"Are you two fighting? Lacey wondered if I'd noticed anything. Journey's been acting a little distracted."

I'm sorry, wrote Calder. *I'm sorry I ever agreed to champion my mother's cause. But I promise you—if you were my champion, that would not be what we asked for as victors. I don't know what it would have been before—but now, we could ask to bring the vampires back to life. A real life. A mortal life.*

"We're just... I don't know," I said to my mom. "She's having issues with her boyfriend—"

"That boy came down with the same thing the Kelly girl did, didn't he?" Mom bit her lip as she executed a turn. "I wonder if Journey will even want to go this weekend."

As if on cue, I actually got a reply from Journey herself.

Devam dumped me. After everything, he had the nerve to DUMP me.

My fingers hovered over the screen, wondering which to reply to first.

No brainer. Journey needed me. She'd reached out to me. And she was the only one who might understand—who wouldn't try to trick me into killing off the entire vampire race. Probably.

What? I typed back. *What happened?*

Mom pulled into a parking lot and took out her phone, asking me what I wanted to order from the restaurant she was right outside of. She'd charge it to her account and then wander around the strip mall until it was ready for pickup.

"The Asian salad," I said, finally bringing the phone out of my purse and forgoing all sense of secrecy.

"What is it?" Mom asked.

"The Asian salad," I said again.

"No, I mean... Is everything all right?"

Where to start? I sighed. "Journey just texted. She and Devam broke up. He dumped her."

Mom scowled. "He got sick and *dumped* her? Talk about strange timing. Does Lacey know?"

I'd been so distracted, I'd almost forgotten about the best friend code. Our mothers were best friends, and anything either of us shared with one could and would be used in a court of judgement against us by the other. "I don't know. It just happened." I turned to Mom, pleading with her. "Can you let Journey tell her mom first? It's all still fresh."

"All right," said Mom, sliding her phone back into her purse. "It's just... I remember she took her last breakup pretty hard."

"Because he was cheating on her."

"And this boy isn't...?"

I opened my mouth to respond, but I didn't really know. Besides, from what I'd observed of him, he *had* been awfully cozy with Yvonne. Ha. As if I could tell Mom her supposedly adult secretary was the other woman. "I'm still... We're still talking about it."

"Well," said Mom, "if you're feeling better, maybe I should take you back to school after lunch and you can talk to her in person."

Right. School. Journey was there. Or was supposed to be.

"I'm still... I don't know," I said, rubbing my forehead dramatically. "The doctor said the shot takes a few days to really settle down, you know?"

"All right, all right." Mom opened her door. "Are you coming?"

"I'll wait in the car."

"It's chilly out."

I hadn't even noticed. "I'm fine."

"Well, take the keys if you change your mind. It should be ready in just ten minutes."

"Thanks," I said, wholly focused on the phone in front of me.

He's a... Journey was still typing but must have erased what she was going to type next. *You know. And I don't want to be.*

I don't blame you, I wrote back. *I'm sorry I ever dragged you into this.*

I'm glad you did, she texted. There was another long pause. *I'm sorry I ever blamed you for this. If you were going to be involved in all of this, of course I'd want to know. I'd want to do what I could to support you through it.*

I wanted to keep you out of it.

What's done is done.

Neither of us wrote anything for a while. A new message from "C" appeared, but I dismissed it for now.

Do you still want to go to Chicago with me and my family this weekend? Journey asked.

Sure, I texted, suddenly feeling confident in my ability to keep my cool around crowds of humans. I'd done just fine at the doctor's without Dean. *If you want me to come.*

Of course I do, she wrote back. *It'll be like old times. No you-knows, no boyfriends... Does Dean need to come, you think? For your safety?*

He's not the boss of me, I texted. *I'll tell him to stay away.*

He can come if you think he ought to.

You-knows can go and rot right now for all I care. Shifting, I clonked my elbow against the car door on accident, breathing sharply through my teeth as my funny bone began to tingle.

Did I miss something? Journey asked.

Talk about it later, I said, noticing my mom coming out of the restaurant, a to-go bag in hand. *Mom will probably make me go back to school tomorrow,* I wrote. *I'll see you then. Unless you want to come over tonight.*

She didn't ask why I'd missed school for a few days, but then again, I'd known she'd seen the messages I'd sent explaining I had "blood-related problems." I figured if the NSA was reading it, they would assume I'd meant Aunt Flo.

Can you meet me at Dad's diner after school?

No car, remember?

Mom got into the vehicle just then and handed me the bag, which I quickly stuffed at my feet. Another message from "C" popped up and this time when I went to dismiss it, I caught the first few words.

We're under attack, he wrote.

"They almost forgot my bread roll," Mom muttered as she started up the car. "And then they handed me a baguette when I'd explicitly asked for multigrain."

I swiped Journey's message aside and took a closer look at Calder's.

I'll do whatever you want me to do to prove it to you, he'd written first. Then, *Alarms are going off. Bloodsuckers with you?*

Then: *We're under attack. Orin and Ivy's sister.*

A new message appeared as I looked at the screen: *None of our safeguards work against the fae.*

"Mom, I'm really feeling sick again," I said. "I might throw up."

Mom's eyes widened as she pulled out of the lot. "Should we go back to the doctor?"

"No! No. Just, uh... Can we get home? Please?"

Where's Ivy? I typed back.

"That's where I was headed." Mom took a hand off the steering wheel to touch my cheek with the back of her hand. "You're a little warm."

Fire was starting to soar through me, at odds with the icy venom that wanted to bring my throbbing pulse to an end.

"It's fine. Probably just a reaction to the shot."

Not here, he wrote. *She's not answering. She might not care to help. Not unless she thinks her sister is in danger.*

Which she very well could be going against a merfolk stronghold like that.

I don't know if I can make it, I wrote back, and my heart was thundering at the thought. What did *I* care if I didn't make it in time to save the merfolk? Or to protect Autumn? Let them all wear each other down. It would make it easier for the vampires to declare victory.

Because that was what I wanted, wasn't it?

Darn it, I thought. There was that part of me—however small—that believed Calder. Believed he could help me bring Raelynn and Devam back to life properly.

Believed he might care... Maybe.

If any man genuinely could.

Don't hurt Autumn, I said, thinking about my little brat of a step-sister. She'd been nothing but cute and fun before I'd realized she'd wanted to choke me to death.

We'll try. No guarantees. Besides, Ivy has to be the one... His message sent without the rest of that sentence. The one what? The one to attack Autumn. To make her surrender. Or it wouldn't count.

Calder? I wrote.

"We're almost there," said Mom, nervousness twinging her voice. I must have looked as panicked as I felt.

Only we weren't almost *there*. I couldn't very well tell her to drop me off where her little step-daughter was attacking the merfolk mansion, could I? *Hey, Mom, be a doll and drop me off at a friend's? I know I said I was sick, but I have a faery's butt to kick and a merfolk army to keep at bay.*

Ivy's here. With Autumn, wrote Calder. *She's behind her. Letting it happen.*

That revelation almost made me swear out loud, but I didn't think Mom would buy I'd dropped the f-bomb because I'd felt nauseous.

———

"I don't have to go to work today, honey," said Mom, tucking me in like a five-year-old.

"Mom, please. I don't want you to miss because of me. I'm fine. I didn't even throw up, right?"

Calder could have been dead by now. Or Autumn and Ivy could have been hurt—and what did he mean Ivy was with Autumn? Was she teaming up with the faefolk?

And if they won, what did *they* want?

I'd never even seen any of them besides Orin.

Mom sighed and got up. "If you're sure. I'll just go in for a few hours and make sure everything's in place."

"That's fine, Mom. Go. Thank you," I added quickly, my palms clammy as I clutched the comforter.

"I'll be back early," she said, heading to the door.

I counted to ten, waited for the sounds of the front door to open and shut, and then jumped up, scrambling to get the door open and run down the stairs after her. In the dark hall-way, I almost tripped over Arty, who darted in front of me and let out a screech as he continued on to my mom's and Easton's room. I stumbled, then grabbed on to the stair railing, my arm wrenching as I shouted in pain.

Before I could blink, Dean was there, holding me in his arms like a princess, saving me from tumbling right down the stairs.

My heart was thundering, echoing loudly throughout my brain. "What are *you* doing here?" I snapped.

"Saving you, apparently." He smiled, but it quickly faltered. "I told you I could follow your ma's car without being noticed."

"And I told *you* to leave me alone." I pushed at his chest, kicking my legs until he put me down. "How did you get in here?"

"Same way I always do." He reached into his pocket and pulled out a keyring with a key. *My* house key.

I bristled and walked toward the coatrack. "I don't have time for this."

"You've looked worried for a while now," Dean said, following me as casually as if going for a jaunt. "Ever since you read something on your phone."

Of course he'd been watching me in the parking lot, too. "If you must know, Journey's devastated because vampire Devam dumped her. Probably for one of your much-older aunts."

"My *aunts* don't date teenagers," said Dean, the disgust plain as day on his face.

Vampires with several extra decades on them didn't date teenagers, apparently. It was distasteful. Nothing wrong with that statement coming from my supposed vampire boyfriend.

"That came out wrong," said Dean.

My jacket was already on and I was slipping on my shoes. I was in no mood for his nonsense.

"So why the rush?" asked Dean. "Miss Slowe is still at school, isn't she? Did she leave early?"

That got me wondering about Ivy and Autumn—and Calder and any of his friends for that matter. None of them went to school today? Maybe the merfolk didn't care anymore. Maybe the Sheppard sisters had just snuck out early to plan this attack when the merfolk would least expect it.

Who cared about school anymore if the world might end?

I ran out the front door, not even bothering to lock it behind me. Why should I? My would-be vampire boyfriend had free access to the place apparently.

"Doll, hold up!" Dean called from behind me. "Where are you going? You're going to walk to meet Journey? I can give you a ride."

A ride would be excellent about now.

But then I'd have to explain I wasn't going to meet Journey.

I didn't think Dean would be happy with the idea of me heading to the Pooles' mansion.

Then again, short of knocking him out—and I wasn't sure *how* I could if I even intended to—it was clear I was going nowhere without him following me.

I swirled on Dean. "I'm not going to Journey's, okay? I'm going to the Pooles' house."

"Why?" A muscle in his jaw clenched.

"They're under attack. Autumn and Orin... and Ivy maybe."

"Ivy's attacking the fishfolk?" A close-lipped smile threatened to break out across his lips.

He probably thought *he* was responsible for her turning traitor. By letting her be the first to know secrets he hadn't even shared with his champion—his girlfriend.

"I need to know what's going on," I said.

"How do you even know this is happening?"

Pulling my phone out of my pocket, I checked to see if Calder had sent any more messages since he'd identified Ivy among the mansion's attackers. He hadn't. I'd left Journey hanging, but I'd explain what had happened later.

"Will you give me a ride or not?" I asked instead of answering the question.

"Not until I ring Minnie and—"

"No."

"I'm sorry?"

"I'm not asking you to bring your vampire army in to swoop into the wreckage of some in-progress battle. I want to see what's going on *right now*."

"It could be a trap," said Dean, his hands sliding into his pockets.

As if I hadn't already thought of that. "Then it could be just the occasion I need to end this. Champion versus champion versus champion, remember? All of the rest of you are supposed to be hanging back."

"We'll hang back if *they* hang back."

"You sound like a kindergartner," I said. "*'They started it.'*"

"Maybe they did."

Growling, I turned around and headed back down the sidewalk.

"Wait!" said Dean after a beat. "I'll give you a ride."

I stomped toward his shiny car, refusing to let him open the door for me, but when I grabbed for the handle I found it locked. Crossing my hands over my chest, I stewed as he unlocked the door and held it open for me anyway.

Fire was raging through my veins as I waited the excruciatingly long time for Dean to find himself behind the steering wheel and start the car up.

"I don't think it's a good idea, going without backup," said Dean. "Last time we took a risk because Miss Slowe was in danger, but this time... Are you worried about your stepsisters?"

I snorted. I was running out of patience when it came to forgiving either one of them, even if Autumn was just a kid.

"Ember, you need to tell me what you're thinking—"

"I don't *need* to do anything." Staring out the car window, I swallowed hard, fighting against the lump in my throat. "I know I'm stuck as your champion—"

"Stuck?" echoed Dean. Cars were honking and there were sirens wailing somewhere up ahead.

"But that's it from now on." My heart was pounding so hard, it almost burst out of my skin. "Okay?" Tears were pooling in my eyes now, tears that sizzled and turned to steam as the venom ventured out and retreated from my heart, my head a mess of confusion. I kept my eyes closed tightly against the rays of the sun penetrating even through the overcast sky. "I don't want to be your girlfriend anymore."

Dean didn't say anything.

He didn't try to win me back. Didn't act hurt or angry or anything.

I'd wanted him to have *some* reaction.

"Glad to know you don't even—" I started, but my eyes flew open as Dean slammed on the brakes.

Police had begun to set up a barricade as firetrucks wove past them, heading down the covered gravel driveway that led to the Pooles' mansion.

Beyond the trees, plumes of smoke swirled up into the air.

A loud thumping from the back of the vehicle practically made me jump out of my seat.

Both Dean and I turned to find Orin pounding a hand against the back window, waving once he got our attention.

I hastened to roll down the window, cursing the crank the car used instead of a single button. The muscles in my wrenched arm ached. I started coughing as soon as the window cracked.

"Bit late for the show," said Orin. "The girls went on ahead home."

"What happened?" asked Dean, all business. A car honked behind us, but Dean didn't move from the middle of the road.

"Had a bit of a tussle with the fish, yeah?"

"You can't attack them like that," I said. "Champion versus champion, not—"

"Since when do any of these younglings pay attention to my rules?" Orin leaned his arms where the window should be. "Besides, it was my champion's idea. And we didn't hurt no one. Possibly. Gave them a fair shake of getting out."

The water. They must have swum away... They had to have. Right?

Why was my heart thundering so much? What did I care if Calder was injured?

"You destroyed their home," said Dean. He didn't have to see it to know. The smoke seemed to be evidence enough.

"They had no use for the thing if they got their way, all right?" Orin shrugged and leaned back. "Just hastening the inevitable. Putting a little *fire* in their veins. Excuse the expression. And the fact that we borrowed your own little trick." He pulled a lighter out of his pocket. "But I don't need a girl who can shoot fire out of her hand when I got me one of these, do I?"

"You're sick," I said, my anger boiling over at the smile on his face. "If you wanted the merfolk out of this, you should have focused on defeating Ivy—"

"Ember," said Dean. He placed a hand on my shoulder, but I shrugged it off.

"Autumn is having a bit of trouble at the idea of attacking her big sis, all right?" Orin's eyes narrowed at me as he stood back. "She wasn't so hard to convince to play this little game with *you*."

"You won't win unless you defeat Ivy," I said.

"Or get her to surrender. I'm working on it." Orin rubbed the side of his nose and stepped farther back. "Easier to have them unite against the common enemy first, no?"

The common enemy. Me.

If Ivy could turn even on her army of mersoldiers...

"Ember, let's go," said Dean, the car making a sharp turn as we turned around at the police barrier and made our way back.

Orin walked casually along the edge of the woods, giving me another nod as we drove away. Bringing two of his fingers up to his eyes, he then pointed them right at me, like some threat straight out of an action movie.

And then with just the slightest crack in the air, he vanished out of sight.

CHAPTER TWENTY-THREE

Dean had insisted he didn't know anything about faeries vanishing.

Minnie had seemed contemplative when I'd brought it up, after we'd given her a full report. Well, I'd left out *how* I'd known about the attack. Minnie hadn't seemed to notice, her usual confident demeanor cracking as she'd paced in front of the fire.

She hadn't seemed surprised Orin had vanished, but she hadn't offered an explanation, either.

Nor had she seemed pleased that the merfolk were nowhere to be found. They'd indeed lost their home, we'd found out the next day on the news, though the fire had been contained by the moat and the woods had escaped undamaged.

"There are more of them," Minnie had said, brushing my dad aside as he'd come to offer her a goblet of blood. "Orin isn't the only one. Watch your back."

She'd reached out and grabbed the goblet from my chastened father, swallowing it in one throaty gulp.

Dean had seemed confused, contemplative.

And not at all bothered about what we'd discussed right before Orin's little confrontation.

I kept checking my phone, but even if it were true that Calder was all right, there was no way he'd thought to bring his phone under the water with him. It was hopeless.

"We need to regroup," said Dean as he pulled into my driveway. "Think through the next stage of the plan."

"You do that," I said, opening my door before Dean could. "I'm going out of town this weekend."

"What?" *That* seemed to snap Dean out of his thoughts. "You can't."

"I *can*," I said, "and I don't need a vampire entourage. I'm going to Chicago with Journey's family."

I'd given Journey as much information as I could about what had gone down, and she'd been insistent we get the heck out of town as long as we could. Away from these "consummate lands." Away from all this... mess.

I didn't know if Calder was all right. I wasn't entirely sure why I cared, unless it was because without him, I wasn't sure how I could change the vampires back to human beings.

Dean would never agree to make that our wish if we were to win this thing together. He wanted *more* vampires, not fewer.

"You can't go anywhere," said Dean, but I was already out of the car. He appeared next to me in a flash as I made my way toward the front door. I hoped no one had been looking out the window, though the lack of Mom's car in the driveway eased some of my worries. No need to explain why I'd been "so sick" and had just been dropped off by the boy she'd known to be my boyfriend.

How did I explain he no longer was? He'd probably be hanging around here endlessly because I was his champion; I'd have to keep up the charade until this whole thing was over.

"I didn't ask your permission," I said. "And I don't need to."

Dean stood in front of me. "You do," he snapped. "You're just a girl—"

"I'm a *champion*," I said. "And I don't appreciate you pulling this 'overprotective man' thing on me—"

"It's what you wanted," he said, standing straighter. "I've been the man you've dreamed of, *exactly* how you've wanted me to be, since this whole thing started."

That lump in my throat was back and I clenched my phone in my hand. It was as good an admission of the fact that he'd been tricking me this whole time as any. "Don't flatter yourself."

"Ember, you may be my champion, but that doesn't make you invulnerable. It makes you a *target*."

"Then come." I sighed. "To Chicago with me. But hang back. Skulk in the shadows like the overprotective monster you are." I didn't stop even when Dean's bright blue eyes flashed coldly, when he stepped back unconsciously. "I don't want to even know you're there."

"Doll—" He grabbed for my shoulder.

I whipped it away. "Don't call me that." We'd reached the front door now and I stepped inside, remembering I hadn't bothered to lock the door.

Dean followed me inside. The old man could not take a hint.

I spun on him. "Where's Lyric?"

"Huh?" Dean seemed surprised by that question.

"I didn't see Raelynn or Devam when we went to your place."

"They're at school." Dean checked the old-timey wristwatch on his forearm. "Dr. Gibbons cleared them both for attendance, so long as the other vampires are keeping an eye on them—"

"And Lyric is just okay with all of that?" I asked. "Journey told me she wasn't at school today. She also told me Minnie had made them an *offer*, to become bloodbags, to *wait their turns* to become vampires—"

"I told you we're trying to get them on our side. Smooth over the... *accidents* that led to their sweethearts making the trip over to our side a little sooner than planned."

"You promised me," I said. "You promised me Journey and Devam would never become vampires."

Dean tossed his head back. "Things change. We adjust to those changes. Hey, you were the first one to turn a kid from your school, not any of us—"

"Don't talk to me anymore," I said, ripping my coat off and hanging it haphazardly atop the coat rack. "Unless it's directly related to something to do with this stupid, endless war you dragged me into—"

"Ember," started Dean.

"I mean it!" I shouted, turning around at the bottom stair. "Leave me alone."

Dean's jaw clenched. "I never meant to hurt you."

"Then you never should have made me believe you cared." Dragging myself up the stairs, I didn't look back.

———

"School wearing you two down?" asked Mrs. Slowe as she looked up from her smartphone.

"Yup," said Journey, her voice clipped and to the point. She didn't even move from where her head rested against my shoulder, the two of us sharing a bench seat on the Metra to Chicago. Her dad was sitting in the row next to us, chatting about football with Dante. He and Journey were going to visit their grandmother while in town.

"If it's a couple of *boys* making the two of you mope like this..." started Mrs. Slowe.

I was pretty sure Dante's ears perked up at that, though Mr. Slowe went on undaunted about numbers and trades I didn't understand.

"Hmm," was all Journey said.

"Hmm," I added.

I didn't know where to start even if I *had* wanted to talk about it with Journey's mom. Which I certainly did not.

"If a man doesn't make you feel appreciated, he's not worth

a second of your time," said Mrs. Slowe. "Do you think they're sitting somewhere right now moping about you?"

"*Mom*," said Journey.

She had a point, though. Journey shifted upward, crossing her arms over her chest and stretching her legs out.

Wherever Devam was, he was more focused on blood than an ex-girlfriend.

And Dean... Well, he was somewhere on this train. I supposed he *was* thinking about me. Only not like I was his ex. Just the champion he was stuck with.

We'd both agreed that my mom was probably not a target, considering she was carrying Ivy and Autumn's sibling, too. But just to be safe, Herbert and some of the bloodbags were taking turns keeping an eye on her.

My father had actually volunteered to help.

In case Orin somehow convinced his little child soldier to do to our house or Mom's business what they had done to the Pooles'.

"I'm just saying," said Mrs. Slowe. "Moping about a man never helped anyone." She tugged up the zipper on her jacket and shivered. "It's cold on these things in the fall."

I had to agree. My nose was growing numb. But still... Chilly as late November was in the Windy City, it was nice to be getting out of town. Even if a cadre of vampire bodyguards was on another car, even if I wasn't *totally* getting away from all of this.

At least I could pretend I was.

"We should see the Christmas decorations at Macy's," said Journey. "Or the Christkindlmarket." She sniffled. Whether from the cold or "moping about a man," I couldn't say for sure.

"Yeah," I said. "And maybe head to Navy Pier?"

"Are the rides open this time of year?" asked Journey. Her heart was barely in this discussion. But I empathized.

"Who knows?" I said wistfully. "Maybe we can just see a movie."

"Yeah."

"Don't sound so excited, girls," said Mrs. Slowe. She narrowed her eyes as she looked us over. "And don't go anywhere without Dante, all right?"

"What?" Journey shot straight up. "*Mom*, we're not ten."

"I'd feel better if you weren't alone."

Journey opened her mouth, but Mrs. Slowe beat her to it. "Don't argue about this with me, Journey."

Journey huffed and sent her cousin a scathing look, as if he were to blame for this. Luckily, he didn't seem to notice.

The train slowed as we came to another of the thirty or so stops the train would make on the way. It was true that driving might have taken less time, but there *was* something convenient about the train. Better than dealing with Chicago traffic. And weekend passes were a fairly low price. Journey and I had taken the train to Chicago to visit her grandma or just to hang in the city countless times on our own over the weekends in the summer especially.

Now, for some reason, we were too vulnerable to go anywhere in the city without a chaperone. I doubted Mrs. Slowe would buy the fact that I had a stealthy vampire bodyguard force out there somewhere and that we'd be perfectly fine.

Even though there were fewer people on the weekend trains in the colder months, the latest stop adding a fairly teeming throng. I went from cold to warm all at once, the air thick with the odor of living, breathing heartbeats.

"I'm going to use the restroom," I said.

"Ew," was Journey's response.

True. But I didn't necessarily have to *use* it. I just needed to get away from the throng.

There wasn't a restroom on the car we were on, so I squeezed past the assorted people moving from one car to the other to get to the next. The proximity of the family beside me wasn't helping stave away the dizziness throbbing in my head.

The clang of the train doors closing behind me was maddeningly loud, jolting through me like an anvil.

I darted into the bathroom just as a little kid ran out, sliding the door shut.

I didn't have a chance to reorient myself as the train started moving again, sending me stumbling, and the door behind me opened.

"Occupi—" My mouth got stuck open.

Calder had followed me into this cramped, tiny space.

He slid the door shut behind him and locked it.

"How did you—why are you...?" Clearing my throat, I got ready to scream.

"Wait!" he said in a hush. "Your bloodsucker friends are two cars down."

"That's the idea," I said. "I need to get their attention."

"I was careful to avoid detection when I followed you," he said. "I don't think they even know I got on the train."

"How did *you* know I was on it?"

"Your step-dad might have mentioned it to Ivy's mom."

"And you're on speaking terms with her? Considering she was helping Autumn and Orin *destroy* your home?"

The train buckled and we both grabbed for the bars on either side of the small stall, his fingers brushing against mine.

A little thrill shot through me at the touch and I quickly pulled away, cursing my stupidity.

"She hasn't renounced being the champion of the water yet," he said. "I can't just leave her be."

"So you want her to...?" I asked. "If she's no longer your champion, this whole thing is at an end for the foreseeable future."

Calder shuffled best he could to remove a backpack hanging off one shoulder. He unzipped it and the dim lighting of the bathroom stall was instantly bathed in a multi-colored glow.

Green. Blue. Red.

The orb needed to declare oneself a champion. Before sealing the deal with a kiss.

"Denounce the blood," he said, his voice clipped, harsh. The light reflected off his russet eyes to reveal a sense of desperation, a deep kind of longing.

"Why would I do that?" I meant to say it louder, harsher, but it came out as a hoarse whisper, the cold, metal bar on the wall digging into the small of my back.

"You know why," he said. "Become my champion and we'll fix this all. End the war. Bring your friends back—as human beings. We may annihilate *vampires*, but if you wish for them all to be alive again, you won't even be seeing to their deaths."

"And what about the faeries?" I asked.

"Will you really miss Orin?" His eyebrows narrowed. "Can't say I will."

I supposed he wouldn't. "Minnie... Minnie said there were more of them," I said. "More faeries."

Calder pushed the backpack closer. "If that's even true and not some bloodsucker trick, they won't be missed. Ember, *please*."

The bright lights in the dark backpack were soothing somehow, the throbbing of my head fading away as I found my fingers moving without my knowledge to the open bag.

Yanking my hand back, I gripped the metal bar behind me.

"If you drop out, no one can win," he said. "Champions need to *surrender*, not drop out of the game entirely. Ivy might be satisfied and drop out, too. Then you can declare for water before Autumn drops out—"

"Leaving Ivy with no choice but to become the *champion of blood* if she wants to stay in this war?" My incisor pierced a small hole in my bottom lip, the tang of blood seeping to my tongue like a trickle of water after a desert trek. Visions of Dean holding Ivy in his arms started my heart beating wildly again. That was exactly what he wanted, I bet.

I was just a kid to him, but her...

"No," I said.

"It has to be that way," said Calder. "If you want to end this."

"*No!*" I said, louder this time. "Not like this."

The bathroom door clattered as someone tried opening it, the rocking of the train beneath our feet causing me to pitch forward.

Calder caught me, one arm around my back, the other still clutching the backpack between us.

"Dean won't let you wish them back," he whispered into my ear.

"I..." I wanted to lay into him, to ask him if he thought I was *stupid* enough to believe Calder cared. Instead I said, "I want to believe you." It was the truth. My forehead nestled into his shoulder. It was so warm. So sturdy and comforting.

"You want to save them," he said, his deep voice like a feather caressing my cheek. "I want to save my family—*without* flooding the world. Please. You're the only one who can decide to save them both." He clutched my chin, his backpack wholly supported between us. "Ember, I know I seem desperate. I am. But it's true. I'm in love with you. I always have been."

He lowered his face and I closed my eyes as his lips pressed to mine, timid at first, and then harder, greedier, warmer.

His breath was warm, not the icy blast from the chaste kisses Dean had bestowed upon me. His tongue slipped inside my mouth and danced with mine.

I leaned up into the kiss, my arms wrapping around him, my head growing dizzy, strange.

The door clanked again and someone pounded on the outside.

It broke the spell and I pulled away.

Calder's grip on my back loosened, though his eyes remained hard, staring at me. I had to look away.

I heard the zipper on his backpack. "That's a taste," he said. "A taste of what could be."

"What?"

Calder's hand was already on the lock. "Even if you're not my champion, my kiss, my saliva, affords you the ability to experience life as a mermaid for a time."

"*What?*" That was news to me.

"Think it over," he said, clicking the door unlocked and sliding it open.

"*Finally*," said some guy in a White Sox cap as Calder pushed past him. "Took long—whoa!" He shook his head and stared at me. "That explains what took so long. *Kids*."

That loud car-to-car slam of the door made me jump, and I pushed past the man, the heavy scent of sweat from behind his windbreaker almost enough to make me vomit as I went after the mermaid prince who'd claimed to have magically kissed me out of some fairy tale romance.

Only he was nowhere to be found among the crowd of people headed toward the doors as the train came to another stop.

CHAPTER TWENTY-FOUR

After checking into our hotel attached to the convention center where Mr. Slowe's restaurateur convention was taking place, we parted from Mr. Slowe and headed to the south side of the city to have lunch with Journey and Dante's grandma.

It was hard for me to concentrate on the questions Mrs. Johnson asked. My fingers kept brushing my lips as I focused inward on any sign that anything about me had *changed*, but of course it hadn't.

This had to be another trick.

"The plan still being roommates at that upstate college?" Mrs. Johnson asked.

Journey nudged me and I jumped, my eyes drawn to the elderly woman in front of me instead of the window—where I'd been looking for a sign of anyone. Vampire. Merman. Step-sister.

This was supposed to be a weekend where I *forgot* everything.

"Yup," said Journey. "We're both already accepted. Bradview."

"Hmm," said Mrs. Johnson. She tugged her knitted shawl

tighter around her shoulders, and I could feel her eyes boring into me through her Coke bottle glasses attached to a chain. I had to look away, fixing on the china mug she'd filled with tea for me. "And you, boy? You got your post-high school plans all set yet?"

"Nah," said Dante. "Too early." At Mrs. Johnson's sharp look, he stiffened and grabbed his tea cup. "That is, not yet, ma'am. But I may be headed to vocational school."

"You try for some scholarships," said Mrs. Johnson, "before you give up on college entirely."

"Mama, not everyone is destined for another four years of school," said Mrs. Slowe, taking another lump of sugar and adding it to her tea. It *was* awfully potent. Jasmine and citrus.

"Yes, but you went and look at you now." Mrs. Johnson pinched Mrs. Slowe's cheek and it was nice to see that some mothers never stopped seeing their babies in that light. "Your brother does well at his body shop, no doubt, but I do wish he'd have given college a shot. He was smart, that one. And all my grandkids are, too." She narrowed her eyes at Dante and he brought the shaking cup to his lips, sipping and clearly trying to hide his disgust at the taste of the brew.

"Nana, we'll stop by tomorrow, but we have to get going." Journey stood and went over to kiss her grandma on the cheek. "We're seeing a movie at Navy Pier."

"Way up there?" asked Mrs. Johnson. "We can watch something right here. In my living room."

"You don't have an IMAX," said Journey, laughing. "Besides, I haven't been to the Pier in ages."

"It's cold out," said Mrs. Johnson. "Not much to *do* there on the lake. The late fall wind can be biting, child."

"We'll bundle up," said Journey. She stared at me and Dante in turn, her eyebrows arched.

"Right," I said, jumping to my feet and grabbing for my coat and hat. Dante followed suit.

"Be careful," said Mrs. Slowe. "Text me when you get there."

"Mom, we're going uptown, not cross-country." Journey rolled her eyes. Then Mrs. Slowe sent her a look that mirrored her mother's most potent. "Right. Of course," said Journey, clearing her throat.

After saying our *goodbyes* and *thank yous*, none of us spoke during the brisk, quick walk to the nearest Red Line stop.

"Sorry about that," Journey said once we'd ascended the platform and used our daily passes to get to the waiting area. "Nana never wants to let us go."

"I wouldn't have minded," I said, picturing a cozy evening watching a movie from the safety of a couch. Not quite so close to the endless waters of Lake Michigan. In the distance, the gray-ish blue poked through the buildings, sending a sharp stabbing to my gut. There was something about *water*, about the vastness of the lake, that wasn't sitting right with me just then.

"You okay?" asked Journey. "You look pale. Er, *paler*."

"Yeah, yeah," I lied. I looked over my shoulder for any signs of being followed and sure enough, down below on the sidewalk, completely out of place, three pasty men in woolen business coats, trilby hats atop their heads, were clustered with a golden-haired woman with a Carmen Sandiego-like hat. My entourage. Trying to keep a few steps out of sight. I wondered what they'd been up to while visiting Journey's grandma, but I supposed hoping they were freezing outside would do no good, considering the cold didn't bother them.

"Yeah, I saw them," said Journey spitefully.

Dante looked up from his phone at that, but before he could ask anything, the train arrived and we joined the crowd pushing to where the nearest car door would open. The cluster of vintage vampires moved quickly then, heading up the stairs.

"Come on," I said, grabbing Journey's hand. We found open seats, Dante taking the end of the bench just as the vampires stepped on a few cars behind us.

I sighed.

"Well, it's not like you *really* want them to leave us be,

right?" Journey twirled a lock of hair around her gloved finger. "Considering..."

"What are you two up to?" asked Dante, a slight grin on his face. "Acting all cloak and dagger? It's freaking me out. Take it easy. I'll protect you two from anyone shady."

"Gee, thanks," said Journey. "I feel much safer now." She snorted and Dante gave her a look to rival their grandma's.

I rested my head against Journey's shoulder as the train made its stops, heading underground at one point as we made our way north. There hadn't been a good chance to tell her about Calder in the Metra bathroom—not a single moment since where the two of us had been alone.

Clutching my purse on my lap, I thought about texting it to her, even if Dante was sure to ask questions. Despite being on his own phone, he seemed pretty observant, his gaze flicking toward us every minute or so.

But how could I explain? I stared at my right hand, wondering if it would glow blue or if there was some other sign of being able to shift to a mermaid.

But no. Blue ice was for his champion. Mermaids... How had it happened for Ivy at first? She'd been in the shower.

Shower. Water.

By the time I got back to the hotel and took one, Calder's spell would likely have worn off. If he was telling the truth at all.

And even if he was—what, did he think I'd care? Oh, joy, I can become a mermaid. Sign me right up for betraying everything I'd fought for over the past couple of months.

It was hard to believe it had only been that long.

"We have to walk a few blocks," said Journey, breaking me out of my thoughts. We'd arrived at our stop already. She stared at my bare hand. "Did you bring any gloves?"

"Uh, no," I said, flexing my fingers. With a brief flash, they glowed red and I clenched my hand into a fist, stuffing it into my coat pocket. "But I'll be fine."

Journey smiled coyly. "Right. Forgot about your... pocket warmer."

Dante shook his head as he slipped his phone into his jacket and we all shuffled toward the door. Through the clear windows separating each car, I noticed my vampire bodyguards headed to their door as well.

Here's to hoping Dante doesn't notice them and ask why my "boyfriend" is stalking me instead of tagging along.

"Come on," said Journey, and as soon as the doors opened, she sprinted past the crowd and up the stairs to the street, not pausing for a second. It was all I could do to follow without resorting to time pause tricks in plain view of a few dozen milling people.

"There's no shaking them," I said, panting once I reached her at a curb.

"I was thinking more my cousin than your bodyguards, but..." Journey looked over her shoulder and lowered her voice. Dante was raising his hands in frustration about a block back as he tried to dart around a slow-moving group of tourists lollygagging and pointing to the buildings around them. "Something's been bothering you for a bit," Journey continued. "Something *other* than everything that's already been bugging you, I mean."

"It's..." I bit my lip. I had just a few seconds before Dante or the vampires—their outfits were easy to pick out from this distance, and they lingered a little behind Dante—were within earshot. Less, if Dean got especially antsy and relied on a time pause.

"Calder was on the train," I blurted out.

"What?" Journey looked taken aback, and she grabbed for my hand, fishing it out of my pocket, dragging us both forward as the crosswalk light turned white.

"He cornered me when I went to the bathroom." My breath was misty in the air in front of me as I hustled to keep up with her pace.

"Why didn't you tell me?" asked Journey, not slowing down.

"Or cave and find Dean? He was a car over. Saw him checking in on us the whole time. Must have missed when you left for the bathroom—"

"He..." I wanted to stop, to let it all out, to explain everything, but Dante and Dean and the other vampires were so close, and...

I wasn't ready for them to know everything just yet.

"It was no big deal," I said instead, my legs pumping as Navy Pier came closer into view. The Ferris wheel was moving, offering rides even in the cool late-autumn weather. "I took care of it."

"I doubt—"

"Cripes, girls, what are you playing at?" Dante screeched to a halt, clearly having jogged the last bit of distance to meet us. "Don't make me run down a busy sidewalk, please." He gestured every which way.

"You could have walked." Journey pouted. "We'd have met you at the Pier."

"Yeah, and if you think Nana and Auntie would accept *that* as an excuse if anything happened to you—"

"We're fine," I said, but I softened when I saw how the words must have hurt him. "But I'm sorry."

Journey growled and muttered something about being sorry, too, but Dante just rolled his eyes and seemed to be biting his tongue to keep from commenting on it.

We walked the last few blocks in silence, the wind from the direction of Lake Michigan tepid but biting, causing me to tug down on my knit hat, as if that would offer my head more warmth.

"Phew!" called Dante after holding the door for us both to step inside. I stomped my feet to get them warmer and looked around. We'd entered near a sit-down restaurant. Up ahead were a few shops and a food court and the movie theater farther back.

"Let's warm up in the Gardens," said Journey, referring to the Crystal Gardens, complete with palm trees and a giant, terrarium-like glass ceiling. "They probably have to keep it warm year-round for all the plants."

Seemed like we weren't the only ones with the idea. Though it was fairly crowded, we found a spot on a bench next to an elderly couple. Dante offered it to me and I sat down, peeling the hat off my head. "Whoa," I said under my breath. "It *is* warm in here."

And the warmth felt nice. At least at first. Soon enough I was unbuttoning my coat, and so were Journey and Dante. My eyes flicked to the glass doors leading back out to the food court and the shopping area. The red hat, the navy and gray woolen coats—they were there. I wondered if they were going to buy tickets to see our movie, too. There was no way Dante wouldn't notice them at some point.

"So we have some time," said Journey as she hung her coat over her arm. "Want to walk on the pier? Take a ride on the Ferris wheel?" She bumped her hip against mine as I stood to peel off my coat. It'd been forever since we'd ridden that—and never in the fall.

"And freeze our behinds off? No, thank you." Dante sat as the two elderly people went on their way.

"*You* can stay here and play on your phone," said Journey as her cousin moved to pull his phone out of his pocket.

He frowned at her but looked at his phone anyway. "Just stay where I can see you."

Sure. It wasn't exactly like much of the pier was visible from this bench. Journey looked at me and shrugged.

"Yes, Mr. Chaperone, sir," said Journey. She tossed her coat beside Dante and I did the same. "Shall we take a walk around the Gardens, my lady?" she asked in her most ridiculous hoity-toity voice.

Chuckling despite everything, I wove my arm through hers and we walked around, warming up. The hot and sticky air had steamed up the windows overlooking the lake and the pier and the humidity was starting to stick to my skin, too. I pulled at my burgundy vintage cardigan sweater, fanning myself. I'd paired it with a knee-length pencil skirt and thermal leggings poking out of UGG boots.

"Wool and humidity don't mix," said Journey, observing me.

I swallowed, looking down at my outfit. Part of me had been reluctant to put on any of my chic clothes provided by the vampires, considering everything... But I remembered how *confident* I'd felt the first time I'd dressed up to fit in with them. How sure of myself I'd been that I'd made the right decision. How happy I'd been to have such a handsome, considerate boyfriend who'd treated me like a queen.

I'd just wanted to capture a little of that happiness again.

I sighed as a couple of kids ran past in front of us, giggling, a harried dad apologizing to us while on their heels.

The scent of iron wafted through my nostrils as they passed, my head warm and heavy with the thought of their blood.

"Em?" asked Journey quietly.

"It's nothing."

"Okay, I'd *think* after everything we've been through together lately, you'd know better than to lie to me like that." A grimace lingered on her lips.

I was about to tell her. I was working up the courage, my thoughts full of Calder and what he'd promised me. Calder and the love he'd professed. Calder, his kiss, his warm lips on mine.

The children squealed and I jumped—only they were shrieking in joy as a spurt of water from the leapfrog fountains shot out over their heads. They raised their arms up to hit the water, splashing each other's faces.

"Stop that!" shouted the father, snatching one by the arm. "If you get wet, you'll catch your death of cold—"

A child screamed again and wiggled both of his arms into a spurt of water, the stream fanning out and spreading every which direction.

Journey dropped my arm and jumped back, her hands instinctively shielding her face. I held out my arm and felt the toes of my boot get soaked.

Soaked. Water. Calder. Slippery.

I fell to the ground, my boots shooting outward, my tights ripping as my legs snapped together.

They *ached*, and my throat—my throat was sore, parched, as if it needed water.

Water, water, water, or I would die.

CHAPTER TWENTY-FIVE

"Ember?" shrieked Journey.

But I was crawling toward an emergency exit, making my way through the overgrowth of flora, between two little areas of plants and shrubs toward the misty window and the promise of the lake beyond that would quench my need... For water.

"Ember!"

Journey's voice buzzed through my brain, but I was already there at the door, my arms reaching up and clutching the bar as if for dear life. I was breathing air, sure, but it didn't feel like enough. I needed to get out—out of this hot place, out of this muggy oxygen, away, away, and to the water.

I pushed through, ignoring the flashing light, the little whoop of sound that rang out with the movement.

The cold air hit my face like a shot of adrenaline to my veins, a relief soaring through every fiber of my body, right down to... I stared at where my toes should have been.

Fins. Pale red fins at the edge of a scaly, red fish tail.

The door opened behind me, the alarm going off once more. "Ember, what the...?" Journey gasped.

I sent her an apologetic look and tugged myself up over the railing separating the walkway from the edge of the pier.

Water. I needed water. More than air. More than anything.

"Ember, don't, just wait a—"

But I'd launched myself up and over and leaped down into Lake Michigan, my hands breaking the surface of the water that should have been deathly cold but felt so cool, so refreshing, so *nice.*

I submerged myself completely, just floating there upright in the murky waters, bouncing gently with the soft movement of the waves.

I was breathing underwater.

I stared down at my tail. I was a mermaid.

Calder had been telling the truth. But why...?

My torso *itched* with the sudden noticeable weight of the sweater, thick and soggy. I peeled it off, leaving nothing but my camisole and bra.

"You did it," came a husky voice from behind me. There was a sonorous quality to it, even in its familiarity—a melodic tone.

I opened my mouth to answer, not sure if I could even speak.

"Go ahead," said Calder in his merman form, swimming from who-knew-where up beside me. A grin tugged at his lips. "Say something. You belong here."

"What did you do to me?" I barked, the anger evident even beneath the harmonic quality of my strange voice through the liquid surrounding me. I banged on his chest with a fist as he approached, my eyes darting to the glowing orb he'd tucked under one arm.

He looked entirely nonplussed by my assault. "I told you I granted you the powers of a mermaid. For a time."

What was he talking about? Why was he doing this? Was this all just some trick—did he really not love me? Of course, he didn't, he...

Something *strange* happened then. Well, even *stranger.* Instead of seeing Calder in front of me, I saw... *me.*

At school, laughing next to Journey at a cafeteria table. Me at a dance, looking awkward as I danced with Dante—my arms stiff on his shoulders. Me slamming into someone's broad chest—a chest that seemed my own from my point of view. Me with Dean in the dark outside the woods in my backyard, my cheeks dashed with red, tucking a strand of hair once, then twice behind my ear.

And through it all, I felt... Love. Envy. Joy. Jealousy. Self-hatred. For not... For not speaking up sooner.

Only those weren't my *feelings.*

Someone let out an exasperated breath under her lips beside me. Ivy. Hugging her arms to her chest, ready to go into the woods with Calder. With me?

I snapped back to the moment, the waters of Lake Michigan all around us. "What was that?!"

Calder studied me and nodded. "You must have used our subconscious mindreading."

"What? That's how it works?" My beautiful mermaid voice didn't match my anger at all. "So what did I just see?"

"I don't know," said Calder. His pale green eyes searched me, and he was either a good actor or he wasn't lying. "The person whose mind is read never knows what the other saw."

"I saw... Me."

Calder seemed noticeably taken aback. "You must have wanted to know... how I felt about you."

"I..." I *had* wondered.

"And did you get your answer?" Calder moved closer, his hand hesitatingly floating beside my cheek.

I wanted to lean into it, but a jolt of reality came crashing down over me.

He was my enemy. He... He ought to be my enemy.

I wondered if Dean had noticed the problem by now—how could he not have with the alarm going off—but he couldn't do a thing about it. He hadn't packed his diving suits. Hadn't thought them necessary in the middle of the city, I was sure.

And I'd walked right into—*swum* right into—Calder's trap.

That became clearer as his comrades appeared from the

murkiness all around us, the teens who'd fought alongside Ivy, some adults I barely recognized lingering behind them.

Wanting to help me had been a *lie*. Going against his people—how foolish I had been to ever believe him!

Calder didn't seem ready to gloat just yet, though. "We've been living underwater," he said, "for the most part. Our river leads here, to the lake. The bloodsuckers can't touch us here and the faefolk wouldn't know where to find us."

"Stop!" I shouted. "Stop trying to confuse me."

"Confuse you? I'm not—"

I pushed away at him, my tail tingling as I struggled to get control of where I was, but all these *feelings* overwhelmed me at once. I clutched at my hair, screaming, yanking it at its roots.

"Ember, be careful—" said Calder.

My tail was *peeling*, ripping apart, as the venom moved out from my rapidly beating heart to the rest of my body.

"Ember! Ember, you have to stop. You have to let me kiss you. Your mermaid powers are—"

But I couldn't hear what else he had to say. With a sudden tide-like *yank*, I felt my body torn asunder, the weight of a thousand anvils weighing me down. I stared at my hands to find a red mist oozing out from my pores, looked down to see my feet returned, the red coming from every inch of my bare legs.

I opened my mouth, but no sound came out. The long incisors scraped against my lips and I realized my eyesight had sharpened even more than it had before, the murky details of litter beneath me as clear as day as the lake bed rose up to meet me.

As I sank down to meet *it*.

I could barely keep my eyes opened.

"Ember!" Strong hands took hold of me, but I was dragging, dragging the body down with me to the depths. It wasn't that I needed to *breathe*—there was no need for that. But I couldn't move in the water. I was so *heavy*. So *tired*.

Something hard pushed up against one of my hands. Something warm. The glow was evident even through my closed eyelids. Red. Green. Blue.

"You have to renounce being the champion of blood," came the singsong voice in my ear. "Ember, you *have* to. I can't lift you. You're suddenly so heavy—"

My hands fumbled weakly for the hard orb.

"Help!" shouted Calder, yanking me. "Help me get her to the surface! Bay—Llyr! *Come on*!"

No one seemed to be coming. But I was fading fast.

Calder's tug on my torso barely did anything.

His lips grazed mine again—no love in this kiss, just desperation.

"Think about water. Think about mermaids," he urged, trying to yank me backward.

What I meant to be a choppy laugh escaped my lips, but it was just an air bubble. I was thinking about water, all right. And how it would pull me down to my doom.

Forcing my bleary eyes open, I stared at the orb, at the pulsating red.

I don't want to be champion of blood, I thought to it. I stared hard, willing it to hear me. I opened my mouth, the words muffled as they fought past the water getting into my lungs. "I... am... not... blood... champion."

The orb slipped from my fingers as a bitter, bitter cold slapped against my skin, as the water sliding down my throat began to choke me...

And then with a mighty red glow that penetrated even through my closed eyelids, I was out.

———

"Ember!"

Something hard pushed against my chest and I felt suddenly suffocated, my eyes popping open to find hazy figures hovering above me, someone's strong hands compressing repeatedly on my sternum.

Water bubbled out from between my lips and multiple sets of hands shoved me onto my side as it spilled out.

Filth and liquid spilled over the coarse sand. I blinked as it finished, saw the Ferris wheel from Navy Pier way off in the distance.

More water spilled from my lips.

"Should we call an ambulance?" asked a strangely familiar female voice—slightly husky, often sarcastic. Right now it was shaky. Nervous.

I spun around, my head dizzy with the rapid movement.

Ivy. Autumn. Orin.

What the...? I struggled to speak. "How?" was all I got out between coughing fits.

Ivy's eyes shifted past the stretch of barren sand toward the lake—it was too cold for most anyone else to be here.

Calder stood there in the lake. Or floated or what have you. His torso was hidden by the water.

"We knew you were headed here," explained Orin. "Thanks to your mum—not exactly a secret. Tracked the merfolk to the lake, too. Thought something interesting might happen." Orin put a palm to my forehead and I slapped it away.

He chuckled. "If she were any other girl, maybe she'd need a hospital, but this here's a former champion."

"*Former?*" said Ivy, all business.

Former? I echoed. I stared down at my hand, as if that would explain. But it did. Because I was shivering, my bones chilled, my skin soaked beneath the heavy, damp camisole and skirt, and I wanted the fire. I *needed* it. And it would not come.

Not even a slight ember.

"You dropped out?" asked Autumn. She was chewing on a pompom attached to the end of her rainbow scarf. "Sorry. About your car... And everything." She looked sheepish, then turned to Orin. "Does this mean I win? Am I the faery princess?"

"Crikey, child, don't get ahead of yourself," said Orin, a mischievous grin on his face. "There's no winner if there aren't three champions."

Disappointment as clear as day washed over Autumn's expression.

Ivy jumped to her feet. "That's what we want, Autumn. Don't believe a word he says."

"If you can't believe a word I say, then you can't believe that there isn't a winner without three champions, either," muttered Orin.

Ivy ignored him and started looking around. "So where is it? The orb?" She stared down at me.

Like I could tell her anything. I shivered, coughing, and Orin peeled off his peacoat, laying it on top of me. I sent him a death glare but accepted it.

"Where's the orb?" Ivy shouted out at the water. "If Ember's dropped out, I will, too, now. It's what you wanted, isn't it?"

One, two, three, four new heads popped out from Lake Michigan beside Calder. One of the girls held the glowing object in her hands. She handed it to Calder, who locked eyes with Ivy.

She crossed her arms and tapped her feet, intimidating even in a blue, puffy down coat. "Well?"

Orin stood and twirled his wrist in the air. Out of nowhere, a sharp gust of wind shot straight toward the merfolk, who cowered in its assault, bending back, and the orb slipped out of Calder's hands, flying up and up and then soaring straight back at us like a giant baseball pitched at record velocity.

Ivy caught it in two black-gloved hands, digging her feet into the sand and glaring at Orin.

Shrugging, he slipped his fists into his khaki pockets, shivering just a bit as his shoulders hunched forward. "Just speeding things up, love."

Ivy looked down at the orb. Only blue and green glowed now. "I renounce being the champion of water," she said.

The blue grew brighter and then with no fanfare at all, it was out, flickering to darkness.

In her hands, she held an orb with nothing but a soft green glow radiating from a third of it.

Ivy crouched down beside Autumn at my side and shoved it toward her. "Now you."

"No!" Autumn leaned backward.

"Autumn, I'm not playing around—" started Ivy.

Autumn was on her feet, jumping back—skipping. "I don't want to!"

Stumbling to her feet, Ivy tucked the orb beneath her arm as she lunged at her sister. "This isn't a game, Autumn!" she shouted. "Get back here!"

Autumn ripped off her mitten and shot a vine at Ivy's feet. "Stay back!"

"Autumn, I'm counting to three..." Ivy stood stock still, her eyes narrowing. Coughing, I got to my feet, shivering as I threaded my arms through Orin's coat.

"Ladies, please," said Orin. "I know there aren't many people on this beach toward the end of November, but there *are* ways we can be witnessed. Bad enough we got some bobbing heads out there in the water, but there are people walking in the park over there. Nutters. It's *cold*." He mumbled the last few words.

"One," started Ivy.

I stumbled toward Ivy, my throat scratchy, my head dizzy.

"Two," she said.

"All right then," said Orin, and with another flick of his wrist, a gust of wind pushed past me and assaulted Ivy, sending the orb flying out from under her arm and gently back to rest atop Orin's fingers.

"We got company, gals." He nodded toward the park, Lake Shore Park if I remembered its name right, the strange zigzag walkway amidst the foliage and trees.

Four sets of sunglasses and vintage hats. And every few

seconds, the lead figure with the sunglasses seemed to teleport even closer. Dean.

Dean.

"Give that back!" screamed Ivy, brushing past me to launch herself at Orin.

I stumbled and before I could lose my balance entirely, I found myself in a pair of cold but sturdy arms. But so cold.

I spun around to find Dean at my side.

"No," he whispered, and it was more a shock than a command. "No..." A muscle in his jaw clenched perceptibly and it was enough. Even without seeing his eyes, I knew.

He knew I was no longer his. In any way, shape, or form.

He let me go and took a step back.

But I was strong enough to stand on my own feet now. Being in his arms had only made me colder.

The other vampires arrived at the beach, the wind ruffling their perfect hair, Zelda clutching her hat to keep it atop her head. And one of the men I'd mistaken for Ernesto—it was Devam.

Devam in a 1940s zoot suit. Devam acting like his whole purpose had been to fight in this war, to bodyguard for the champion.

It reminded me sharply of Raelynn, of what *I'd* done to her. I'd led Devam to his path as well.

"Where's Journey?" I asked. "And Dante?"

Dean shrugged. "We saw you go under and followed the migration." He jutted his chin toward the lake, where Calder and his merfolk cohorts were submerged up to their necks. "There's a whole school of fishfolk down there. We thought... *I* thought they'd taken you. To kill you. But Journey said..."

I finished for him. "I turned into a mermaid."

The sun setting over his shoulder, Dean removed his sunglasses slowly and tucked them into his front pocket. "A vampire mermaid," he said.

"Not anymore." I found my hand clutching my throat. "I had to... I would have sunk."

Dean guffawed, but there wasn't any amusement in it. "Clever plan of theirs."

I opened my mouth, prepared to defend Calder, to tell Dean that it wasn't some *plan*, but I knew he wouldn't understand.

Calder had saved me. The fear in his voice when I'd been sinking—that had been genuine.

I stared at my hand. Besides, I'd *seen* his thoughts. He did love me. He actually did, unlike Dean.

Giggles danced in the air behind me. "This ends now!" shouted Ivy. I turned to find her lunging at Orin, Orin and Autumn both laughing like children as they zigzagged around the beach, tossing the orb back and forth.

"How?" asked Dean. "How did he turn you into a mermaid? There's only one way, and it's only temporary—"

"I assume you know how, then." I lifted my nose in the air, tugging the coat tighter over my torso, willing myself to ignore the cold, cold, cold pricking at my human skin. "With a kiss."

Dean looked taken aback. "Then is that what *you* want?" asked Dean. "To be with him?"

"Yes," I said, still staring after my step-sisters and Orin and this ridiculous game of keep away.

"Ember?" Dean seemed confused.

I wasn't.

The orb went soaring through the air in a pass from Orin to Autumn, who hovered near me, and I lunged forward to snatch it out from her before she could catch it.

CHAPTER TWENTY-SIX

Grinning, Orin tucked his hands behind his back as I held the orb in front of me.

Autumn rushed up to try to snatch the orb from my grip, but I shoved her aside.

"Let go!" she said. "*I'm* the winner."

"Not without other champions, you're not," I said.

"Ember, don't—" started Dean.

"Ember, give it here," said Ivy, her lips in a thin line.

I stared out over her head at the figures in the water and swallowed, the movement tough on my scratchy throat.

"I declare myself the champion of water."

The blue glowed bright—icy in my hands.

The orb was so cold, I dropped it on instinct, but soon enough, the cold didn't bother me, and I stood straight, the shivers dying on my body as I grew accustomed to the dampness.

"What have you done?" screamed Ivy, running toward me.

Only when she moved to tackle me, I whipped out my hand on instinct, ready to summon the fire, but instead, out came ice. A stream of ice—purplish ice—shot forth.

Ivy jumped back just in time, the ice landing like jagged spikes at her feet.

"Well, that's fascinating." Orin stroked his chin as he crouched down beside the growth of icicles. He poked at it. "Come and have a dekko. There are what look like little frozen flames in the ice."

I didn't have time to consider what that could mean or why he cared.

I found myself shaking, all my confidence dissipating.

My hand was so *cold*.

Ivy leaped toward me and snatched the orb away. "It's not too late," she said. "There's that stupid *trial* period, and then—well, you can drop out at any point anyway." She stared me straight in the eyes, her eyebrows narrowing. "Drop out."

The trial period. Right.

I turned toward the lake, eager to get toward Calder.

Whether I trusted him or not, I'd made up my mind. This was the only way.

He was emerging from the lake, his torso gleaming with the moisture even in the frigid cold. Below the torso, his bare legs were emerging out from where his blue scales had been. I tried not to look at his nudity.

I'd made it just a few steps before Dean appeared between us, blocking my path.

"*Why?*" he snapped. "I know you're angry with me, but why would you do this?"

I darted to his side, but he caught me by the wrist.

With a startlingly fast *whoosh*, the air went still. All sound ceased. The wind no longer nipped at my cheeks.

Dean was the only thing moving—everyone else frozen in action—and even when moving, he was so *still*. How could I have never been repulsed by it before? The stillness, the lack of life in him, no matter how handsome.

"Why?" he repeated again, softer this time.

"You never loved me," I admitted, the words more sour on my tongue than I thought they'd be.

"But you know what the fishfolk want—"

"You don't know what they want," I said, tugging on my

arm to try to break his spell. "You're wrong. The world isn't in danger if they win."

"They're lying to you!"

I narrowed my eyes at him. "Just like you lied to me."

"I didn't *lie*," he said, his shoulders slackening somewhat. "I *tried*, Ember. I did. And you... Your friends. Your father. They're with us. You can't fight against us."

"They're your *hostages*." I yanked again—but he wasn't ready to let me go just yet. "And I can do more for them with Calder than I could with you."

"*What* has he said to you?" Dean's voice was cracking, the lips peeling back into a sneer that revealed the tips of his long incisors.

I turned to stare off at Ivy, who still had the orb in her possession, her face contorted into an angry glare at Autumn, who was trying to reach for the glowing object. "Go get her," I said. "The girl you *really* wanted. I can't win without her in the game anyway."

Dean's gaze flicked tellingly toward the Sheppard sisters.

"Goodbye," I said. "Take care of them... until I can save them." With a final tug, I ripped myself free and the world came back to life.

"Ember!" Calder's voice reached me and I plowed forward through the sand.

I didn't have time to focus too much on his nakedness before I found myself in his arms, his lips on mine.

And with a *jolt*, I felt my status as champion sealed into place.

"Ember?"

Calder and I broke apart to find Journey huffing as she made her way down the zigzagging path to the beach, Dante on her heels. Both their faces were a mixture of exhaustion and shock, but we were too far apart, and there were too many enemies between us now for me to go to her—to explain just yet.

"Thank you," whispered Calder from beside me, his warm

breath dancing on my skin as he nuzzled the top of my head. "Thank you for believing in me."

"Calder, what's the call?" one of the mermaid teens—the one with the dark hair—asked, strolling up beside Calder in the nude. She was quickly flanked by three others, all nonplussed about appearing in their birthday suits.

Right. I was embracing a strapping young man in his own birthday suit. And he was a *junior* to boot. What was I doing?

I coughed and extrapolated myself from his arms, surveying the scene. There were more merfolk behind us in the lake, bobbing up and down, but no sign of their haughty queen—Calder's mother, I realized belatedly.

My skin prickled with the memory of her dragging me under the river, of Calder's friends here doing the same to me in their mansion's moat.

I'd decided to trust Calder, but I didn't trust any of them.

"If Ivy doesn't declare for blood, we'll get nowhere." Calder sent me a knowing glance, as if I could somehow make Ivy see.

I bit my lip and watched the crowd across from us on the beach. Dean was retreating backward toward his vampire companions—a number too small to win in a battle against the merfolk just now, particularly with the vast lake behind us. I was sure he knew that, though there was no way he could have foreseen something like this.

Dante was swearing up a storm, his jaw nearly on the ground as he stared my way—at the cadre of naked people who'd come out from the chilly lake. Journey rested her hand on his arm, trying to calm him down. Her gaze was on me, not her cousin, though it flicked every few seconds to Devam, who didn't so much as turn her way.

And then there was Orin, a smirk on his face as he watched Autumn shoot vines toward her sister, trying to knock the orb away.

"She needs to think Autumn's in danger, I think," I found myself saying.

"Makes sense," said Calder, though I'd been prepared to

argue my case. Something about the way his jaw set showed me he already knew.

"Attack the kid!" he said to his companions.

"And don't actually hurt her—" I started.

But the four of them were already racing toward Autumn, their bare feet kicking up the dirty sand.

CHAPTER TWENTY-SEVEN

"Was Ember rescued by crazy skinny-dippers?" shrieked Dante as I ran toward them, hot on the Central High merfolks' figurative tails. "We have to call the cops before someone else does!"

"*Wait*, Dante—" said Journey.

I didn't hear what else either had to say.

The naked teens were on Autumn before she even really noticed them, Ivy lowering her guard just enough so that Autumn could steal the orb from her.

I have to catch up, I thought, Calder already at my side.

I looked to Dean. He kept his vampires at bay with a hand out and a slight nod. They wouldn't jump in to save Autumn—either that or they'd figured out what kind of push Ivy might need to take up their cause.

But Calder's friends didn't seem to share the same hesitance.

"Yuck!" Autumn screeched. "They're naked!"

The redhead girl did a roundhouse kick and slammed her foot against Ivy's forearms, sending her stumbling back.

Orin slid in between Autumn and Ivy, removing his scarf and cheekily wrapping it around Autumn's eyes, then turned quickly to grab the redheaded boy's arm as the boy went to strike him, leveraging his attacker's weight and dragging the merman down.

"Guys, wait—" I cried out. *If only I could still pause time.*

And then the world went quiet once more—for just a second.

I was so startled to see everyone freeze mid-movement that I didn't hold on to it for very long at all, didn't take a single step forward.

Then with a thunderous roar, the world picked up its pace again.

How? That was vampire power I'd used there.

"Cat got your tongue?" asked Orin as he slipped past the dark-haired merman boy to step in front of me. He waggled his eyebrows and cracked his knuckles. "We doing this then? Water versus bloom?"

Calder stumbled and slipped between us, then took a shot at Orin.

Orin caught his fist in his palm.

"Oh, for *her* you're a fighter," growled Ivy. She flicked her hand and let out a curse when nothing came out of it. So *she* hadn't retained her champion of water powers, not so long as she wasn't a champion at all.

I was the only one who was a vampire mermaid here.

Was I still a true vampire?

Blood. Iron. I could *feel* it, the venom pumping outward from my heart. *Dean.* My mind jumbled at his name.

Venom. Blood. My incisors seemed to be growing, but—

With a snap, they were gone as Calder pushed me back.

"Okay, mate, this is really bloody distracting, fighting you in the buff—" said Orin.

"Good," snapped Calder, and he wound up another punch.

"Seriously, though," said Orin. "Maybe your new girlfriend can lend you my coat?"

I was getting rather warm—being cold and damp didn't bother me anymore. Sighing, I removed it and tossed it

Calder's way, averting my eyes as he grunted and slipped it on, buttoning only the bottom button below his torso.

"Thanks," said Orin, and he twirled, crouching to sweep his leg at Calder's calf and sending the merman sideways.

Right. Focus. I could experiment with vampire and mermaid powers later.

I had a hand that shot ice now.

Crouched beneath Calder's extended arm, Orin shot his arm up and a blast of wind met my burgeoning blast of ice. I fell back.

Orin stood and wiped his forehead with his forearm. His hair seemed misty, like he was actually working up a sweat.

"Woo," he said. "I didn't think it'd be so annoying to go back to the basics."

"Basics?" I ventured, immediately regretting taking the bait.

Orin laughed as he straightened, his right hand just a little bit extended, ready to shoot me with another gust of wind at any moment. It hardly seemed fair that their prince had an attack like that, on par with what the champions could do.

Autumn let out a little scream as she stumbled back, ripping the scarf off her face. Ivy stopped fighting the mermaid in front of her and slid in front of her sister, taking a kick meant for the little girl.

Gasping, I covered my mouth as Ivy fell on top of Autumn on the ground.

Orin spared the activity a glance but turned back to me pretty quickly. "Vampires are unnatural, love."

Calder shouted something toward his merfolk companions and the redhead boy who'd kicked Ivy drew back.

"Yeah," I said, half-distracted. "And mermaids and faeries are totally natural."

"They are." Orin shot his wind toward the sand beneath him and I poised, ready to dodge, but he only kicked up a clump of algae into the air and snatched it into his grip. "This war was once... just water against bloom. Millenia ago. Before either of you were a twinkle in your great-great-great-grand-mothers' eyes."

Calder limped toward me now, hovering in front of me, his attention frequently drawn to his friends. They were pulling back, drawing into a line—and Dean and his vampire companions approached the Sheppard sisters. The sun was almost set behind them, and Devam, Leopold, and Zelda took off their sunglasses.

The beach was dotted now with the glow of their bright blue eyes.

I put a hand on Calder's shoulder, clutching the soaked and foul-smelling wool.

"What are you trying to say, Orin?" I asked, my voice exhausted.

"The bloom created the blood," he said. He chuckled. "Alliterative that, right? Should have been telling."

Calder clutched his hand into a fist. "Why?"

Did it matter?

As the vampires flanked the girls, Dean swooped in beside Ivy and helped her up. I couldn't account for the sudden and primal urge for *revenge* that cut through me to the core.

But this was what I'd *wanted*.

"My family—they don't really like it out here much," said Orin, playing with the soggy mess of green in his hand. "It was one thing when it was faeries on land, merfolk in the seas, but then those annoying little apes up and *evolved*, and it seemed like we'd just blinked and boom, all these Neanderthals were walking all over the surface, tearing it to shreds, assaulting the flora that gave us strength." The clump of algae tore in Orin's grip. "I'd say you got off easy underwater, but they went out of their way to spill their garbage into your home, too."

Ivy began hacking in Dean's arms, and he shifted her to allow her to throw up. There was a trickle of blood from her mouth—stars, how badly had that merman hurt her?

My stomach turned.

Even Autumn was no longer smiling, crawling forward to hold her sister's hand.

Zelda let out a hiss, and Devam joined in.

Dante yelped and ran away—Journey shot me a pained expression before she went after him, her gaze lingering a beat longer on Devam before she turned to go. There were people in the distance, at the far end of the park, and I feared if we stayed a moment longer, we'd soon have more witnesses than we could control.

"So the bloodsuckers joined this later," said Calder curtly. "Tell us something we don't know. What does that matter anymore?"

"It *matters* because they owe their second lives to the fae." A vein seemed to throb on Orin's forehead, a strange look on the normally too-cavalier face. "We created them from plant venom—a plant so rare no human had ever encountered it. We flew around the world and chose a curious human girl, made her our vampire princess and sicced her and her newly-made kind on the merfolk."

"Why?" I asked. Dean was whispering something to Ivy now, turning to Autumn, who crawled over to where she'd dropped the orb and shoved it toward her sister.

"Fall back!" said Calder, well attuned to what was going on.

The merfolk did, their bare feet shifting backward through the sands.

Orin smirked as he glanced over his shoulder. "My people don't like getting their hands dirty—let the vampires eradicate the merfolk, then clean up the mess we'd created, we figured. It almost worked once, too. But there were *survivors*." He stared pointedly at Calder. Calder's merfolk friends flanked us now, and Calder grabbed my hand, pulling me back toward the lake, his focus on the blue eyes building a wall around the Sheppard sisters, the blue eyes advancing toward us in the twilight.

"The consummate lands were secure then, the only humans

to cross its path a more respectful kind who'd do it no harm," continued Orin, taking one step closer. I wouldn't let Calder drag me backward, though. "But we knew—wait long enough and we knew that others would migrate here, disrupt the magic of the place where bloom and water first met in agreement to determine the fate of the world—would the merfolk win and drown it or would the fae win and salvage our beloved trees?"

"Ember, just ignore him," whispered Calder. "We have to go."

To where? I wanted to ask. But I knew. Retreating to the lake. The merfolk were always retreating to where they were strongest.

I ripped my hand free from Calder's grip, too curious about why Orin was monologuing now. "The first vampire was Minnie?" I asked.

He nodded. "Wilhelmina. We found her in Europe. And it was there we returned her to sleep, to gather her strength as we waited for new champions. Did she ever tell you she was in love with her first champion of blood? That the loss of the Ho-Chunk girl broke her, made her lash out and destroy as many merfolk as she could, proxy battles forgotten?" His expression soured. "It disrupted the consummate lands' magic. The lands needed time as much as the blood and water itself did—time to recover."

"And she woke during World War II," I said, trying to make sense of it. "Sleeping in Europe—"

"It was the first world war, as you call it. All the blood woke her. The scent of it. The *waste* of it. She spent some decades on her own, groggy and still angry over her champion's loss before she finally made her way back here, back to where a new champion could be named."

"Ember." Calder's arm tugged on me harder. "What are you doing? We need to go."

I found myself approaching Orin, moving closer.

A shock of red glowed out from behind the advancing

vampires. Something *stirred* in me, a rapid beat of the heart, an internal battle against advancing and then retreating venom shooting out from my core.

In the red glow between the shadowy figures with the bright blue eyes, there was no mistaking Dean's lips pressing against Ivy's on the beach, the sealing of her becoming his champion.

So it was done.

"Retreat!" called Calder, and his companions did.

Orin grinned at me, but the smile didn't reach his eyes. His voice lowered. "But the blood will always be a poor offshoot of the bloom," he whispered. "You've chosen well—the only other ancient side of this conflict, the only side that can offer any real challenge to ours."

"*Ember!*" pleaded Calder. "It's done—we have to go."

"No," I said, raising a hand. "No, I can take them now—get this over with. There are only a few of them."

"That's where you're wrong, love," said Orin. With a flick of his wrist, a burst of air shot forth and whipped up in a frenzy behind him, rattling even the clothes of the vampires, sending their hats flying.

"Autumn, princess!" called Orin.

Autumn jumped up from beside her sister, taking a few wary steps back as Dean attended to Ivy.

Ivy looked better now. Paler, angrier—but better. Her eyes sparkled a bright blue.

"Is it time?" asked Autumn, trotting up to Orin's side, the wind seeming to part for her and not hinder her way.

"It's time," he said.

Autumn's brows narrowed and she shot out her vines. I sent a stream of ice out to meet it, stopping the first vine's advance, but then Autumn let go of that one and shot out another. I moved to blast ice at it—and with a firework-like screech, a ball of fire swung out like a curve ball and slammed right into my ice.

The flame was a violet-blue, not red, crackling and misting as it ate away at my spiky ice trail.

Ivy stared me down, her hand glowing purple. I looked at my own. The light was purple as well.

The distraction was enough. Autumn shot out another vine and with a grunt, the vine bloomed on the beach, little buds growing outward and peeling open, turning to blossoms. And from each blossom, a small green glow emerged, dotting the dark air above our heads.

Calder cursed and slid in front of me, picking me up and slinging me over his shoulder before I could do more than let out a gasp of surprise.

"What are you *doing?*" I demanded as he ran toward the lake. "What's going on?" I struggled to shift on his back, to take a look at the little balls of green.

They looked like *bugs*. There were little flapping wings everywhere.

The Central High mermen and mermaids bolted into the water, their bare ankles kicking up the shore as they ran full-throttle. Calder and I were a few steps behind, my weight bringing Calder's pace to a crawl.

The green lights shot forward, advancing toward us just as Calder's ankles were submerged in the water.

Without ceremony, Calder plucked me from his shoulder and tossed me farther into the lake.

He screamed as a green light darted at him, and my mixed-up senses could smell the blood, taste its tang in the air before my back crashed against the lake water.

My legs snapped together into a tail as my heart wrenched for Calder—as the water embraced my skin, weighed down my skirt and camisole. I reached toward the shore, toward the dancing lights, and then one light zipped right above my head, lingering just above the water's surface.

It was a little *person*. A faery. Of course. Her brown skin matched Orin's, her hair dark and curly woven through with ribbon-like strands of green. Her green eyes glowed, brighter than the green light that surrounded her. In her hand she held a twig sharped to resemble a sword, its point fine enough to draw blood. The rocking surface of the water gave her a ripple-like filter, enough to make me question whether she were real or just a vision.

The water was tainted with blood beside me as a dark form collapsed.

Calder. I flipped my fins and swam toward him.

"Calder!" I called out in my singsong mermaid voice.

I had him in my arms and he winced but smiled. "We have to go deeper," he said, pointing above.

Hundreds of green lights darted out above the waters. I wondered what anyone looking out at Lake Michigan just then would see.

I wondered what Journey would say to Dante.

How they would explain my absence to her parents.

I wondered what Ivy thought of me—how she and the vampire who'd always preferred her would fight against me.

Calder took my hand. It was warm, even in the chill of the waters—but the chill didn't bother me.

"Come on!" shouted one of the mermaid girls, and I saw them—so many of his people just beyond the shore, deeper in the lake, waiting for us.

"They can't follow us here," I said, feeling safe, feeling welcomed—ready to retreat. To figure this out.

"They're not the blood," said Calder, his hand gripping one of the many cuts on his arm. The green lights were swarming above us now, joining together into one large glow. "They may not be able to breathe down here, but they're not weighed down by the water, either. They—"

With a splash, the mass of green lights shot down into the waters, straight for us.

It was like being swarmed by hornets, only the little stinging creatures were bigger and faster, streaks of light torpedoing, leaving trails of bubbles in their wake. They came for my arms first, bare as they were, slicing with those sharp twigs before I could register what was happening. My skin stung, the water peppered with wisps of red, a tangy iron taste permeating the liquid around me, causing my heart to thump loudly in my ears. It was all I could do to shield my face, offering my arms up for more of the attack.

"Ember, swim!"

Lowering my limbs, I opened my clenched eyes to take in the scene around me. Calder swum toward me, his friends flanking him, stopped every few seconds by another assault. More dexterous merfolk than I were zipping through the murky waters, this way and that, leading the green lights on a chase. Still others held their positions, whapping their tails at the lights or swinging their fists toward them. But it didn't matter. The faeries were faster. More agile. Not a single hit connected, not a solitary merperson was able to swim faster.

Calder darted through the chaos, kicking up a force of water that whapped against my body as he came to a halt beside me. "We need to leave." His deep voice was harried despite the aery, magical quality.

"And go where?" I screamed as another green light flit past, slicing across my side.

Calder seized me in his arms, our torsos' scales chafing up against each other and my cheek resting against his warm, broad chest. "My mom's waiting outside of Chicago—" He grunted and grit his teeth as a pair of green lights crisscrossed over his back. My nostrils were overwhelmed with the particles of blood tainting the water around us, my head growing dizzy with an insatiable ache at war within me.

I couldn't open my mouth to express it to Calder, to explain about the vampire venom still oozing inside me.

"Retreat!" called Calder over my head, his voice carrying through the waters around us like a hollow echo.

The dark-haired teen mermaid let out a yelp. "We'll never make it that far north with these pests on our—ow!"

"They won't follow us that far," added the dark-haired teen merman. Calder had called him "Bay." He spoke in Spanish to the mermaid, and they took off northward, rolling and zigzagging ahead at an impressive speed.

"Calder—Laguna!" said the redhaired merman Calder had called "Llyr." A swarm of green lights pulled together into one large mass, all heading toward the direction Llyr pointed.

Calder pulled back, his palms still flat on the small of my back, and whipped his head around. A screech rung out in the waters and I instinctively covered my ears, writhing in place.

Llyr bolted past, Calder trailing after him toward the sound, like a scream and a song and a chorus all at once. A cadre of merfolk joined them, heading toward the endless screeching as I finally let loose some of the tension in my shoulders to stare at the source of the cacophony. The redhaired mermaid, "Laguna," I supposed, was emitting the sound all by herself, the waters shaking around her as vibrations soared outward in all directions, grinding the fast-moving green lights surrounding her to a halt.

"It's working!" shouted Calder. He let out a relieved laugh, but all too soon, his face went grim, his eyebrows narrowing. He doubled back as quick as if his life depended on it, grabbing me by the hand and pulling me northward. It took a few flaps of his tail before my own fins were working just the same, before the strain on my arm felt more like guidance instead of jerking.

The sound cut out sharply, and I was left with the eerie sensation that the song was unfinished.

Sparing a glance over my shoulder, I saw the merfolk swimming after us in a line, the redhaired Laguna cradled in Llyr's sculpted arms, the two lagging slightly behind the rest. Behind them, what few remaining green lights there were shot upward, breaking out from the surface of the lake.

"What was that?" I asked, facing forward once more.

Calder grunted, his expression dour. "A siren's death shriek," he said. "Pray we never hear that again."

The prickle tingling up from my fins to my spine made me uneasy as I pushed forward, swimming on, Calder's firm grip wrapped around my hand.

He didn't explain if the shriek heralded the death of the siren or their foes.

I was too exhausted—too frightened—to ask.

"I know," said Calder's mom as he limped, propped up by Bay on one side, toward the massive RV that idled for us.

We were somewhere north of Chicago, having swum as far as we could before Calder's wounds had been too much for him to keep going, his grip on my hand growing weak. Several mermen had caught up to us and dragged him the rest of the way.

The dark-haired teen mermaid was my support as we pulled ourselves from the craggy lakeside to the road. I wasn't as wounded as Calder, but my camisole and skirt were torn, my blood pooling out from little faery stick scratches mostly on my arms.

I felt nauseous with Calder's and my blood in the air, with everyone's, my head throbbing with contradictory thoughts, the repulsion of the blood, the *need* for it.

"Come on, come on." Calder's mom waved her hands rapidly toward the motorhome and Calder and his friends settled inside, Llyr carrying an exhausted but conscious Laguna into a bedroom in the back, Bay and the Latina mermaid guiding their wounded prince and new champion to the couch before scrambling for blankets and clothing. The mermaid girl whose name I didn't know yet headed to the bathroom and emerged with a first aid kit as Bay joined the freckled redheads in the back.

I stared out through the RV window as Calder's mom conversed with a naked merman, both their expressions dire.

As some of the other merfolk bustled about the space, I stared at Calder, whose bare chest rose and fell rapidly as he seemed to readjust to breathing the air.

"She wants something we don't want," I whispered. "Your mother."

He nodded and bit his bottom lip.

"So why are you still with her?"

I stopped myself from prodding further as the dark-haired mermaid plopped the kit on a small table in front of us and opened it up, rifling through its contents and drawing out bandages.

"Wait, Cascade," said Calder, holding up a hand. "Get dressed and cleaned up—just give us a minute."

"The queen won't like if we don't attend to you first—" she started.

"Please." Calder's eyes narrowed, his breaths shallow, and Cascade nodded, stepping back to join the others in the back of the motorhome.

Calder's eyes flicked toward the tanned man with blond hair in the nearby driver's seat. He looked more like Calder than his mother did. His father? No. He'd told me his father had died.

"We need their help," Calder said softly. His shaking hand reached out to grab me by the chin, to lock my eyes with his own. "We can't do this alone."

"But they—"

He put a finger to my lips. "They don't make the wish if we win," he said as quiet as could be. "*We* do."

The driver's gaze burrowed into mine as he adjusted the mirror above him.

"Trust me." Calder squeezed my hand. "We'll figure everything out," he said louder.

"I..." There seemed to be a lump lodged in my throat. I didn't know where to begin. I had so much I needed to answer for—so much to worry about just then. I could hardly go home and pretend everything was fine now, could I? But I couldn't... I didn't want to be on the run with these merfolk, either, whatever they were up to in their RV.

"Why aren't you dressed?" Calder's mom sneered as she reentered the motorhome and shut the door behind her. "And staunch those wounds." She recoiled back as if in disgust, her eyes narrowing on me. "I won't stand for blood in this home."

Calder meekly grabbed for the first aid kit without a word of protest as his mom sat in the seat beside the driver.

"Go," she barked, and the tanned man put the RV into drive, taking us down a dark and deserted road.

A sting on my side made me jump and I realized Calder was holding an alcohol swab to one of the larger holes in my camisole. "You should undress," he said. "Cascade can help you if you want. Make sure you get all the wounds."

"Okay," I mumbled. I took over pressing the swab from Calder, our fingers brushing. "Calder, what's going to happen now?"

"Now... the war begins anew." Calder sullenly picked up another moist toilette and cringed as he patted down the biggest gash on his arm.

The blood was making me woozy. I stood, my feet unsteady in the moving vehicle, one hand clutching the swab against my arm.

I caught sight of my face in the reflection of the window.

My hair was plastered to my skin, my face ghastly pale. And as the scent of blood assaulted my nostrils, there was a flash of two bright blue eyes staring back at me.

I gasped, almost forgetting we were moving, that it wasn't Dean or another vampire out there staring back at me—that it was just me.

The vampire mermaid.

Give me enough time and I'd figure this out, figure out how

to win against bloom and blood—even if they may have combined forces.

As I marched down the narrow walkway, adjusting better and retaining my balance, I thought I saw a flicker of green floating out there beside the RV—a soaring ball of light that bobbed up and down and then floated out into the night sky, blending in with the twinkle of stars in the distance.

the means. Though smitten with her merman prince, she's not certain they can keep their plans to save those she's wronged secret from the friends and foes alike who would stand in their way.

Ivy Sheppard never saw herself crossing sides to become the champion of blood, but it's the only way to protect her little sister from their traitorous step-sister. What she doesn't expect is to fall in love with an undead prince whose days might be numbered.

The fourth book in the Blood, Bloom, & Water series sees friend become enemy and adversary become lover in the climax of the battle between vampires, mermaids, and faeries. After the events that unfold, things will never be the same.

ABOUT THE AUTHOR

Amy McNulty is an editor and author of books that run the gamut from YA speculative fiction to contemporary romance. A lifelong fiction fanatic, she fangirls over books, anime, manga, comics, movies, games, and TV shows from her home state of Wisconsin. When not editing her clients' novels, she's busy fulfilling her dream by crafting fantastical worlds of her own.

Sign up for Amy's newsletter to receive news and exclusive information about her current and upcoming projects. Get a free YA romantic sci-fi novelette when you do!

THE DAUGHTERS OF MORRIGAN
ANNIE COSBY

Three sisters. A magical castle. And a legend as old as Ireland.

The day the Doyle sisters are attacked by a monster on the foggy shores of the Atlantic, they're saved by a mysterious boy who stumbles out of the waves. That's the first sign that nothing in their small world will ever be the same again.

Striking, vain Bríd, caring but brusque Moira, and sweet, silent Ríona invite their injured savior into the crumbling castle they call home, only to find he's prepared to challenge everything they think they know ...

About themselves. About their family. About their upbringing here on the edge of the world. And about the magic that permeates the castle. For the girls are keeping secrets of their own.

When a second attack takes them all by surprise, they'll have to decide what to believe, what to reveal, and just how to stay alive.

Will the old walls of the castle be enough to keep the Doyle sisters safe, or will they be forced to flee?

The Daughters of Morrigan is the first in a contemporary YA fantasy series steeped in Irish legend. If you like a sweeping setting and characters to fall for, you'll love the first installment in Annie Cosby's haunting new series, Souls Out of Ireland.

CAPTAIN BLACK SHADOW
JANINA FRANCK

The life of a shipwright's son is a quiet one, always staying in one place while sailors of all sorts pass through, telling tales of their daring escapades to any who will listen. For the young Griffin, stories of adventure aren't enough; he longs to see the world for himself, to have adventures out on the ocean, and to captain his own ship. Even if that means abandoning his old life and running away. But the seas of Jianlah are a dangerous place, filled with strange creatures, treacherous waters, and most dangerous of all: pirates. So when Griffin finds himself aboard the Bat, the most notorious pirate ship of all, his adventures are only beginning.

READ MORE FROM AMY MCNULTY

THE NEVER VEIL SERIES

"The story is fun and engaging, featuring a female protagonist who will resonate with young teens." -School Library Journal

"...A whirlwind of time-bending adventures that immerse readers in a maelstrom of plot twists and allusions to "Beauty and the Beast" and other fairy tale love stories, while Noll's understanding of gender-based social and cultural dynamics develops." -Publishers Weekly

Nobody's Goddess (Book One in The Never Veil Series), winner of The Romance Reviews Summer 2016 Readers' Choice Award for Young Adult Romance:

> In a village of masked men, each man is compelled to love only one woman and to follow the commands of his "goddess" without question. A woman may reject the only man who will love her if she pleases, but she will be alone forever. A man must stay masked until his goddess returns his love—and if she can't or won't, he remains masked forever.
>
> Seventeen-year-old Noll's childhood friends have paired off and her closest companion, Jurij, found his goddess in Noll's own sister. Desperate to find a way to break this ancient spell, Noll instead discovers why no man has ever chosen her. She is in fact the goddess of the mysterious lord of the village, a man who refuses to let Noll have her right as a woman to spurn him.
>
> Thus begins a dangerous game between the choice of woman and the magic of man. The stakes are no less than freedom and happiness, life and death—and neither Noll nor the veiled lord is willing to lose.

The complete The Never Veil Series is out now and is free on Kindle Unlimited!

Terror. Callousness. Denial. Rebellion. How the four teenage children of leaders in the duchy and the neighboring empire of Hanaobi choose to adapt to their nefarious parents' whims is a matter of survival.

Rohesia, daughter of the duke, spends her days hunting "outsiders," fugitives who've snuck onto her father's island duchy. That she lives when even children who resemble her are subject to death hardens her heart to tackle the task.

Fastello is the son of the "king" of the raiders who steal from the rich and share with the poor. When aristocrats die in the raids, Fastello questions what his peoples' increasingly wicked methods of survival have cost them.

An orphan raised by a convent of mothers, Cateline can think of no higher aim in life than to serve her religion, even if it means turning a blind eye to the suffering of other orphans under the mothers' care.

Kojiro, new heir to the Hanaobi empire, must avenge his people against the "barbarians" who live in the duchy, terrified the empress, his own mother, might rather see him die than succeed.

When the paths of these four young adults cross, they must rely on one another for survival—but the love of even a malevolent guardian is hard to leave behind.

The complete Fall Far from the Tree duology is out now and is available widely.

BALLAD OF THE BEANSTALK

A Library Journal Self-e Selection.

As her fingers move across the strings of her family's heirloom harp, sixteen-year-old Clarion can forget. She doesn't dwell on the recent passing of her beloved father or the fact that her mother has just sold every-thing they owned, including that very same instrument that gives Clarion life. She doesn't think about how her friends treat her like a feeble, brittle thing to be protected. She doesn't worry about how to tell the elegant Elena, her best friend and first love, that she doesn't want to be her sweetheart anymore. She becomes the melody and loses herself in the song.

When Mack, a lord's dashing young son, rides into town so his father and Elena's can arrange a marriage between the two youth, Clarion finds herself falling in love with a boy for the first time. Drawn to Clarion's music, Mack puts Clarion and Elena's relationship to the test, but he soon vanishes by climbing up a giant beanstalk that only Clarion has seen. When even the town witch won't help, Clarion is determined to rescue Mack herself and prove once and for all that she doesn't need protecting. But while she fancied herself a savior, she couldn't have imagined the enormous world of danger that awaits her in the kingdom of the clouds.

A prequel to the fairy tale *Jack and the Beanstalk* that reveals the true story behind the magical singing harp.

Ballad of the Beanstalk is available now in e-book, paperback, and audiobook.